"Will remind readers what chattering teeth sound like."
—*Kirkus Reviews*

"Voracious readers of horror will delightfully consume the contents of Bates's World's Scariest Places books."
—*Publishers Weekly*

"Creatively creepy and sure to scare." —*The Japan Times*

"Jeremy Bates writes like a deviant angel I'm glad doesn't live on my shoulder."
—Christian Galacar, author of GILCHRIST

"Thriller fans and readers of Stephen King, Joe Lansdale, and other masters of the art will find much to love."
—*Midwest Book Review*

"An ice-cold thriller full of mystery, suspense, fear."
—David Moody, author of HATER and AUTUMN

"A page-turner in the true sense of the word."
—*HorrorAddicts*

"Will make your skin crawl." —*Scream Magazine*

"Told with an authoritative voice full of heart and insight."
—Richard Thomas, Bram Stoker nominated author

"Grabs and doesn't let go until the end." —*Writer's Digest*

FREE BOOK

The Dancing Plague 2

World's Scariest Legends 6

Jeremy Bates

The Dancing Plague 2

PROLOGUE

2022

White cinderblock walls and heavy industrial doors. Tiny cell-like rooms without windows. Psychotic patients roaming fluorescent-lit hallways in their pajamas, either screaming crazily or staring blankly into space. Burly staff tackling the unruliest ones. Sadistic nurses forcibly medicating them.

These were the images the movies liked to use to portray psychiatric wards. And maybe it was like that in some of the poorly funded and overcrowded inner-city hospitals. But those kinds of scenes were unrecognizable at the Oasis Mountain Academy, a privately run healthcare center on the outskirts of Camp Verde, Arizona.

As Dr. Nancy Glonti walked through the juvenile ward on

the building's second floor, she passed large windows filled with sunlight and walls covered by canvas prints that she had purchased at her own expense showing locations from around the world: a traditional market in Japan; mist-covered mountains in China; an aerial shot of New York City; the stone statues in front of Angkor Thom; a snowy Scandinavian village; an old church in Cuba; the Sydney Opera House; and many others. She believed they helped the kids she treated to see that the world was a much bigger place than Camp Verde (where many of them had never stepped foot outside) and to give them perspective on the problems that consumed them, which for the most part involved depression, generalized anxiety, social phobias, substance abuse, eating disorders, and suicide ideation.

She entered the communal area and stopped before a fifteen-year-old boy sitting in a beanbag chair and reading a book. "How are you doing today, Teddy?" she asked him.

"Okay," he said without looking at her. Diagnosed with bipolar disorder, he was one of the more troubled children in her care. He'd been admitted to the facility on several previous occasions, each time with new self-inflicted cuts on his arms and legs. To say he came from a troubled household was a gross understatement. His father was serving a life sentence in Florence State Prison for the murder of a corrections officer, while his mother was currently awaiting trial in a murder-for-hire plot that led to the death of a Phoenix-based meth dealer.

"What are you reading?" Dr. Glonti asked him.

He flashed her the cover of *Harry Potter and the Chamber of Secrets.* Despite the nearby bookcase being filled with an impressive collection of titles, the Harry Potter books were always a hot commodity, often causing tempers to flare among the children who wanted to get their hands on one. It was amazing—and heartening—how much these young kids took to old-fashioned reading when they didn't have their phones.

She said, "Everybody seems to like that one."

Teddy shrugged. "Harry Potter's a wimp. But the story is

okay."

"I'm glad you're enjoying it."

Dr. Glonti's next stop was seventeen-year-old Fiona Greenwood, who was lying stretched out on the lounge. She suffered from schizophrenia and could become a real handful on the occasions she believed someone other than herself was sleeping in her bed. But right then she seemed content watching *The Price is Right*. There was a DVD player on the cabinet below the TV, but nobody ever seemed to use it. This wasn't surprising since the available titles were esoteric eighties fare such as *Fraggle Rock*, Richard Simmons's *Sweatin' to the Oldies*, tutorials on Tai-Chi, and the like (the modern Hollywood blockbusters were kept locked in a drawer at the nurse's station and reserved for Tuesday and Friday Movie Nights).

She said to the girl, "I used to watch this show when I was your age."

"Yeah?" Fiona said.

"The Showcase with the car is always the best one to bid on."

"Sure."

"I think you're going to like who's going to be visiting us at pet therapy today."

Fiona looked up at Dr. Glonti, showing some interest in the conversation for the first time. Amongst the several therapeutic group sessions scheduled throughout each day, pet therapy was everybody's favorite. "What is it?"

"Can't tell you that. It'll ruin the surprise."

"It's not another hamster, is it?"

"You don't like hamsters?"

"They're cute, but they're getting boring. Can't you bring in a coyote or something?"

"Coyotes are wild animals, not pets."

"I'm sure *somebody* has one as a pet."

"I'll look into it," she said with a laugh.

Dr. Glonti's final visit was to the Games Corner, where the younger patients liked to gather. Russell Robinson and Stuart

Glascock were playing Scrabble despite the fact several of the most important letters, such as X and J and Z, were missing (though this wasn't a big deal as Russell was dyslexic and Stuart couldn't spell anything longer than four letters). Andrea Buchanan was assembling a jigsaw puzzle. Julie Hatfield and Camilla Gryski were setting up the Monopoly board. And the rest were using the art supplies, some weaving colorful gimp friendship bracelets, others playing Cat's Cradle with a looped length of string. Four more were playing M*A*S*H with construction paper and crayons. One of the latter, Laura Torres, insisted that Dr. Glonti play a round with her. She obliged...and learned her fate was to live in a mansion with Dwayne "The Rock" Johnson, have 101 kids together, and drive a Tesla.

"It's not a bad life," Dr. Glonti kidded. "Except I think I might adopt."

"Dr. G? Can I ask you something?" Laura was eleven with a face full of freckles and crooked teeth. Like most girls her age experiencing puberty, she had her ups and downs. But unlike most girls her age, she had a lot more downs than ups, leading to withdrawal and disobedience and other mental health issues, which had landed her in the ward for two weeks.

"Of course, Laura. You can ask me anything."

"What's appendicitis?"

"Appendicitis? Well, it's a kind of pain that begins down around your belly button. You're not feeling anything like that, are you?"

"No, but I heard some of the older girls talking about it. When they go back to school, and their friends ask them where they've been, they're going to tell them they were at a regular hospital with appendicitis."

Dr. Glonti understood the stigma of mental illness, and the fear many of these children had of telling other people, especially their peers, what they were going through. "Is that what you're going to tell your friends when you go back to school on Monday?"

She twisted her mouth. "I don't know. I'd be lying…"

"I'd think of it more as a little fib than a lie, and sometimes little fibs are allowed if they're only told once in a while."

"Thanks, Dr. G. I'm going to miss you when I leave here."

"I'm going to miss you too, Laura."

"Maybe I can come back and visit sometime?"

She smiled. "Anytime you like."

△△△

Dr. Glonti made a perfunctory knock on the open door as she stepped inside the small, sparsely furnished room. Young Mary Porter lay on the bed's thin mattress, the white covers bunched around her waist, revealing the pink camisole top she wore. Her hair fell to either side of her hollowed-out cheeks like two greasy brown curtains. Her eyes were open, but they weren't focused on anything.

Nurse Deleuze collected a tray containing empty medication cups from a wooden desk. "She's just taken her pills," she said. "I don't know if she's had any bowel movement yet."

"Thanks, Genie," Dr. Glonti said. "Can you do me a favor and put this somewhere." She handed the nurse a yellow hair elastic. "I took it from Georgie. He wouldn't tell me where he got it."

"Georgie? His head is practically shaved!"

"He was using it to snap his skin."

"I'll talk with him when I see him."

When she left, Dr. Glonti went to the radio by the window. It was playing a song by Frank Sinatra, but the station was staticky. She adjusted the AM/FM analog tuner until the reception cleared.

Mary Porter continued to stare into space. The girl was unlike many of the other children in the ward who came from broken and impoverished and drug-riddled households. Her parents were wealthy and well-respected, and they visited her religiously during visiting hours each day. They brought her snacks, magazines, and pictures of her Golden Retriever. They shared the latest news and gossip. They treated her to a lavish chocolate cake for her sixteenth birthday last week —a sixteenth birthday that had been anything but sweet. No hairstyling, no makeup, no expensive gown. No laughter—at least, no genuine laughter.

Mary's parents put on upbeat faces, but there was nothing to be upbeat about. Mary hadn't spoken a single word to anybody since she was admitted to the facility at the end of last month. She barely ate anything either—she would have starved herself by now if the nurses didn't force something into her at each meal—which explained her gaunt frame. She would allow herself to be led around the facility but wouldn't participate in any of the daily activities. She was a shell, empty inside.

Dr. Glonti didn't understand the cause of the girl's catatonic state. Nobody did. But something terrible and traumatic had clearly happened to her last month during a hike with her best friend, Elise Becerra, and Elise's parents. They had planned to spend a Saturday hiking along West Clear Creek, camp overnight at Indian Maiden Falls, and then hike back in the morning.

However, when Mary didn't return home by Sunday afternoon, her parents grew concerned and contacted the police. They discovered the Becerra's SUV where they had parked it at the trailhead, deserted. It would be another two days before they found Mary in a rocky ravine about three miles north of West Clear Creek. She was uninjured yet unresponsive, dehydrated, and shivering. They never found any trace of the Becerras, despite the help of a large group of volunteers, and the official search was ultimately called off a week later.

What might have happened on that Saturday or early Sunday morning in the wilderness to the east of Camp Verde had been the talk of the town ever since, and speculation involved everything from an alien encounter of the fourth kind, to satanic cultists, to a lone serial killer.

Of course, the only person who knew the horrible truth was Mary, and unfortunately she wasn't talking.

"How are you doing this morning, Mary?" Dr. Glonti asked her.

The girl didn't reply.

"Here's your schedule for today." She set a piece of paper she'd printed on the desk near the bed. "Nurse Deleuze will be back shortly to help you get changed and bring you to breakfast. Smells like it's going to be crepes and waffles. How does that sound?"

No response.

"You're safe here, honey. Whatever happened in the desert... you're safe now. We just want to help you."

Nothing.

Dr. Glonti left the room.

△△△

"Doctor? You'd better come see this."

Dr. Glonti looked up from the psychological test of a potential patient she'd been reviewing. Nurse Deleuze stood at the door to her office, appearing uncharacteristically flustered.

"What is it, Genie?"

"Like I said, you'd better see it for yourself."

Dr. Glonti got up from her desk and followed the nurse to the ward's communal area. She stopped on the spot when she saw what awaited her. Half of the children in her care were dancing in the middle of the room, while the others kept their distance, watching in a kind of bemused fear. This didn't appear to be some sort of rebellious dance party to get a rise out of the staff. Not only was there no music playing on the radio; there were no cheeky smiles, no knowing looks on any of the dancers' faces. Yet perhaps strangest of all was the participation of previously catatonic Mary Porter, who was also dancing animatedly.

"My God," Dr. Glonti breathed softly. "How did you ever get

Mary to join them?"

"That's the thing," Nurse Deleuze said. "She *started* it."

Dr. Glonti blinked at her in surprise. "Excuse me?"

"She got up from where she sits in the corner during free time and started dancing. Andrea and Laura joined her after a few minutes, and then the rest of them, one after the other. I don't understand it. I tried to get them to stop, but they're...I don't know...they're in some kind of *trance*."

"Trance? Don't be silly." But even as Dr. Glonti approached the group of dancing children, their unseeing eyes and emotionless faces told her that Nurse Deleuze was right. They had indeed been swept up in some kind of trance. She touched Laura gently on the shoulder. "Honey? Can you hear me?"

Laura kept right on dancing.

She tried communicating with a couple of the other children.

They ignored her.

She looked back at Nurse Deleuze. "I've never seen anything like this before..."

"I haven't either, Doctor. What should we do?"

For the first time in her professional career as a clinical psychiatrist, Dr. Glonti felt out of her league. "I suppose," she said, shaking her head, "we let them dance."

PART 1
Camp Verde, AZ, One Week Later

"*And those who were seen dancing were thought to be insane by those who could not hear the music.*"
—*Friedrich Nietzsche*

CHAPTER 1

A SURPRISE VISIT

Sally Levine snapped awake at 4:30 AM, the bedroom dark, the nightmare fresh in her mind: deadly, wolfish creatures pursuing her through an endless forest. At one point she found help in a rundown hunter's cabin, where she and an old man barricaded the windows and door with furniture. She thought she was safe for the time being…until she began turning into one of the creatures herself.

Exhaling shakily, she pushed aside the covers, swung her bare feet to the oak parquet flooring, and sat on the edge of the bed for a long moment, thinking.

Finally she stood, flicked on the wall light, and began packing a small travel bag.

△△△

By 7:30 she was angry at herself for running behind schedule. Initially believing she'd had plenty of time, she'd taken a leisurely bath instead of a shower; cooked a large breakfast that included eggs, bacon, a muffin, and yogurt; and sat down with a coffee to watch the local morning news. When she checked the time again, she was shocked to find three hours had passed since she'd woken from the nightmare. This threw her into a panic, and the last fifteen minutes were a frantic whirlwind of activity: adding last-minute items to her travel bag (how had she forgotten her toothbrush?), charging her phone (which she'd been dismayed to see had only a five-percent charge left), changing her outfit (for a third time), and hunting for her apartment keys (which had been on the kitchen counter where she usually left them, hidden beneath a discarded paper napkin).

Now Sally hurried across the lobby of her co-op, telling Hugo the concierge that she would be away for a few days. Outside on Avenue of the Americas she hailed a taxi.

"Where to?" the cabbie asked, looking at her in the rearview mirror.

"Broadway Plaza Hotel, please," she said.

While watching the news earlier, she'd called several hotels within reasonable walking distance to Rizzoli's Bookstore. She'd gotten lucky with the fifth one she'd contacted. When the front desk agent asked if she wanted to be patched through to Ben Graves' room, she declined. She wasn't sure how Ben would react to her revelation that she would be accompanying him to Camp Verde today, which was why she wanted to tell him in person, not over the phone.

If he hasn't already left...

Sally checked her wristwatch. 8:05. What time did the first flight depart from La Guardia to Arizona? Nine o'clock? Earlier? Yet why would Ben be on the first flight? What was the rush? He wouldn't have to check out from the hotel until ten or eleven...

No, he hasn't left. I have plenty of time.

Still, she silently urged the cabbie to drive faster.

ΔΔΔ

"Would you like me to try again?" the woman behind the front desk at the Broadway Plaza Hotel asked.

Sally shook her head; the woman had already rung twice. Either Ben was passed out cold and didn't hear the phone, which she found hard to believe, or he had already left for the airport.

"Thanks anyway," she said, and headed for the hotel entrance, wondering what she would do now. Take a taxi to LaGuardia and hope to bump into Ben there? Fly to Camp Verde and find him *there*? She didn't like either option. Surprising him at his hotel was one thing; it was only a few blocks from her apartment. But following him to the airport without his knowledge? Flying halfway across the country? He would think she was a stalker.

Sally stepped outside onto the corner of Broadway. The sidewalk was congested with construction pylons and scaffolding and fast-walking pedestrians going about their morning routines. She started along West 27 Street toward Avenue of Americas, in the direction of her apartment, despite not having made up her mind on her plan.

Maybe she should take a taxi to the airport, after all? Yes, it was stalkerish. But Ben would likely be grateful to see her. He truly believed a pack of werewolves was holed up in Camp Verde. She might think it was nonsense (as she'd made clear to him outside Rizzoli's Bookstore the previous evening), but she didn't have to bring up werewolves or lycanthropy. She could tell him she wanted to investigate the inexplicable dancing that had been reported out there. Which was true. She *was* curious about it. She had experienced a bout of inexplicable dancing in Chatham thirty-one years ago. If something similar was happening in Camp Verde, she wanted to check it out herself.

Or you can just forget the entire thing, she thought with a tired sigh. *Go home, put your feet up, enjoy your Saturday.*

Not only did this option sound appealing; it sounded rational. The truth was, Sally didn't care about the dancing mania in Camp Verde. It would be due to some sort of mass hysteria, as had been the case in Chatham—and as had been the case for every episode of dancing mania recorded throughout the centuries. Because unlike werewolves, mass hysteria was real. It happened. It was an illness, a strange one admittedly, but an illness nonetheless. Case closed.

So why did she want to accompany Ben to Arizona? The answer to that was simple: she had feelings for him. She didn't know what exactly to make of those feelings, or how deep they ran. However, seeing him again yesterday after more than three decades had been a gut punch. He didn't much resemble the boy he had been. The gangly body and unkempt mop of brown hair and shyness were gone, replaced with an athletic build, a short haircut, and quiet confidence. Yet the kind, inquisitive blue eyes and the lopsided grin that she remembered were enough to tug at her heartstrings. She and Ben might have only bonded for a few short days in September of 1988, but their feelings for each other had been intense and real and trialed by fire during the night they were imprisoned in Ryders Field. In the years since, whenever Sally thought back to Ben and that forever-ago autumn, those three or four days they spent together seemed magical. Despite all the time that had passed, she felt as though she knew him better than she'd known anyone else in her life.

Of course, much of this could be attributed to nostalgia for her youth, a longing for a time when her life had been on track and her future had looked bright. Since then, her life had felt like one long downward slide. A crazy part of her—a part that thought there was purpose and meaning in the universe —flirted with the idea that she and Ben had met at Rizzoli's Bookstore for a reason. They were meant to be together, or something along those star-crossed lines.

The saner part of her understood their encounter was simply the result of a stroke of luck and a choice. The luck had been when she came across a review of Ben's latest book *The Dancing Plague* in the New York *Post*, and the reviewer had mentioned the launch party at Rizzoli's Bookstore. The choice: her decision to attend.

A stroke of luck and a choice.

Not very romantic, but what in life—at least, her life—ever was?

"Sally?

She stopped, surprised to hear her name.

"Sally? It's Ben."

She peered into a black SUV parked alongside the curb. The passenger-side window was down. Ben sat behind the steering wheel, grinning at her.

"Ben?" was all she could manage, squinting to make sure it was him. Then, "What are you doing…?"

"I'm about to head to the airport." His eyes went to her small travel bag.

"What are *you* doing?"

"I'm, uh—going to the airport too. Care to give me a lift?"

CHAPTER 2

THE FLIGHT

Sally climbed into the SUV, squeezing her bag into the footwell next to her feet.

Ben was frowning at her.

She smiled back. "Well?"

"Well?" he said.

"Shouldn't we get moving?"

"Where are you going?"

"LaGuardia."

"I mean—where are you flying?"

"Arizona."

"*Arizona*?" He laughed, though his confusion was clear. "Is this a joke?"

"No joke, Ben. It's why I came to your hotel. I've decided to go with you to Arizona."

"Ah, I don't think so..." he said, shaking his head.

"You don't want me to come?" Speaking those words out loud made her feel panicked and angry.

"No, I..." He ran a hand through his hair. "I mean, I haven't thought about it. But...*why*?"

"Yesterday we learned of a dancing plague in Camp Verde. They're not exactly a dime a dozen, are they? This is the first one I've heard of since what we experienced as kids. I want to check it out for myself."

He studied her for a long moment. "And the werewolves?"

"We have different recollections of '88," she hedged. "You say we were held captive in Ryders Field by werewolves, I say a cult of crazies. Tomayto, tomahto." He didn't appear amused. "Look, Ben, regardless of who—or what—held us captive in Ryders Field," she went on, "well, that's one thing. The dancing plague is another—"

"No, Sally, it's not," he said sharply. "It's related, all of it. That gypsy woman made people dance—made my *mother* dance—so they wouldn't turn into—"

"Werewolves. I know, Ben. I know what you believe. And it makes for good fiction—"

"It's *not* fiction, Sally!" he snapped. "What I wrote in my book is what happened."

"What you *think* happened. We were kids—"

"I'm not having this argument again," he said dismissively. He pressed a button and started the SUV's engine. "I appreciate your willingness to join me, Sally. But this is something I need to do on my own. I can drop you off at your apartment—"

"Why does it matter whether I believe in werewolves or not?" she demanded. "Why should that stop me from coming to Arizona with you?"

"It matters," he said tightly, "because you clearly don't appreciate what you would be getting involved in. Just like you didn't back in Ryders Field. I let you come with me then, and that decision almost got you killed. I'm not letting that happen again."

"And if there is a pack of werewolves in Camp Verde? Or a cult of lycanthropists? You're going to confront them?"

"I'm going to gather the proof they exist. If that involves confronting them, then I guess I'm going to confront them."

Sally did her best not to roll her eyes in frustration. "I'll be careful, okay?" she said, feeling disingenuous (and a little childish) for implying danger lurked in Camp Verde when she knew very well that it did not.

"No, Sally—"

"You can't stop me from coming, Ben! You want to uncover

werewolves, fine. I want to learn more about the dancing plague." She had more to say but held her tongue. She'd said enough; anything more would be going in circles.

A tense silence ensued. The air conditioner hummed, blowing cool air from the vents. The vehicle smelled brand new, and the engine purred smoothly. Outside their bubble the sounds of the city—jackhammers, traffic, a car horn—seemed muted and far away.

Reluctantly, Ben put the SUV in gear and pulled onto West 27 Street. "Were you always this stubborn?" he grunted without taking his eyes from the road.

Sally turned her head to look out the passenger-side window —so he wouldn't see her smiling.

∆∆∆

As the Boeing 737-700 soared at thirty-thousand feet, Sally preoccupied herself by skimming through a duty-free magazine. Ben, seated to her left, was listening to music on his phone through a pair of earbuds. The passenger to her right was a large man with a ruddy face whose beefy forearm and clumsy elbow took up most of their shared armrest. A few minutes after the jet had reached cruising altitude and the seatbelt sign had pinged off, he'd grabbed a backpack from the overhead bin and produced a mammoth LED-emblazoned laptop that occupied his entire lap. He wore a bulky headset over his ears and held a gaming controller in his hands as he played Fortnight. The laptop's fans sounded as loud as a hair dryer, and the constant mashing of the buttons on the controller was driving Sally crazy. She gave up on the duty-free magazine, stuffing it back into the pocket on the seat in front of her. She considered getting up to stretch her legs but decided not to, given the inconvenience of getting past the big man and his gaming setup. Instead she took out her iPhone and purchased a two-hour WiFi pass. She checked her emails and then did a Google search for "Camp Verde Dancing Plague."

Halfway down the first page of results (most of which seemed attributed to a French recording artist) a headline announced: DANCING OUTBREAK REPORTED IN AZ TOWN.

Sally clicked the link and began reading:

In a saga gripping the small Arizona town of Camp Verde, nine patients at the Oasis Mountain Academy, a mental-health facility that serves both adolescents and adults, have been dancing in a continuous, trance-like state for multiple days, showing no interest in food, water, or rest.

According to Camp Verde sheriff Russell Walker, pastors in the area have gathered at the health center to embark on spiritual intervention, offering special prayer sessions while purifying the area of negative energy. "The Lord works in mysterious ways," Walker told reporters at a news conference earlier in the day. "Right now sustained prayer is our best bet to counter whatever unseen forces are at play in our town." When questioned about the cause of the dancing outbreak, the sheriff said he had seen no evidence to suggest that either a communicable disease or environmental factors were involved. "The investigation is ongoing. But we'll get to the bottom of it, don't worry about that."

Cindy Finke, a cocktail server at the local Cliff Castle Casino, told The Verde Valley *Independent* that her younger sister, Anna, was one of the patients affected by "the dancing bug," a moniker that many in Camp Verde have begun using to refer to the unusual behavior of the patients. "When I went out there after my shift to visit, she was just there, in her tiny bedroom, dancing like a fool, not a care in the world. She wouldn't talk to me. I don't think she could even hear me. She was just…not on drugs but way out there if you know what I mean? I couldn't stop her either. I tried, but she threw a fit, swinging at me and screaming. She's never done anything like that before. I was a little scared, to be honest."

As strange as a "dancing bug" may sound, it is not a completely unknown phenomenon. Several documented episodes of this kind of dancing mania date back to medieval times. Perhaps the best known was the Dancing Plague of 1518, during which hundreds of people began dancing together spontaneously, many of whom collapsed in exhaustion, or ultimately died from the exertion put on their bodies.

While this may sound like something out of a paranormal movie, one expert from the Arizona Department of Health has a more plausible explanation. Dr. Amelia Gloyne told the *Independent* that she believes the dancing is a form of mass hysteria based on a syndrome of acute fear. "Mass hysteria is not as rare as you may believe," she explained. "In 2002 students across various grade levels at a rural North Carolinian high school began having unexplained seizures. In 2007 students in Virginia experienced an outbreak of headaches and fainting that lasted months. More recently, an epidemic of hiccupping spread through two high schools in Massachusetts. Make no mistake, these are genuine symptoms. They have nothing to do with a TikTok challenge or any of that nonsense."

Sally sat back in her seat. Now that was a theory never contemplated in Chatham in 1988: a TikTok challenge. It reinforced just how much the world had changed in the last thirty years. In 1988 there were no mobile phones, internet, or social media. What happened in a small town like Chatham stayed there, gaining little attention outside of the local airwaves. Today, of course, you could find out what was happening in any corner of the planet with a simple Google search, as she had just done. In fact, she wouldn't be surprised if there were videos of the Camp Verde dancing plague on YouTube or Instagram.

A chill slipped beneath her skin as she recalled the woman she had seen dancing on the night that she, Ben, and Chunky had gone to Light Beach. How many other dancers had there been in Chatham? There was the elementary school teacher that she and Ben had seen on the news. And the assistant teacher in the apartment across Main Street from Ben's friend's place. And of course Ben's mother, who had been sedated and taken to the hospital. Two people had died in Chatham that same week. Ben had overheard his father and the sheriff saying that they both had bruised and bleeding feet.

Fortunately, Sally thought, it seemed nobody in Camp Verde had died yet.

But how long until someone does?

She was about to open the YouTube app on her phone when the big man next to her slapped the lid closed on his laptop. The fans, thank God, shut down.

He tugged off his headset and grinned sheepishly at her. "Battery don't last too long while gaming," he said.

"I imagine not," she told him.

He looked past her to Ben, who had nodded off, his head leaning against the porthole window, the earbuds still in his ears. "What brings you and your husband to Arizona?"

"He's not my husband. We're old friends."

"Ah," the man said, and Sally recognized the change in his eyes. Although she was getting on in years—forty-four already, if you can believe that (she couldn't)—she had remained in shape and kept a rather youthful appearance through exercise and eating well. Consequently, she still got a lot of looks from men. This pleased her—it was nice to feel attractive—even though she never gave them too much thought. She'd been there, done that, and it had led to sixteen years of marriage hell.

She had met her husband while in her sophomore year at college, where she had studied political science. His name was Mortimer Adler, a bright, charming law student. The following year she got pregnant. Mort wanted her to get an abortion. She ended up keeping the baby, a beautiful girl they named Valerie. While she dropped out of college to raise their child, Mort earned his law degree and passed the bar exam. Soon after they married during a small ceremony in upstate New York. Although she didn't love Mort, she was scared to death of becoming a single mom. And if Mort loved her, he rarely showed it. Why he proposed to her, she didn't know. Maybe he believed being married would help him climb the ranks in the close-knit, family-run law firm he had joined. Whatever the reason, their marriage was a sham.

Sally woke early and went to sleep early, mirroring Valerie's daily routine; Mort, on the other hand, worked extremely late hours, including most weekends. The result was that they often went an entire week without seeing one another. She was confident he was seeing other women, although she turned a blind eye to his infidelity. He was providing for Valerie and, well...Sally realized she didn't really care. She'd learned during those early years of their marriage that you didn't need to love your husband to lead a fulfilling life. Her daughter was her everything, and that was enough to get her through each day.

Ten days after Valerie's fifteenth birthday, she was struck by a car while walking home from school. She died hours later at the hospital. The eighteen-year-old driver tested positive for crystal methamphetamine and was currently serving an eight-year prison sentence.

Sally's grief was indescribable. She moved in with her mother, as Mort was no comfort to her. He sent her divorce papers through the mail two weeks later. Sally's black depression lasted years, during which she often thought about taking her own life. It was only earlier this year when she gave up the anti-depressants and other medications she'd been taking that she started to feel a little bit again like her old self. She still thought about Valerie every day, but she no longer cried when she did so.

So...dating again? A relationship? Thanks but no thanks.

Which made the feelings she had discovered she had for Ben so remarkable.

"You're not from Arizona, I take it?" the large man said.

"I'm from New York," Sally replied.

"I'm from Phoenix. Was in New York on business. So, err... if you're interested in seeing some of the sights, I have the day off. I'd be happy to show you around?"

"We're not sightseeing," she said pointedly.

"Oh no? What are you doing then?"

Sally realized the man wasn't likely to take a hint. God forbid, he might spend the next five hours chatting her up. "We're, um, going to..." She was about to make up a fib—a friend's wedding? a visit with relatives?—when she changed her mind. "We're investigating a dancing plague."

The man raised his eyebrows. "A dancing plague? What the hell is that?"

"Some teenagers in Camp Verde have started dancing in a trance. They can't control themselves or stop. They've been going for days."

"Jesus Lordy Christ. I've never heard of such a thing! What's wrong with them? They having some sort of nervous breakdown?"

"They're most likely werewolves," she deadpanned.

He blinked at her. "Werewolves?"

"They're dancing so they don't change into beasts during the full moon tomorrow night."

The man chuckled mirthfully. "Is that so? What's so bad with changing into a werewolf?" He winked at her. "They *ethical* werewolves? They don't want to feast on the blood of innocents, huh?"

"The master werewolf doesn't want them to. Too many werewolves on the loose will blow their cover. So it's tracked down everyone who's been infected with the disease, probably by a rogue member of its pack, and put them in a dancing trance. That stops you from turning."

The man chuckled again, though he now seemed uncertain as to whether she was pulling his leg or not. "And this master werewolf can just put people in a trance like that, huh? How does that work?"

"It has psychic powers. It can make you do things just by looking at you."

"Gotcha. And how, err, do you know all this, missy? Are *you* a werewolf?"

"When my friend and I were kids, a dancing plague occurred in our town. We traced its origin to the master werewolf. It caught us and locked us in a circus wagon during a full moon. We saw people turn. It was pretty horrific."

"This the same master werewolf that's now in Camp Verde?"

"We don't know yet. That's why we're going there. To get some answers."

"All right then!" the man said with put-upon blitheness. He shifted his bulk in his seat and took a hardcover book from the backpack at his feet. "You folks have a good time in Arizona, you hear? Good luck with...everything."

He didn't speak to Sally again for the rest of the flight.

CHAPTER 3

MONSTER'S WORLD

Eugene "Monster" Bailey packed the bowl of the glass bong with marijuana and took a hit. He held the smoke in his lungs for a good five seconds, exhaled, then wheeled the chair he was seated in across the floor to the red bar fridge. He took out a Monster Energy drink (he drank a half dozen of the cans each day, hence his nickname), then wheeled the chair back to his computer desk.

The desk was decked out with all the latest technology. An ultra-widescreen monitor with a fast refresh rate and curved display. A custom-made tower PC boasting a state-of-the-art CPU and GPU, which allowed him to play all the latest video games. A wireless mouse and a backlit mechanical keyboard. A professional microphone and a top-of-the-line webcam.

Monster cracked open the energy drink, chugged a good amount, then turned up the volume of the Jefferson Airplane song streaming on Spotify. The LED lights on the Logitech speakers flashed with the beat.

Despite being a straight-A student, Monster had dropped out of school last year when he was sixteen. He'd decided he wasn't going to learn anything he couldn't simply look up on his phone. To make some cash he got a part-time job at McDonald's. However, he had been fired six months ago for consistently showing up late. He suspected his manager had also known he was high all the time, which more than likely factored into her decision to can him. Monster hadn't cared one way or the other. It had been a shitty job, and the other staff had been shitheads. They were either kids his age, working weekends or after school on weekdays, or older fucks who couldn't find better work elsewhere. The only person he'd liked had been a seventy-year-old grandpa named Mike who was working there for something to do with his days. He had some form of dementia because he could never remember anything (which was likely why his main responsibility was flipping burger patties). Yet despite his patchy short-term memory, he had been able to recall the Vietnam War as though it had happened yesterday, and he had often regaled Monster with some pretty dope stories.

Anyway, getting fired turned out to be the best thing for him, allowing him to dedicate his time to becoming a YouTube content creator. His channel focused on streaming the latest triple-A video games. Viewers found his content and humor and laid-back personality interesting because he was gaining about ten thousand new subscribers a month. This had earned him enough cash not only to purchase the baller gaming rig and top-of-the-line accessories but to grow his savings account (especially since he lived in his parent's basement and didn't pay room and board).

Monster had been experimenting with podcasts as well. His current weekly series was called Monster's World. He typically invited other popular gamers onto his show, but he had also begun branching out to include chats with indie musicians and authors.

Today's show was special. It featured an interview with a bestselling author from Seattle who had written a book on the so-called Dancing Plague of 1588. Monster was looking forward to the chat enormously since a dozen girls from Camp Verde High School had recently been afflicted with a dancing bug themselves (the reason he'd sought out the author in the first place).

The computer beeped, indicating his guest had joined the scheduled Zoom meeting.

Monster closed the Spotify app, hit the bong again, then started the video conference. His profile picture was a selfie he'd taken a few weeks ago. For the most part it looked like him: rusty-colored hair, black-rimmed glasses, pug nose, thin lips. He'd also used a few filters to erase his acne and give his sallow complexion more warmth.

"Yo, yo, yo," he said into his microphone. "Can you hear me, Luke?"

"Yes, Monster, I can hear you. Thanks for having me."

The podcasts were always audio only; Monster didn't want to risk interrupting the sound quality by streaming video.

"Thank *you* for agreeing to chat today, my man. As you know, your book is pretty damn timely given what's been happening here in Verde. So let me do the spiel for those listening, and then we'll dive right into it." He hit a button on the keyboard that played some canned intro music. "Today I'm thrilled to have the Wall Street *Journal* bestselling author, Luke Meyers, on the program to talk to us about dancing. That's right, dancing. But not the foxtrot or salsa. We're going to be talking about some much stranger shit than that, so sit tight and get ready to have your mind blown." He ended the music. "All right, Luke, why don't you start by telling us a bit about your book? Why were you interested in writing about something that happened five hundred years ago?"

"Well, Monster, I'm a historian first and foremost, and I've always been drawn to the more esoteric topics not usually covered by others in my field. When I retired and began writing novels full time, the dancing plague in Alsace, France was too irresistible to pass up."

"Can you give us some background on... Okay, let's speak bluntly. What the hell *is* a 'dancing plague'? It sounds so ridiculous."

"Dancing plague, dancing epidemic, dancing mania, call it what you want, Monster. However, I believe the best way to understand the phenomenon is to think of it as a kind of mass hysteria, which in medicine is referred to as a mass psychogenic illness. It occurs when symptoms of an illness, whether real or imaginary, are transmitted through a population or society at large, even though there is no bacterial, environmental, or pathogenic cause."

"They just make the shit up?"

"That's one way to put it, sure."

"But why?"

"Well, that's the question, isn't it? Understand, Monster, the human mind is an incredibly powerful and complex organ, one that we don't know as much about as we may like to believe, one that often works in mysterious ways. Yet having said that, the theory about the cause of mass hysteria is some sort of root fear and anxiety that prompts individuals to believe something that isn't real. Let me give you a relatable example. We've just been through Covid-19, a once-in-a-century pandemic. This fast-spreading virus came seemingly out of the blue. Nobody knew anything about it, which made people anxious. It's a natural human response to fear what we don't know, to try to put answers to what we don't understand. So it wasn't surprising that you had a lot of people, including well-educated folks, buying into conspiracy theories. A Satanic cabal released the virus as part of their preparation for the global Antichrist takeover. It escaped from a Chinese lab. It was a plot by Big Pharma. It was created as a biological weapon. It was the evil machinations of Bill Gates to depopulate the world. Moreover, people's anxiety and fear, and paranoia of catching the virus, became so acute that you then basically had people throwing common sense out the window and ignoring recommended precautions by reputable agencies such as the CDC. They became fear-mongers, panic-buying groceries and toilet paper and spreading misinformation online. It was a vicious circle: the more this went on, the more anxiety and fear was generated in the general public, ultimately building into what became a kind of worldwide mass hysteria."

"But nobody started dancing in the middle of the streets."

"There are many subbranches of mass hysteria. The one

you are referring to—people spontaneously dancing in the street—is an extreme case of motor hysteria. That is, the fear and anxiety in a group of people become so great, so overwhelming, that this kind of irrational, physiological, externalizing behavior, is the only way they can process it."

"They lose their shit."

"They believe, Monster, at least subconsciously, that they need to express their stress bodily because it allows them to sort of say, 'Hey, look at me, I'm suffering here! I'm not simply depressed or withdrawn. I'm really hurting and need help.' Consequently, when you have other people experiencing extreme stress, they—again, subconsciously—copy the symptoms they see. It's important to note, Monster, that motor hysteria does not always involve dancing. It can manifest itself as laughter, fainting, nausea, vomiting, weeping, anything. Any kind of abnormal physiological behavior. And if you're curious about the demographics, those affected are more commonly—not always, but more commonly—young rather than old, female rather than male, and employee rather than employer."

"Do you have any examples of non-dancing stuff?"

"How long do we have on this podcast?" The author chuckled. "To name an episode off the top of my head—it happened not too long ago in Lafayette, Indiana. Some workers at a DMV became sick with the same respiratory disease. The building was repeatedly shut down, but when no contaminants were found, the DMV was ultimately moved to a new location. In the end officials determined a mass psychogenic illness was to blame. The DMV had been such a terrible place to work—the environment, the managers—a low-level employee convinced himself he had respiratory disease. All his coworkers collectively and subconsciously began copying the imaginary symptoms he manifested. It sounds crazy, right? But it's not as crazy, or as rare, as one would think."

"It *is* crazy," Monster said. "Batshit crazy. So let's talk about

Camp Verde, yeah? Let's walk through this for those who don't know what's been happening here. There's this girl, Mary Porter, from the high school. I used to know her. Very normal chick. She goes camping with her friend, Elise Becerra, and Elise's parents, in the desert east of town last month, and something fucked up happened. Something really fucked up. 'Cause when they found Mary hiding by some rock, she was sent to a psych ward, and Elise and her parents have never been seen again. What happened that night? Nobody knows. Something happened though. Something pretty fucking awful, 'cause the Becerras, you know, they're probably dead, and Mary is, like, insane. Pretty much a vegetable."

"What you've described, Monster, is extremely tragic, and my heart goes out to the victims and their families. After you got in touch with me, I did some research myself. There wasn't much online except a few stories by the local paper. The police still have no idea what might have happened in the desert?"

"No, man. There was a big search, but they found nothing. And like I said, Mary won't talk because she's so fucked up. Then last week she just broke into dancing in the psych ward."

"Which is how most cases of mass psychogenic illness usually begin, with one individual."

"Right, so she starts dancing, and then so do half the kids on the ward."

"Troubled children dealing with higher levels of stress and anxiety than most of us. In other words, a high-risk population for this kind of thing."

"Well, a couple of girls at the high school, friends of Mary, visited her a few times at the psych ward, and then they started dancing two days ago. By noon yesterday, there were about ten or eleven girls and a couple of dudes, all in the same grade, my age, dancing. Like, what the fuck? They're all super stressed too? About what?"

"I can't answer that for certain. As I mentioned, the mind works in mysterious ways. But as I also mentioned, females, especially teenagers, are more susceptible to this kind of behavior than other demographics. Interestingly, not too long ago, about twenty students in a New York high school, almost all of them female and friends with one another, began experiencing involuntary Tourette Syndrome-like jerks and tics. Their limbs, neck, or face would suddenly spasm, or they would twitch, grunt, or shout uncontrollably. Some had seizures. They were examined by the school nurses, doctors, and even officials from the CDC and Columbia University. There was no biological explanation for their behavior. The school was checked for mold, lead, carbon monoxide, and other environmental contaminants. All the tests came back negative. Nobody ever figured out what caused their symptoms."

"But they all recovered?"

"Within a few days, yes. So I wouldn't worry too much about your friends."

"Okay, but the girls in Camp Verde aren't just having tics and seizures. That's fucked, I know. But the girls here are *dancing*, man. That's really fucked. I guess this is a good lead into your book?"

"Sure, so my book—*The Dancing Plague of 1518: An Incredible True Story*—focuses on the dancing plague of 1518 in what was then the Holy Roman Empire, which is now France. To give you some context, the earliest recorded outbreak of a dancing epidemic occurred in Europe in the 7th century. Since then, it's reoccured numerous times across Europe, from England to Germany to the Netherlands, until about the 17th century, when they seemed to peter out. Now the one I wrote about, the one in July, 1518, in Strasbourg, involved a woman named Frau Troffea. She began dancing in her street unwillingly and uncontrollably for days on end. At one point she collapsed from exhaustion, but then she got up again and continued dancing. The city elders believed she was possessed by madness or demons. But then one of her neighbors began dancing too. Then another one. By the end of the first week, more than thirty people were dancing night and day on the streets of the city."

"And there's actual proof of all this?"

"That's a good question, Monster, and the answer is, yes, there is a surprising amount of documentation. The event was chronicled by the civic and religious authorities of the time. There are even medical records of some of the dancers who died from heart attacks and strokes. For some inexplicable reason the cure for the dancing was believed to be more dancing. So the authorities erected a wooden stage for the dancers, musicians were called in, and professional dancers were hired to encourage the dancers to keep dancing. In the end, as many as four hundred people were afflicted. And then finally, in early September, the mania stopped just as mysteriously as it began."

"And you believe it had something to do with, like you said, some kind of serious fear and anxiety?"

"Extreme stress, yes. Even by the standards of the 16th century, the people in Strasbourg had it rough. Famine and malnutrition were rampant then, as well as smallpox and syphilis and numerous other diseases. It wasn't a great time to be alive."

"You mentioned the dancing plagues petered out about a century or so later. Any ideas why?"

"It turns out they haven't petered out completely, have they, given what's happening in Camp Verde? But in general, what happened to them? If you ask me, I don't think they have so much disappeared as been replaced with other behaviors."

"Like?"

"Laughing. You see, laughter serves the same cathartic purpose as dance. Both reduce stress hormones and increase endorphins, providing physical and psychological relief from distress. It sounds like a classic Freudian theory, doesn't it? We build up psychic pressure, which is released through dance or laughter, through whatever metaphorical valve we have for that."

"So laughing manias...I haven't heard of any of that shit."

"They are, in fact, rather commonplace in modern times. The most famous case happened in Tanzania, then Tanganyika, in 1962. The laughter began, once again, with a small group of young girls, teenagers, before spreading through much of their school. Their symptoms—incapacitating laughter that in some cases led to fainting, respiratory problems, and severe pain—lasted anywhere from a few hours to a couple of weeks. The school shut down, but the epidemic spread to other villages and, eventually, more than a dozen other schools, affecting a thousand students and ensuing for several months."

"What could stress out so many students?"

"Tanzania had just won independence before the outbreak, so the students—who had been enrolled in British mission-run boarding schools—were facing a lot of uncertainties. But again, who really knows for sure? Now, what's even more fascinating is that similar laughing epidemics, admittedly on a much smaller scale, occur weekly around the world. You don't hear much about them because they occur largely in impoverished and neglected regions such as Kosovo, Afghanistan, and Southeast Asia."

"Well, Luke," Monster said, "you've been awesome, man, and I think a lot of people in Verde, if they've been listening, they're gonna be really grateful. They're gonna appreciate you telling 'em what's been going on, man. So…I guess we can wrap things up now, but I'd love to have you on again sometime. Maybe in another week or two when we see what happens with all the dancing here?"

"Hopefully everything will be back to normal in Camp Verde by then."

"I hear ya. Definitely. Fingers crossed this bug is squashed sooner than later. Peace out, Luke." Monster played his canned closing music. "And that's it for today's episode of Monster's World everyone! Thanks for tuning in, and let me end on this note. The next time you decide to get down and boogie, feel free to do it like nobody is watching—but for fuck's sake, stop when the music stops."

CHAPTER 4

CATCHING UP

The Hertz at Sky Harbor Airport had been short on rental cars. Aside from those in the economy class (which Ben had described as sewing machines on wheels), there had only been a Toyota Tacoma pickup truck and a Chevrolet Camaro convertible. They opted for the Camaro... and discovered in the parking lot that it had a fluorescent yellow paint job that very well might have glowed in the dark.

Now they were speeding along a highway that cut straight through the Sonoran Desert. Ahead, heat phantoms shimmered across the blacktop, and mirages of other cars and bodies of water popped in and out of existence. The land, baked under months of unrelenting heat, was mostly flat and brown and dotted with hardy shrubs and the occasional gray tumbleweed. Far in the distance rounded foothills rose against the brilliant blue and cloud-streaked sky. The sunlight was so bright that Sally's eyes felt tired and abraded if she looked too long in any direction.

They had been on the road for nearly thirty minutes now. Sally was sipping the dregs of a Starbucks latte and found that she was enjoying herself. It was good to be out of New York, on a road trip, doing something. It sure beat her dreary routine of...well...did doing nothing each day count as a routine? She supposed it did. Moreover, she appreciated the change in environment from the East Coast. It might be rugged and inhospitable, but it was also quietly sublime and calming.

"So—what the hell have you been up to these past thirty years?" Ben asked her abruptly, breaking the comfortable silence that had settled between them over the last few miles.

Sally had known this question was coming at some point, and although she didn't want to talk about her past, she nevertheless settled on bluntness. "I got married when I was young, still in college. We had a daughter named Valerie. She was beautiful, smart...and just such a damn good kid." Sally paused, her throat tight. "She was killed five years ago. She had just turned fifteen."

"I'm sorry," Ben said, glancing momentarily at her. "I'm so sorry, Sally..." He seemed about to ask what happened but didn't.

She told him anyway. "She was struck by a car while walking home from school. The driver was an eighteen-year-old kid on drugs." She couldn't keep the bitterness from her voice. The Christian thing to do was to forgive and move on—and Sally was Catholic, albeit non-practicing—but how did you forgive a meth-head who got behind the wheel of a car while high and ran over your daughter?

Ben squeezed her leg, just above the knee.

It was a simple gesture of support, but Sally felt it in her heart. Steeling herself against tears, she said, "My husband filed for divorce shortly thereafter. Not that I cared. He was an asshole. I didn't love him. I would have arranged the paperwork myself...but I wasn't in the mindset, not then. I moved in with my mother. It was only going to be temporary, but somehow it stretched into four long years. God, I love her, but she lives in this little two-bedroom apartment in the Bronx and...I don't know how well you remember my mom, but she can be a handful, to put it mildly."

"Your parents sold the big place in Chatham?"

"That's right. You skipped town before all the drama began."

Ben frowned. "What drama?"

"Do you know what my mother did for a living?"

He shook his head. "Just that she made a lot of money."

"She founded a technology company in the early eighties that promised to be a big player in the home computer market. She raised millions of dollars from investors, though she was a much better salesperson than CEO, because the core technology she was bragging about never worked. Faking it until you make it, sums up my mom, I guess. Unfortunately faking it in this case and making false claims also meant defrauding investors. Worse than that, it was alleged she knew about the problems and lied to cover them up. Cover-ups are always worse than the crime, right? She settled the civil action by giving up her majority stake and voting rights in the company and paying a massive fine that pretty much bankrupted her. Later, she was charged criminally with wire fraud. That earned her two years in prison. While she was locked up, my dad married someone my age and moved to Mexico. I haven't seen him since."

"Christ, Sally. I had no idea. Your mom and dad always seemed so happy."

A tear came—for Valerie, or for her mom, she didn't know —and she wiped it away. "You know what Chunky would say right now? 'Aren't you full of cheery news, shithead.'"

They both laughed, and she felt a little better.

She exhaled sharply. "I'm sorry," she said. "I'm just...a bit emotional about this stuff."

"It's good seeing you again," Ben told her. "I'm glad you came down here with me."

"That's a relief. I was feeling a bit...unwanted for a while."

"Unwanted? Never. I was just... Well, we've already discussed all that." He overtook a white sedan that was doing eighty and returned to the right lane. "So Donut Boy, huh? What the hell ever happened to that guy?"

"Do you remember that time at my house? He actually guessed every single flavor in the box of donuts."

"A man of many talents. Do you keep in touch with him?"

She shook her head. "After you left Chatham, I never really spoke with him anymore. He was your friend, not mine."

"You must have seen him around?"

"Sure. Chatham's not a huge place. We'd say hi and stuff but that was all. We never hung out. We're friends on Facebook now though. You should see his friend list. It's like a who's-who of everybody from Chatham in those days."

Ben huffed. "Why am I not surprised? He didn't have many friends at school. Guess he's trying to re-write history."

"He's a doctor now."

Ben shot her a skeptical look. "A doctor?"

Sally nodded. "A pediatrician." She couldn't help but feel a tinge of jealousy at Chunky's success. She wasn't surprised that Ben had become a famous novelist. As a kid he had been thoughtful and imaginative and had a good head on his shoulders—characteristics she believed applied to herself too. Chunk had been the underachiever. Wily, yes, but lazy and a bit dense. He was the one you'd expect to be unemployed and adrift at your high school reunion. Yet there he was, a pediatrician with his own practice, a beautiful wife, and two kids.

Ben still seemed unconvinced. "Chunk went to *med school*?"

"You should see his profile picture. White lab coat and stethoscope and all."

"Is he still fat?"

She shook her head. "Not like he used to be. And he has a really pretty wife. He's always posting pictures of them together. I'm surprised he never sent you a friend request."

"Maybe he did. I don't use Facebook."

Sally knew that; she had stalked Ben online once, curious to see what he had been up to with himself. That had been several years ago, and his last post had been years before that, a link to his first published book on the publisher's website.

"Why not?" she asked him.

He shrugged. "Don't know. Feels too much like looking back, I guess. Too many people I used to know."

"You're not interested in what they're doing with their lives?"

"I'm interested in people who are in my life now. And if I want to know what they're doing, I'll go out and have a good bottle of wine and a nice dinner with them."

Sally thought she wouldn't mind having a good bottle of wine and a nice dinner with Ben. Back at Rizzoli's Bookstore she had noticed he wasn't wearing a wedding band. Nevertheless, she asked, "Is there a Mrs. Graves?"

"There is not."

The tautness in her chest eased. "Take it from me," she told him, "marriage is overrated."

"I was married once. Young like you—just out of college."

"Really?" she said, surprised they had this in common. "What happened?"

"I didn't live up to her expectations."

"Must have been some pretty high expectations?"

"I did well in college, grades-wise. Stephanie, my ex, thought I had a good future after I graduated. It was her idea to get married so young."

"Wanted to lock you in."

"I suppose. And in fact, I got a solid marketing job right off the bat. But after a year I decided I couldn't do that kind of thing."

"What kind of thing?"

"The office thing. The suit-and-tie thing. I decided to take a break and travel through Canada, where I ended up living in a camp and planting trees for four months. Steph and I stayed together, did the long-distance thing. She thought when I returned I was going to get back into marketing. I didn't. I had about twenty grand saved from the tree planting—there wasn't anywhere to spend it where I was stationed in northern Ontario—so I just bummed around for a while. When the money ran out, I started waiting tables. By then, our friends were getting good jobs like the marketing one I had. Steph wasn't impressed that I'd gone backward. We started fighting more and more. Eventually...we got divorced. It was sort of mutual. We just weren't on the same page."

"Did you know you wanted to be a writer then?"

"Nope. That was the problem. I knew what I *didn't* want—I didn't want a boss, someone telling me what to do for the rest of my life—but I didn't know what I wanted. But fuck it, I was twenty-five. I felt like I had a lot of time to work things out."

"You must have been about...what, thirty, when you wrote your first book?"

"Twenty-nine. I was working the front desk night shift at a hotel. There was this one creepy guy staying in a room on the top floor. Each night he returned from wherever he'd been between three and four in the morning with this huge backpack on, like those backpackers in Europe have."

"Was he a backpacker?"

Ben shook his head. "The hotel was in downtown Boston. Where was he going sightseeing every day that he needed that much stuff? And why wasn't he getting back until the early hours of the morning?"

She was intrigued. "So...?"

"So I began bantering around ideas. One that I liked was that he was a kind of anonymous, Batman-like vigilante. He went out at night and fought crime. He couldn't wear his costume in or out of the hotel obviously, so it was in the bag, along with all his weapons and stuff."

"Did he change in a phone booth?" she teased.

"Well, somewhere. The scenarios I made up in my head were amusing, and I began to write them down, mostly because I had nothing else to do all night. Then one night, the last night I saw the guy, he came back like he usually did when just about everyone else in the city was still sleeping. Only this time he had blood on his face and shirt."

"Holy moly! Did he get in a fight?"

"I have no idea."

"You didn't ask him what happened?"

"I asked if he needed any help. He ignored me, and I never saw him again. But I couldn't stop thinking about him. And you know, sitting by yourself for hours in the middle of the night in a small, empty hotel lobby—the hotel was probably a hundred years old and had a haunted-house vibe to it—gets your imagination going. But then my thinking turned darker. That's when I came up with the idea for—"

"*The Sack Man,*" she said.

"You read my first book?"

"I've read all of them. I never knew *The Sack Man* was based on a true story."

"The guy with the backpack was real. Everything else was made up."

Sally remembered the plot from his book and quipped, "You mean, there's no such thing as a bogeyman that feeds on human children each night?"

"Before I started working at the hotel, I spent a year or so traveling through South America, teaching here and there. I heard about the Sack Man from some of my students. It was their version of the bogeyman. It hauls naughty children in its sack back to its lair, where it eats them. So when I saw this guy with this big bag coming and going from the hotel each night, I thought—well, what if a bogeyman was holed up on the top floor of the hotel? It wouldn't be able to run around downtown Boston snatching children off the streets; it would need a servant, a familiar, to bring it food." He shrugged. "That was the basic idea. I spent each night working out the story and writing it down. I finished the final draft in about six months."

"Did you think it would be published?"

"No chance in hell! I'd never written a book before, and I didn't think the writing was great. Also, I didn't think the story was commercially viable. You've read it. Some pretty sadistic stuff went down in the Sack Man's room. And the violence was toward kids."

"But only really naughty kids."

"Still, kids are kids. I figured that would be too disturbing or extreme for a general audience."

"Yet you found a publisher?"

"One of the first agents I queried requested the manuscript.

She got back to me in a few days. You know what she said? 'I don't think anyone will *enjoy* reading this book, but I think they *need* to.' I didn't know what she meant back then."

"But now?"

"The story might have been brutally violent, but it wasn't violence for the sake of violence. It was an allegory about human nature, and the depths of depravity that we're capable of doing to one another, especially to children. It shone a light on issues that nobody would talk about because they're just too disturbing, but they're issues that we should be talking about, or at least acknowledging."

"To be honest," she told him, "I almost couldn't finish the book. But I did, and I haven't been able to forget it either. None of your other books are that dark."

"That wasn't a conscious decision. Another plot that dark just never came to mind. But as tough as *The Sack Man* was to write—I mean, getting into that kind of headspace—it was nothing compared to the last book." He hesitated. "Whether what happened Chatham in '88 was supernatural or not, Sally —we disagree, and that's fine, I'll leave it at that—something *still happened*. We were held captive and subjected to…I guess you'd call it a kind of psychological torture. People died, my dad died. That night was real and traumatic. Reliving it to get it down on paper was the hardest thing I've had to do in my life."

Sally quietly absorbed that, while at the same time acknowledging the unreality of the moment. This morning she had been in New York with nothing more interesting planned for the day than a stroll to the nearby café for her daily coffee. And now she was speeding through the Arizona desert with someone she hadn't seen in thirty-one years yet with whom she felt completely at ease, discussing what had happened all those years ago.

What made everything even more unreal, however, was just how different their recollections from their childhoods were. How could Ben—clearly an intelligent man—truly believe that they had been held captive by a pack of werewolves? She kept waiting for him to tell her this was all a gag. He didn't believe in werewolves. He was just down here to investigate the dancing plague, perhaps as research for a sequel to his last book.

Of course, she knew it wasn't a gag. Ben really did believe in werewolves, and he really did think he was going to find a pack of them in Camp Verde, perhaps the same pack he was convinced had been in Chatham.

In any event he was right about one thing: that night in Ryders Field had been real and traumatic. In the immediate aftermath she too had believed that their captors had been werewolves. She'd had nightmares about them for months. Her parents had been concerned enough about her mental well-being they'd arranged for her to see a psychiatrist in Boston. The woman assured Sally that the werewolves didn't exist, that they were the product of her imagination, her mind's way of coping with the horrible event she had endured.

Clearly Ben hadn't received that kind of therapy, and his childhood imaginings had stayed with him ever since. Rather than fading with time, they had strengthened so that even now, as an adult, he continued to blend reality with fiction.

So what would come of this trip to Camp Verde? What would they find there? A case of mass hysteria, certainly. That had already been reported in the media. But gypsies? Werewolves? Of course not. Ben would have to accept the same conclusion that she had come to all those years ago.

Monsters do exist, yes, but they are always human.

The other kind lives solely in one's mind.

A green road sign announced that Camp Verde was two miles away.

"Almost there," she said, for the sake of saying something.

CHAPTER 5
THE DETOUR

Ben slowed down and said, "What the hell is this?"
Ahead of them more than a hundred cattle blocked the two-lane highway—and there wasn't a rancher in sight.

"Honk the horn," Sally suggested.

Ben hit the Camaro's horn. Some of the animals looked nonchalantly at the vehicle. None moved out of the way.

"Great," he said.

"Can you go around them?"

"Off-road in this car?"

"Should have rented the pickup truck."

"We're going to have to find another way into town," Ben said as he put the car in reverse. After completing a three-point turn, he accelerated up to the speed limit.

"Can farmers simply let their cattle roam like that?" Sally asked, amused. She took out her phone and opened her map app. Two highways fed into the town, the one they were on and another angling northwest to southeast. She zoomed in on the area. "If you make a right onto…State Route 169 in about a mile or so, it looks like you can make another right onto a little road that leads up through…a place called Cherry. The road branches off here and there"—she followed the winding line with her finger—"but, yeah, it looks like it continues up to Camp Verde."

△△△

The single-lane dirt road cut northwest through the desert. The landscape was surprisingly alive with grasses, chaparral, and other shrubland plants that thrived in the harsh environment. Saguaros towered dozens of feet into the air like green alien hands. Far above in the sky a hawk wheeled in a predatory circle.

After a few miles the road transitioned from dirt to gravel— not ideal for a low-slung sports car. Small rocks rattled against the undercarriage like gunfire, while Ben constantly slowed to navigate around potholes and ruts.

An imposing tree-covered plateau that had originally been on the distant horizon now loomed directly before them. As they drove higher up it, more and more conifers crowded around them until, quite suddenly, the car was swallowed by a scenic green forest of piñon pine and juniper. As the elevation rose, Ponderosa pine became the dominant species, their huge branches crowding over the road and casting it in shade.

Ben pushed a button that retracted the car's roof. The pine-scented air was wonderfully refreshing, and Sally found it a treat to have the wind roaring around her. She'd never been in a convertible with the top down before.

Never been this far south. Never been in a convertible. You're on a roll, girl—and it's only day one.

When they reached the top of the plateau, they came to Cherry. Judging by some of the abandoned buildings, it had once been an old mining town; now it appeared to be a small vacation home and retirement community.

On the other side of Cherry the road wound along the edge of an escarpment that dropped precipitously to a rugged ravine far below.

"Oh wow!" Sally said. "Check out the view."

"I'd prefer to keep my eyes on the road," Ben said.

"You're afraid of heights?"

"I'm afraid of careering off a cliff and exploding in a fireball at the bottom of a canyon."

"Watch out!" She grabbed the door grip in alarm. A pickup truck on oversized tires had just rounded a corner and was careening toward them on the narrow trail. "Pull over, Ben."

"Where am I supposed to pull over?"

"Pull over!"

He slowed to a crawl and squeezed as far to the right of the one-lane road as he dared. Sally couldn't bring herself to look out her window. She was mere feet away from the sheer drop.

As the pickup truck approached them, she could hear a song by The Eagles blaring from its stereo. The guy in the passenger seat—gaunt face and long, unwashed hair—stuck his head out his window while chugging a can of beer.

"Nice car, assholes!" he cackled. As the truck roared past, he chucked the empty beer can onto their back seat.

Ben angled the Camaro back into the middle of the road. "Jerks," he grunted.

"We really should have chosen the pickup truck," Sally said.

"Didn't know we were going to be off-roading up a mountain."

"I don't know if I'd call this a mountain." She finally asked what she'd been wondering about. "So what's the plan when we get to Camp Verde?"

"We find where the gypsies are camped out," he said matter-of-factly. "Then we wait until tomorrow night, the full moon, and see what happens to them."

"The last time we spied on the gypsies, things didn't turn out so well for us."

"I'm well aware of that," he said, his face tight. "Which is why I would have preferred that you remained behind in New York—as much as I enjoy your company."

"Well, I'm here now."

"You are indeed."

"How do we go about finding the gypsies?"

"In Chatham they set up shop in Veteran's Field for a few

weeks in the summertime. I'm hoping they're doing the same thing here."

"You're talking about thirty years ago, Ben. Things are different now. People don't travel around in caravans and sell stuff in parks anymore."

"If they're forced to travel each month to remain incognito, they need to be mobile."

"Maybe they've all become YouTube influencers? They'd just need a computer and internet connection for that."

Ben scowled. "I understand we're not on the same page, Sally, but can we cut out the sarcasm?"

"Let's take a step back then. How did you find the gypsies before? How did you know they were in Ryders Field?"

"When I described the gypsy woman to the sheriff, he mentioned she'd applied for a permit to camp out there."

Sally twisted her lips.

"What?" he asked.

She recalled a scene from his semi-autographical book. "This was after the gypsy woman went to your house...and made your mom dance?"

"That's right."

"And you're sure...this happened?"

"Of course I'm sure, Sally!" he said. "I was there. One minute my mom was fine, the next she was dancing. The gypsy woman made her."

Sally held back a quick retort. She didn't want to upset Ben, even though this was the part of his...werewolf theory...which was the most far-fetched and frustrating for her. Because if you wanted to believe that the gypsies were not a cult of crazies who believed they were werewolves, but were *actual* werewolves, well, fine. There was a lot of strange stuff in the world. Ghosts, mermaids, Bigfoot—who was to say for certain whether any of these creatures existed or not? So had werewolves remained under the radar for centuries until now? Logic told her no. But she could at least keep an open mind.

However, Ben wanted her to do much more than

that. He wanted her to believe that the gypsies weren't only werewolves, but they had gone around Chatham compelling regular folks infected with their disease to dance uncontrollably for days on end as some sort of cure for lycanthropy.

And Sally just couldn't go there. It was one step too far, so to speak.

So here was the rub: Why had the gypsy woman—regardless of whether she was a crazy or a werewolf—gone to Ben's house?

It made no sense.

That made Sally wonder whether Ben had misremembered this event too. Perhaps she had never gone to his house. He'd simply latched onto the idea while writing his book because it fit his narrative.

But if that were the case, he never would have been able to describe the gypsy woman to the sheriff, and the sheriff would never have mentioned the permit.

So how the hell did Ben know the gypsies were in Ryders Field?

Sally began rubbing her forehead. She didn't know what to believe. She only knew what she *didn't* believe, and that was giving her a headache.

She said, "Why don't we just go to the police station in Camp Verde and ask the sheriff if a caravan of people has applied for a permit to stay around town?"

"I've thought of that," he replied. "But I'm not convinced the sheriff would offer a stranger that information." He shrugged. "I'm leaving that option as a last resort. After we eat, we'll drive around town ourselves. Camp Verde isn't very big. If we don't see the gypsies set up anywhere, then I'll ask around. The locals would know if a dozen or so out-of-towners have been camping out somewhere for a month or two."

The road continued to zig-zag along the canyon rim. Several paths branched off it into the forest, presumably leading to ranger cabins or campsites. The only other vehicle they passed was a red sedan parked at a lookout spot. A couple seated in folding chairs waved at them as they drove by.

When they approached a junction at the base of an unused fire tower, Sally checked her map app and instructed Ben to go right. Eventually the road started its twisty descent out of the forest and back to the sun-scorched desert. About five miles later they entered a large roundabout and took the first exit south.

That was how they came to Camp Verde, Arizona.

CHAPTER 6

BULLIES

Gabriela sat at her desk in the fourth-grade classroom of Camp Verde Elementary School, listening to her teacher, Mrs. Robinson, read aloud from the novel *A Wrinkle in Time*. Gabriela had a copy in front of her and was supposed to be following along, but her mind was a galaxy away, back when she'd lived in Mexico. She felt a sharp pang of regret that she would never be returning to Guadalajara. She didn't necessarily miss the ranch or the nearby neighborhoods; she missed the simplicity of her life, and she missed her father.

He had been murdered about three months ago, stabbed in the heart while walking back from the markets with a sack of maize seeds. Gabriela's mom believed it was a botched robbery, but she didn't know for certain because the police never bothered to investigate his death. Even so, if it was a robbery, the thief wouldn't have gotten much money; her father had likely spent all his pesos on the seeds.

Gabriela's mom cried off and on for a full week afterward. Gabriela knew her mom loved her dad, and some of the crying was for his passing. But a lot of it, Gabriela suspected, was for the uncertain future they both faced. With *Papá* dead, there was no one to run the ranch.

A few days after her mom stopped crying for good, she sat Gabriela down and told her a story about a clever but poor ant who worked hard gathering food in the forest every day.

This ant deserved a better life than the difficult one she was born into, but to achieve this, she needed an education. The problem, however, was that to get an education, the ant needed money, and to get money, she needed an education.

Gabriela's suspicion that the little ant was her was confirmed when her mom told her that if Gabriela studied hard in the United States, she could earn a scholarship to attend college and one day become anything she wanted: a doctor, a lawmaker, or even the President of the United States itself.

The tricky part would be getting into America, but her mom assured her that she had a plan. The trip would be difficult and dangerous, but once they were across the border, everything would be different. They would no longer live in poverty. They would have opportunities. They could be happy.

"What do you think, *nena*?" her mother had asked her. "Should we go for it?"

Gabriela had nodded, knowing that her mother's mind had already been made up.

The next day Gabriela's mother put their two dairy cattle down with *Papi's* rifle and turned the beef into jerky that she sold at the markets, alongside containers of homemade salsa. She used some of the money to purchase the Greyhound bus tickets to Tijuana. The more than two thousand-kilometer trip had taken nearly two days. It had been incredibly boring, even though Gabriela's mom had allowed her to sit in the window seat. But the novelty of the passing scenery hadn't lasted long, as there wasn't much to see other than fields.

Stepping off the Greyhound bus in downtown Tijuana was like stepping into a new world. This new city was much noisier and more colorful than Guadalajara and pulsed with energy: laughter, conversations, jeers, and raised voices, all set against a backdrop of honking car horns and music playing from several unseen locations.

Gabriela and her mother started down a chaotic street lined with handicraft and souvenir shops, kiosks hawking statues of Jesus and sombreros, restaurants and cafés, and a large number of pharmacies, which seemed to be patronized mostly by Americans. Gabriela had been fascinated by the foreigners. It had been the first time she'd seen Americans in real life. Although they seemed to be mostly minding their own business, they were treated like celebrities, with many shopkeepers urging them to check out their shops. One shopkeeper offered two young white men free shots of tequila if they would come into his silver shop.

They continued through the bustling, intimidating crowds, eventually ending up in a dark and smelly bar. Gabriela didn't hear what her mother had asked the barmaid, but the woman had nodded at a man drinking a beer by himself at a table beneath a noisy fan. He looked up when they approached. After her mom explained what she wanted, he said, "*El Norte*, huh? *Si*, I can help." They followed him—he'd introduced himself as Diego—through a maze of streets to an old house where a middle-aged couple lived. He told them he needed until tomorrow to organize the trip, but they would be safe there until everything was ready. The middle-aged couple (the chubby wife was dressed in too-small clothing and the husband lacked one of his front teeth) let Gabriela and her mother shower and scrub their dirty clothes on a cement washboard. They gave them spare clothes to wear while theirs dried on the clothesline (which didn't take long in the mid-afternoon heat). After what passed for dinner—a raw egg mixed into a cold glass of milk—the couple showed them to a room on the second floor. It featured a single window, some pillows and sheets dumped on the floor, and a bucket in a corner to serve as a toilet.

Both Gabriela and her mother were so exhausted from the cross-country bus ride that they curled up on the sheets (even though it was still light out) and promptly fell asleep.

They woke at an unknown hour to darkness and several voices downstairs speaking and laughing loudly. This continued for a while before the people ascended the creaky steps to the second floor. There was a perfunctory knock on the door to the room before it opened. The middle-aged couple stood silhouetted against light filtering up from the first floor. Beside them was a man Gabriela had never seen before.

Smoothing his goatee with his forefinger and thumb, he said, "Oh ya...oh yes—*provocativo*. Ya, ya ya. How old is the young one?"

The woman shook her head. "Not her, *señor*. The older one only."

"No!" Gabriela's mother cried, leaping to her feet.

"You want to cross the border, don't you, *princesa*?"

"I can't! I won't—"

"Didn't Diego mention this? It's part of the deal. One night of service for a new life."

Gabriela wasn't sure what "service" was required of her mother, but she looked scared to death. And then her defiance faltered, her shoulders slumped. Her hand wrapped around Gabriela's cheek, pressing it reassuringly against her thigh.

She let go and left the room.

With a wink at Gabriela, the woman in the too-small clothing closed and locked the door.

Gabriela didn't see her mom again until the morning. She looked pale and upset when she entered the room, though she wouldn't answer any of Gabriela's questions, including where she'd been and what she'd done all night. She simply went to sleep on the sheets. Gabriela loitered by the window and watched the activity down on the street.

At some point in the morning, Diego returned. Gabriela excitedly woke her mom—she couldn't wait to leave the unpleasant house—and they followed the coyote downstairs and through a back door into an alleyway. He opened the trunk of a white Peugeot sedan and told them to climb inside. It was for their own safety, he assured them.

The ride was stuffy and hot and claustrophobic. Gabriela's mom held her hand the entire time. After about an hour the car stopped and the trunk lid opened. They climbed out into light so bright it temporarily blinded Gabriela. When the spangles cleared from her vision, she saw they were in the middle of the desert. The dry and stony soil stretched in every direction for as far as she could see, supporting little more than scraggly shrubs, feather grass, and the occasional prickly cactus.

"What now?" her mother asked.

"We walk," the coyote told her.

"Gabriela?" someone said, and it was neither her mother nor the coyote. Sharper now: "Gabriela."

Gabriela realized she had fallen asleep at her desk. She rubbed the sluggishness from her eyes with her small fists.

"Yes?" she said.

"Am I boring you, Gabriela?" Mrs. Robinson asked her.

"No, ma'am."

"Then Madeleine L'Engle's writing is boring you?"

"No, ma'am."

"She just can't understand it," one of the other kids in the class snickered.

"She needs a Mexican version," someone else said.

"That's enough, Tiffany," Mrs. Robinson said. "And they don't speak Mexican in Mexico."

"What do they speak?"

A knock at the door interrupted their conversation. It was the vice principal, a tall, gray-haired man wearing a suit and tie. "Sorry to interrupt, Mrs. Robinson," he said. "May I have a word with you for a second?"

When she stepped outside the classroom to speak with him, most of the students took the opportunity to chat with their neighbors or whip out their phones (which weren't allowed to be used in class). Gabriela simply sat quietly at her desk and tried to remain invisible. This rarely worked because Katie Weiss, one of the meanest girls in the class, sat directly behind her.

As if reading Gabriela's thoughts, Katie kicked one of the metal legs of Gabriela's chair and said, "Move up, alien! I don't wanna catch your alien germs."

Gabriela dragged her chair forward until her tummy pressed tightly against the hard edge of her desk.

This wasn't good enough for Katie. Another kick. "I said, *move!*"

"I *did*," Gabriela shot back quietly. She didn't know why Katie and a lot of the other girls hated her. Was it because of her dark hair and dark eyes? Because her skin was a different shade than theirs? Because her English wasn't perfect (though it had improved tremendously in the short time she'd been in the United States)? Or did they simply hate her because she was an outsider, born somewhere other than the small, remote community of Camp Verde? Whatever the reason, she was teased on a daily basis.

"Move it all the way back to Mexico!" Helen Appleford said from her desk next to Gabriela's.

"She's an alien," Katie said. "Maybe she can beam herself back?"

Helen snickered at the joke. So many freckles covered her face that they almost formed one big freckle. And when she laughed like she was doing now, she always covered her mouth with her hand so you couldn't see her pink gums and metal braces. Helen loved announcing how ugly Gabriela was, and she didn't pass up the opportunity, telling Katie, "Do you think she knows how gross she is? If I looked like her, I'd wear a paper bag over my head."

"Everybody in Mexico is ugly," Katie said knowingly. "They can't help themselves."

"Is your mom as ugly as you are?" Helen asked.

Gabriela didn't reply.

"I asked you a question, *Hag!*"

They'd started calling her that after she forgot to comb her curly black hair one morning. When she entered the classroom right before the first bell, Katie Weiss had pointed a finger at her and squealed, "Eww! Look! It's *Hagrid!*" (even though the Hagrid she was no doubt referencing from *Harry Potter* was a monstrous, overweight man). "Hagrid" had only lasted a day or two until, out of laziness or perhaps inspired wit, Helen Appleford had shortened it to "Hag."

Gabriela locked her jaw. "My mom's pretty."

"I bet she works in McDonald's," Helen said.

"I bet she's the janitor in McDonald's," Katie said.

"The *ugly* janitor."

"Is that right, *Hag*? Is your mom an ugly janitor at McDonald's…?"

And so it went. Katie and Helen only stopped the teasing when Mrs. Robinson returned to the classroom and told everyone to hush down. Gabriela wiped a tear from her eye and went right back to trying to be invisible.

CHAPTER 7

SCOOBY'S BIG PLAN

Scooby sat on a limb of his favorite tree along the bank of the Verde River. The leafy canopy shaded him from the deadly hot sun, and the six-pack of beer in his backpack was giving him a good buzz. It was only two o'clock in the afternoon, but he'd already been drinking for an hour. Some shitheads might think that was too early to start on a binge; for him, the middle of the day was the best time to drink. The sun was out, the sky was blue, and there was something nice about getting smashed while you knew everybody else was either in school or at work wasting their day away.

Scooby, seventeen, had dropped out of school in grade nine. He had never set foot in an office or other workplace, and he never planned to. Why would he when he could walk into the welfare office and get all the cash and food stamps he needed? He would never become rich, but it allowed him to pay the rent on his studio apartment, feed himself, and most importantly, get shitfaced every day. In the *middle* of every day.

What a fucking life. He wouldn't trade it with anybody.

He finished what was left of the Miller High Life in his hand, then launched the bottle into the river. It hit the calm surface with a loud *plop!* before sinking out of sight. That was the graveyard where all his bottles went. Why not? He was probably making homes for all the little organisms that lived down on the muddy bottom—all rent-free. He was a real philanthropist, he was. He gave and asked for nothing in return. Shame more people weren't like him.

Scooby reached for his backpack that was hanging from a nearby branch. Somehow his hand swept past it, and he lurched forward. At the last moment his hand caught a slightly lower branch. Karma wouldn't let him fall out of the tree, he knew. Shit like that didn't happen to philanthropists like himself. It wouldn't be fair.

Even so, he gave himself a little time to let the dizziness pass. *Gotta be the sun. What is it today? A hundred and ten fucking degrees Fahrenheit? Sure feels like that.*

When he felt better, he hawked a loogie at the ground below and yanked a fresh beer out of the bag and got comfortable on his branch again. He twisted off the cap and flicked it at Lizzy Bane, who sat at the base of the tree, screwing around on her phone. The cap boinked off the top of her black-haired head.

"Ah ha!" he cried triumphantly. All his previous caps had missed her.

"Fuck off, Scoob!" she shouted up at him.

"You fuck off, bitch! This is my tree, you know what I'm sayin'?"

"Fuck off!"

"*You* fuck off!"

"Fuck off!"

Laughing, he gulped the lukewarm beer.

They were dating, him and Lizzy. He didn't really like her, but it was better hanging out in his tree when someone else was around. He could definitely do better than her. Everybody said he looked like Kid Rock because he was a skinny white kid with blond hair that touched his shoulders. He also had a wisp of a goatee (what he could grow at seventeen) and sleepy, stoned eyes. All he needed was a black leather fedora and he would probably have the paparazzi chasing his ass. So, yeah, his problem with girls wasn't his good looks; his problem was that he lived in Camp Verde. There were maybe three hot bitches his age in the entire town: Cathy Nolan, Jessica Petzal, and Stephanie Haw. They were all still in school and probably thought they were too good for him. Thought they were going to go to college somewhere like Phoenix or Tucson, or maybe even out of state. Thought they were going to marry a rich prick of a husband and live in some big house. They'd probably end up as hookers on some street corner or strippers in some sleazy bar while he kicked back in his tree every day with no worries. That was what happened when you believed you were better than other people. The world shit on you.

Karma.

So Lizzy might be a bit on the ugly side, but at least she was company, and she fucked pretty good for an ugly chick.

"Hey, Lesbo!" he called, using the nickname he'd made up for Lizzy when he realized Liz Bane sounded a little like Lesbian. "What's your mom look like?"

"*What?*"

"She hot like you?"

Lizzy snorted. She knew when he was being disingenuous because he always did it to her.

"Don't be like that, bitch. How old is she?"

"What the hell are you talking about, Scoob?"

"I'm just asking, you know what I'm sayin'?"

"No, I have no idea what you're saying. Are you high?"

That reminded Scooby that he had a joint his boy Monster had given him the other day, just sitting in his pocket, waiting to be smoked on a beautiful afternoon like this one. He wedged his beer between his legs for safekeeping, took the joint out, and lit it up with a pink Bic lighter he'd lifted from the Dollar General in town.

Lizzy looked up at him. "You gonna share?"

"How am I gonna pass it to you with you being way down there?"

"I can't climb up. I'm wearing a skirt."

"I don't see anyone around wanting to look up your skirt." He took another long drag and made a loud show of satisfaction: "*Ahhhh...*"

Lizzy started to monkey her way up the tree.

He took another drag. "Not much left..." he taunted, blowing smoke down in her direction.

"Hold off! I'm coming!"

About a minute later she reached his branch. She stopped within a couple of feet of him, and he passed her the blunt. "Don't slobber on it."

They passed it back and forth a few times until it was finished, and he flicked away the browned roach.

Monster's pot was always good stuff, and it had worked its magic on Lizzy; she looked completely blitzed.

"Dude...we're in a tree..." she said, as though this was some grand epiphany.

"Damn right we are," he said. "And it's *my* tree."

"You don't own it."

"The hell I don't. Squatter's rights."

"How are we going to get down?"

"Just like how you got up. Climb!"

"I don't think I can get down."

He laughed at her.

She started to panic, looking this way and that like a trapped animal. "I'm serious, Scoob! I can't get down!" Her voice turned screechy. "How am I gonna get *down*?"

"Marinate, bitch! You're ruining my buzz."

Lizzy shut up then, and Scooby turned his attention to a line of ants crawling along his branch.

"Ants, yo," he said vaguely, profoundly. "The little mo' fo's got the right idea. Dick around in their tree all day, doing whatever they want, enjoying the view. If I wasn't me, I betcha I'd make a good ant."

Lizzy snorted in that way of hers when she disagreed with him. "You're no ant."

"I'm in a tree, aren't I?"

"What the hell does that mean? Anyway, ants *work*. You're more like a grasshopper."

He frowned. "Grasshoppers don't work?"

"Don't you know that story?"

"What story?"

"Forget it."

He glowered at her. "Tell me the story or get the fuck out of my tree!"

She scowled back, defiant. "It's not your stupid tree!"

He raised a hand threateningly. "Say that again, and I'm gonna slap you out of it."

"Fine, Scoob, fine. It's your tree. Okay? Every branch and leaf. They're all yours, Scoob." She began giggling.

"What's so funny?" he demanded.

"Most normal people own houses and cars and stuff. You own branches and leaves."

"I own the *tree*. It's more than just the branches and leaves. It's like the forest and not the tree, you know what I'm sayin'?"

Lizzy went quiet and seemed to find something fascinating about the branch they were sitting on because she just kept staring at it. Then she began swaying a little, and he wondered if she might actually fall out of the tree on her own. That would be a buzz kill. Not only would he have to carry her all the way into town, but he'd also have to deal with all the stiffs at the hospital. His entire day would be ruined.

"Yo, don't fall," he told her.

She blinked at him. "Huh?"

"I said don't fall, bitch!" He took out another beer from his backpack.

"Can I have one?"

"Hell no." He twisted off the cap and decided not to flick it at Lizzy in case it knocked her out of the tree.

"You know Kitty's got like a thousand views on TikTok?"

Scooby took a swig of the beer. "What are you talking about?"

"Kitty Appleton. Her older sister Cindy uploaded a video of her dancing to TikTok this morning, and it's already got like a thousand views."

"She's not locked up at the community center with the rest of them?"

"I guess not. In the video it looked like she was in her bedroom."

He took another swig. "Who just starts dancing like that?"

"They caught it from Mary Porter at the mental hospital."

"I know how they caught it. But *how* do you catch a dancing bug? Did Mary sneeze on them or something?"

"They say it's mass...mass...mass something anyway. Like those flash mobs on YouTube, right?"

"Nah, it ain't like that. Those shitheads *know* what they're doing. All those bitches at the high school are like in a different world."

"What were we talking about...?"

"How ugly you are."

"Oh, right!" she said, appearing not to hear him. "A *thousand* hits. Imagine a thousand people, a lot of them you don't even know, just sitting there and watching you. Oh my God, that's crazy! Like, what if you had a *million* people, a million strangers, watching you? Oh my God!"

"Imagine you're a porn star and you got a million people watching you *and* jerking off to you."

"You're gross."

"That's just how it is, you know what I'm sayin'? But a thousand people? Yeah, that's dope. And all her sister did was just film her? Shit, *I* could do that."

"I'm sure you'd find a way to screw it up." She began giggling again. "You'd probably delete it before you posted it."

Scooby took a long sip of beer, then said, "Let's do it."

"Do what?"

"Film Kitty and get *us* a thousand views." He'd spoken the idea out loud before he'd thought it over, but now that it was out of his mouth he realized he was onto something. "Seriously. It would be *easy.*"

Lizzy appeared skeptical. "How are you going to film her? You just gonna walk up to her house and knock on her door?"

"You said she was dancing in her bedroom, right? So we just sneak up to her window and film her through it. Booyaka!

A thousand views. We might even make some cash too like Monster does with his gaming shit."

"I don't think TikTok works that way..."

But Scooby was ignoring her, preoccupied with what he'd do with all the money they were going to make.

"Scoob?" Lizzy said.

He looked at her. "What?"

"I said I'm not doing it. Forget it."

"You wanna get rich, or you wanna just sit in a fucking tree all day?"

"You like sitting in a tree all day."

"Yeah, but now I got a *plan*." He chugged what remained of his beer, tossed it into the river, and got to his feet. "Move your ass, bitch. I'm gonna do this. You coming or not?"

"I guess," she said, getting carefully to her feet. "But I'm going down first. I don't want you looking up my skirt."

△△△

Lizzy drove them to Kitty Appleton's house in her 1971 BMW 2500 sedan she was so proud of. In fact, it was a shitbox. Its faded paint was the color of puke, and it had rusty wheels, a torn headliner, no radio or air conditioning, a leaky clutch, and an interior that looked as though a pack of rats had lived in it. Having said all that, at least she had a car, which was more than Scooby could say for himself.

Kitty, it turned out, lived in the northern part of town. Lizzy parked next to a chain-link fence, on the other side of the desert that belonged to the Yavapai-Apache Nation Reservation. She and Scooby got out of the car, the doors squawking as they slammed them shut. The slightly elevated road allowed them to look down to the back of a large single-story house.

"You sure that's Kitty's place?" Scooby asked.

"I've been friends with her since I was like two," Lizzy said. "Of course I'm sure."

"You don't speak to her anymore. What if she moved?"

"She's got a younger sister. Look at all the toys in the backyard. It's her house, Scoob."

"Aight. So where's her bedroom?"

"I can't remember. I think it might be on that side." She pointed to the right side of the house. "You sure you really wanna do this?"

"No chickening out, bitch." He descended the slope without looking back, knowing Lizzy would follow him.

A chest-high fence surrounded the property. He climbed over it. Lizzy had more trouble, mostly because she was fussing with her skirt.

"Nobody's looking at your red undies," he told her.

"Then how do you know they're *red*?"

Crouching, Scooby hustled across the yard to the back of the house, stopping next to a three-foot-tall pink plastic dollhouse. Next to it was a glass sliding door. Beige curtains were pulled closed across it, though they didn't meet in the middle. He peered through the gap into a spacious living room. Nobody there. He hurried along the wall to a smaller window that looked into a laundry room. Again, nobody there, but the wall-mounted dryer was on, suggesting somebody was home. He rounded the corner of the house and peeked in the next window.

Bingo! he thought when he saw Kitty Appleton dancing in her bedroom...though he wasn't sure he'd call what she was doing dancing. He'd expected her to be doing some crazy shit like the Moon Walk, the Bunny Hop, spinning on her head like a break-dancer, or maybe even pole dancing without a pole (that had been his hope). But all she was doing was stepping flatfooted from one foot to the other while swaying a little.

"What the fuck is this?" he whispered.

"She's been dancing for more than two days now," Lizzy said. "She's probably exhausted."

"Is this how she was dancing in her sister's video?"

"She had a bit more energy then."

"And she still got a thousand hits?"

"People don't care *how* she's dancing. They're interested because she can't stop."

"This is lame-ass." He whipped out the Swiss Army knife he always carried with him.

"What are you doing with that?" Lizzy asked him.

"Spicing things up." He opened the largest blade and jammed the tip in between where the aluminum edge of the window's screen met the wood frame. He applied pressure to the knife, and the screen popped free.

"What the hell are you *doing*, Scoob?"

Ignoring her, he set aside the screen, put away the knife, and attempted to open the window. It wasn't locked and slid upward.

"Scoob!"

"Hush, bitch! Just get your phone ready to film."

Scooby scrambled inside the bedroom. The décor was typically girlish with white furniture, pale pink walls, a bed stacked with more pillows than anybody would need (including some furry pink ones that matched the walls), and cheap canvas prints (the biggest one featuring a pair of puckered gold lips on a white background).

Kitty Appleton continued her lame-ass dancing without paying him any notice. He waved a hand in front of her face. She didn't even blink.

He looked back at the window. Lizzy was holding her phone up in front of her, presumably filming. He gave her a thumbs up. She nodded.

Scooby went to a little makeup desk with a LED mirror and two silver pots with enough different-sized brushes sticking out of them to make Picasso jealous. He yanked open the drawer, revealing everything from Q-tips to eyeliner pens to lotions and creams and powders.

Scooby rustled through all the shit, grabbed a tube of lipstick, then returned to Kitty. She continued dancing without acknowledging him. It was trippy because her eyes were open so she had to be able to see him. He removed the lipstick cap and twisted open the waxy bit. He looked back at Lizzy again.

"Hurry up!" she whispered.

Scooby attempted to apply the lipstick to Kitty's face. She began shaking her head back and forth, which caused most of it to go on her cheeks and chin instead of her lips.

Now for the big finale, he thought. He whipped his white wife beater off, then shoved his Hawaiian board shorts down around his ankles. Standing there in only his boxers, he began thrusting and gyrating against Kitty while waving his arms above his head like he was some raver.

He grinned at the camera filming them, and all he could think about was all the clicks the video was going to get—

Suddenly a man shouted, "I'm not taking her, dammit! She's fine where she is!"

Then a woman's voice: "She's sick, John! She's worse every day! She needs help!"

Scooby flinched in surprise, then yanked up his shorts.

"Who knows what those doctors will poke her with!" It was the man again, and he was now on the other side of the bedroom door.

Scooby flattened himself against the wall next to the door right before it swung open. He couldn't see who entered the room because the door was blocking his vision, but he heard him.

"Kitty? Kitty? What the...?" Footsteps moved further into the room, all the way toward the window. "Hey, you!" the man roared. "Get back here!"

Scooby knew Lizzy had left him, and he had about three seconds before he was busted, so he slipped out from behind the door just as the man—a stocky, bearded guy with a barrel chest and tree trunks for arms—turned away from the window. Upon seeing Scooby, his beady eyes, already black with rage, went apocalyptic.

"Stop!" he shouted.

Scooby darted from the room and ran down a hallway. He emerged into a kitchen where a large, doughy woman stood at an island counter with a knife in one hand and a red pepper in the other. Her confused look vanished at the sight of him. She screamed. He screamed too, witless with fear. But he didn't slow until he reached the front door.

"Stop him!" the man bellowed from somewhere behind him.

Scooby knew if the door was locked he was dead meat.

It wasn't, and he burst outside into the blue afternoon. He sprinted down the sidewalk. When he reached the corner of the block, he heard car tires screech. He risked a glance back and saw the pickup truck that had been parked in Kitty's driveway swing onto the road in reverse.

Shit! Shit! Shit!

Scooby knew there was no outrunning it, so he cut across the front yard of the house on his right, ran down the side of it, through the backyard, and up the incline to the street where Lizzy had parked her shitbox earlier. It was gone.

Bitch!

He ran to the end of the road. He ducked around a beige car with cardboard taped over a busted window, jumped over a rotted sofa sitting on the curb, and followed a footpath that weaved between the chain-link fence that bordered the reserve and a junk-heap of a house. About a hundred feet later he emerged in a different neighborhood—with no crazy dad coming after him.

Breathing heavily in the scorching afternoon heat, Scooby headed back to his tree.

CHAPTER 8

THE DEVIL'S WORK

There wasn't much to see as they rolled down Camp Verde's Main Street. A Circle K gas station; a barber shop and laundromat; an Ace Hardware; a brewing company and a few cafes; a couple of shops with FOR LEASE signs in the front windows; and of course the requisite small-town tourist information center.

Sally didn't see many people out and about, aside from a few shoppers and a crew of two changing the banners on the streetlamps. The lack of activity was a little unsettling.

"It's like a ghost town," she said.

"Wonder where everyone is?" Ben said.

"At home dancing?" When he didn't respond to her attempt at levity, she added, "We haven't seen any more places to stay. We might have to double back to the Days Inn we passed." The hotel was located at a major intersection on the outskirts of the town, surrounded by all the usual suspects: Subway, Starbucks, Denny's, McDonald's, Burger King, and an ethnic restaurant with a 24-hour drive thru.

"What's that place over there?" he said, pointing past her to a single-story building. It had a giant American flag out front and featured a fence of roughly hewn and pointed logs that resembled those that the early settlers used to barricade their forts.

Sally spotted a sign. "Fort Verde Suites," she said.

"Sounds good to me."

Ben parked in the half-filled lot, and they entered the front office. An old man was seated behind the counter, reading a newspaper. He looked up at them as they approached. Beneath a large-brimmed leather cowboy hat, his deeply tanned and lined face suggested he spent much of his time outdoors.

"Howdy, folks," he said, getting to his feet with some difficulty and setting aside the paper. "How can I help you?"

"We're hoping you might have two vacancies?" Sally said.

"Sure do. But the rooms aren't next to each other. That okay?"

"That's fine," Ben said, taking his wallet from his pocket. "Is there somewhere I could get a local paper?"

The man slid the newspaper he had been reading across the counter. On the front page, beneath the title *Camp Verde Bugle*, the headline announced: DANCERS MOVED TO COMMUNITY GYM. "On the house," he said. "I'm done with it. Now—you paying with cash or card?"

△△△

Sally's room was furnished with rustic, hand-carved furniture. A braided leather bullwhip, coiled in a circle, decorated one wall as a nod to the town's agricultural roots. She unpacked her suitcase, transferring the few articles of clothing she'd brought with her to a dresser. She spent a few minutes in the bathroom touching up her make-up, then knocked on Ben's door.

"It's open," he called.

She entered and found him sitting on the edge of his bed, the newspaper on his lap. He was shaking his head as he read the main story above the fold.

"What does it say?" she asked.

"Kids," he said, looking at her, his eyes distant. "Jesus Christ. The dancers are *kids*—how's that possible?"

Sally frowned. "What do you mean?"

"The article I read online about the dancing here, the only

one I found, mentioned a dancing outbreak at a mental-health facility. It never specified that the dancers were a bunch of kids. That doesn't make sense."

"What doesn't make sense?" she asked, confused.

"Lycanthropy is transmitted through a bite or intercourse. That's what I thought anyway. But..." He wagged the newspaper. "Kids? And most recently, a dozen teenagers, ten of them girls? How would they become infected? *It doesn't make sense.*"

Sally nodded, but she took no satisfaction that the bottom had finally, inevitably, fallen out of his werewolf theory.

According to the semi-autographical book that Ben recently wrote, he believed in 1988 that a young male gypsy infected with lycanthropy had sex with a housekeeper at a Chatham hotel, passing on the disease to her. She in turn infected someone else via intercourse, who infected someone else the same way, until seven or eight people had the disease, his mother included. To prevent these people from shapeshifting into werewolves on the next full moon, the gypsies, or at least their leader, tracked down the individuals and put them in a deep dance trance, which shut down their minds and prevented the transformations.

It was ludicrous stuff, even for fiction. But Ben believed it— or at least he had.

Sally sat next to him on the bed. "What we went through as kids was traumatic, Ben. It was traumatic for all of us— you, me, Chunky. I had to see a shrink for a year. That helped a lot, helped me to understand, maybe not why, but *what* happened. Some people are just messed up. They do disturbing things. And those gypsies were majorly messed up. They were in a cult. Not a devil-worshiping cult. A werewolf-worshipping cult. They dressed up like wolves and..." She hesitated. This was where her memory was suspect. Had the gypsies only murdered their victims? Or did they do worse? Did they butcher them? Eat them? Were they cannibals? One image that had never left her was of the deputy lying on the floor of the yellow circus wagon, his flesh stripped to the bone. Had the gypsies done that to him? Or was that her imagination in overdrive? She didn't know and would never know for certain. What she did know, however, was that five people went missing that night, and nobody ever saw them again. "I guess what I'm saying," she went on, "is that I know how much that night screwed with my mind. For you, it would have been even worse. You lost your father to those assholes. Did you ever see a shrink?"

He shook his head.

She patted his thigh. "Well, you seemed to have turned out all right on your own—mostly."

"You think I'm crazy, don't you?"

She smiled. "Crazy but cute."

He shook his head again. "I honestly don't know what to think right now."

"Then don't think," she said. "Let's go get something to eat, then we'll head over to the community center and see what's going on in this dustbowl for ourselves."

ΔΔΔ

They walked back through the scorching heat along Main Street and entered a steakhouse that occupied half of one block. The industrial décor featured brick walls (one sporting a huge stag head next to a road sign depicting the Arizona flag and the slogan THE GRAND CANYON STATE WELCOMES YOU), a high open-rafter ceiling, and a string of blue fairy lights above the bar. Thankfully the place was air-conditioned.

They'd only taken a few steps inside when a waitress in a flannel shirt called to them from behind the bar. "Hi there! You folks looking for food? Because we were just about to close for the day."

"Right before dinner?" Ben said, checking his wristwatch.

Sally checked hers too: it was 5:15 p.m.

"We've only had two customers all day. Everybody's been

staying home so they don't catch that damn dancing bug." She emerged from behind the bar holding two menus. "But have a seat. We can stay open a little longer. It's just me and the cook here anyway."

Ben and Sally settled into a black booth, and the waitress handed them the menus. She had a bullet-like body, canary-yellow press-on nails, and platinum-blond hair. Blue eyes greeted them warmly from above a medical mask.

Protection from catching "the dancing bug"? Sally wondered.

"Have you heard anything about what is causing those high school kids to dance?" Ben asked, setting aside his menu without looking at it.

Sally was surprised at his bluntness, even though the waitress nodded easily. "A doctor at the town hall meeting last night suggested it might be due to a kind of...mass hypnosis or something, I think he called it."

"Mass hysteria?" Sally offered.

"Yeah, could be that. It wasn't like any other town hall meeting I've been to, and I go to them all. Everybody was real worked up, everybody shouting questions. The doctor talked a lot about them Salem witch trials. You heard about them, right?"

Sally assumed the question was rhetorical. Who hadn't heard of the Salem witch trials? However, she likely knew more about what occurred between 1692 and 1693 in Salem Village than most. One, it happened in her home state of Massachusetts. And two, she had taken a history course in college dedicated to the subject.

She said, "They're an example of one of the most famous—or infamous, I suppose you would say—cases of mass hysteria in the country's history."

Nodding, the woman said, "Mass hysteria. Yeah, I think you're right about that. Not hypnosis. 'Hysteria' has a better ring to it, don't it? But, yeah, Doc Brown told us them trials began when two kids started screaming and twisting their bodies and throwing things around for no reason at all.

Everybody thought it was the devil's work."

"And because you can't haul the devil himself into a courtroom," Sally told Ben, "they went after three marginalized women, whom the children had accused of casting a spell on them."

"I don't see how what happened then," he said, "and what's happening now, in Camp Verde, is comparable. The strange behavior of those two kids could have been something physiological or psychological. Something as simple as asthma, Lyme disease, epilepsy, child abuse. Hell, maybe they just ate some psychedelic mushrooms they found while wandering through the forest. On the other hand, none of that can explain all those schoolgirls in a trance-like state."

"Except for the fact the strange behavior of the kids spread to other kids in the community," Sally pointed out. "Like what's occurring here with the dancing."

"Then what got into them? What kicked off their initial hysteria?"

"They most likely thought they *had* been bewitched. One of the three women they blamed for their condition practiced voodoo. They might have seen her performing one of her religious rites, which could have seemed like witchcraft to them, and their imaginations took it from there. The other kids saw them acting out and convinced themselves they were bewitched too."

He frowned. "So what happened in Salem, and what's happening now—it's just people...completely wigging out for no reason?"

The waitress bobbed her head. "A case of monkey see, monkey do, that's what Doc Brown called it. One of those girls starts dancing for some reason or another. Her friend sees her and starts dancing too. It keeps going like that, with more and more friends jumping on the bandwagon. That's what's so scary about it. There's no rhyme or reason for who gets affected. You never know if you're going to be next."

Sally nodded in agreement. "Except people aren't 'wigging

out' for no reason, Ben. In Salem—and Puritan society in general in the 1600s—people were uprooted literally and figuratively. They were struggling to survive on a new continent already inhabited by other, often hostile, peoples. At the same time their deep religious faith and way of life were being challenged by science. Given all of this and the inherent supernatural beliefs and superstitions of the time, it's not surprising that fear and paranoia swept through their community, making rational people act irrationally. Not just the kids with the odd symptoms. After all, two hundred men, women, and children were accused of witchcraft in a few months. Of those, about thirty were found guilty and twenty were hanged. All of this without a shred of evidence that anybody was truly a witch or had committed any crimes."

"In any event," the waitress said, adjusting her mask, "I betcha it's a lot more people dancing than the poor girls they're telling us about."

Sally was surprised. "Why do you think that?"

"Because the students that got moved to the community center, they're only the ones we know about. They're others, you can count on it, that are just inside their houses dancing by themselves. One of our staff here, Claire, a young girl—but not friends with any of the girls from the high school—didn't come into work this morning. We sent Benny our dishwasher over to check on her, and sure enough, she had the dancing bug. Benny said he saw her through a window, both Claire and the boyfriend she's living with, dancing together. So how many more people are dancing we just don't know about? We got twelve thousand people in town. How many are dancing... and how many have already dropped dead?"

"People have died?" Ben said, exchanging a concerned glance with Sally.

The waitress bobbed her head again. "Two older folks, yup. I didn't know neither of them. Both retirees, both living on their own. According to the sheriff last night, they'd been dancing for days and nobody was the wiser. In the end they just exhausted themselves, like two houseflies banging their heads against a window on a cold winter morning. That's why the sheriff told everyone to keep in pairs, if you can, in case one of you starts dancing, the other can report it. You two are lucky you got each other. Me, my husband died last year. Fell off his tractor and ran himself over trying to stop it. So if I start dancing in the middle of the night, who's going to know? Who's going to know if I go right on dancing straight to my grave?"

"Hopefully if you started dancing," Sally said to the woman, who was getting worked up, "one of your colleagues would check in on you, just like you did with the girl you mentioned."

"Except the boss says we're not opening the restaurant tomorrow, or the next day. Not until things are back to normal and there are customers again. But when's that going to be? You ask me, right now, this is the calm before the storm. Things are going to get a lot worse before they get better." She shrugged helplessly, as though she believed God had a vendetta against all the poor townsfolk of Camp Verde, Arizona`. "Now, what can I getchas to eat?"

CHAPTER 9

A CHANCE ENCOUNTER

After they finished their meals (pulled pork tacos with cheddar cheese and pico slaw), the waitress gave them directions to the community gym, which was only a short walk away. From the sidewalk, you wouldn't know anything unusual was occurring inside—or anything at all, for that matter. Blinds were drawn across the windows that faced the street, and cardboard had been taped behind the windows in the double front doors.

Ben tried one of the doors. It was locked. He knocked loudly. Nobody answered.

Sally pressed her ear to the wood and heard nothing inside.

"Is this the right place?" she asked.

"It's definitely a gym," he said.

They walked to the east side of the building. A strip of windows looked onto a field. All were blinded with cardboard.

"It's got to be the place they're keeping the dancers," Ben said. "Why else would they cover all the windows like that?"

"I don't hear any music," Sally said.

"They don't dance to music...they just dance. Don't you remember that woman on Seaview Street in Chatham? The one we saw dancing on our way to Light Beach."

"Yes," she said. "But you nearly drowning in the ocean is what I remember most about that night."

"Chunk puking in your swimming pool?"

"Yes, I remember that too."

And dancing with you to "Stairway to Heaven" and waiting for you to kiss me—which you never did.

"Anyway, the woman wasn't dancing to music," Ben said. "Neither was my mom, for that matter. This kind of dancing has nothing to do with music."

They returned to the front doors.

Sally was going to ask what their plan was when Ben said, "Over there." He pointed across the street to a small stone-and-mortar building. CAMP VERDE JAIL 1933 was carved into a weathered wood sign.

"What about it—?" she asked, puzzled, before she saw the van with a satellite dish and telescoping antenna on the roof. It was in a dirt parking lot next to the jail. A colorful livery on its side read *7 News*. "A news crew! Maybe they've had a look inside the gym?"

"Can't hurt to ask."

They crossed the street. The van's side door was open, revealing a mobile production control room with computers, monitors, audio and video mixers, and other electronics. A man and woman sat outside on folding chairs, sipping coffee.

"Hi," Ben said, waving. "Mind if we ask you guys a few questions?"

The man sported long hair and an unkempt beard. Despite the heat of the day receding as the evening shadows lengthened, a sweat stain ringed the neck of his tee shirt. The woman—sporting wavy blonde hair, a trendy pink jumpsuit, and peep-toe pumps—looked like a Barbie doll straight out of the package. She was clearly the on-air talent, and she was the one who answered. "Depends on what the questions are."

"I'm Ben. This is my friend, Sally. We arrived in town this afternoon."

"Welcome to the bottom of the rabbit hole."

"Have you seen inside the gym?"

She shook her head. "They've buttoned it up like Fort Knox and won't let us in, even without the camera."

"Who's they?"

"The town's top brass. The sheriff's clearly on board too. He came by earlier in the afternoon. Tried to get us to leave. Told us not to broadcast anything on TV...or else."

"Or else?"

"It was an empty threat. What's he going to do? Throw us in jail for reporting the news?"

"What's the big secret?" Sally asked. "Boarding up windows? Threatening the media? What's happening is beyond their control. So what do they have to hide?"

"The town elections are in two weeks," the woman told them. "Our thinking is that the mayor and trustees up for reelection hope the hysteria that's causing all these people to dance will sort itself out on its own by then, and they can claim victory, say it was their policies and prompt action that saved the town. On the other hand, if the story goes national, they're not going to be able to control the narrative. There will be questions about everything. The legality of rounding up the teens the way they're doing. The older people who've died. As you said, there might be nothing they can do about it, but it's not a good look. Every decision they've made will be picked apart by journalists and reporters and pundits. Also, who knows what dirty laundry might be uncovered in the process?"

"They're not cracking down on the local paper," Ben pointed out.

She shrugged. "Because it's not challenging their MO; it's only reporting what everybody already knows. It's a small town, after all. And it's too small to have a digital edition, so they don't need to worry about the story going viral online."

"You're right about that," Ben said. "I've only found a single story online so far. I think it was from a Phoenix newspaper."

"That would be the Phoenix *New Times*," the woman said.

"That's the story I read on the plane this morning," Sally said.

"A journalist for the paper, who's a friend of mine, was returning to Phoenix from a weekend in Flagstaff. While getting gas at the interchange in Camp Verde, he heard about the dancing. He did some investigating and wrote a short piece that was published in the *New Times*. He sent me a link because he knows of my interest in cases of mass hysteria...and here I am. By the way, I'm Amanda Smith. That's Ralph." The man tipped his head in acknowledgment. "We've interviewed a number of people around town," she went on. "We've even gotten footage of a couple of dancers. But our producer hasn't aired what we've sent back to the station yet. She's worried it's all some kind of prank. That, or the town's cooked it up as a publicity stunt...even though publicity, ironically, is exactly what the town doesn't want."

"You've seen other dancers?" Ben asked.

"Earlier this morning. They were over at the Outpost Mall, a man and woman in their thirties. A crowd had gathered around them like they were buskers putting on a show."

"What's your interest in mass hysteria?" Sally asked her.

"Five years ago—my first week on the job... Ralph, you were with me for that?"

The man nodded. "Was some strange shit."

"Roughly fifty workers at a meat packaging plant in Phoenix developed symptoms similar to a fictional virus that had been a plot point on a popular TV show," Amanda explained. "The symptoms included unexplained rashes over the majority of their bodies, severe stomach pains, and excessive flatulence. The plant shut down for a week until medical experts declared the cause was mass hysteria. After being on the frontlines of that, seeing the extraordinary behavior with my own eyes, I've been fascinated with mass hysteria."

"When I was doing research for a book I was writing, I read about something in England in the 1980s," Ben said. "Around three hundred people—adults, children, and even babies—spontaneously fainted at an outdoor marching band event." He snapped his fingers. "Just like that, all at the same time."

"There have been bigger incidents than that," Amanda said. "You've probably heard of them; you just haven't recognized them as cases of mass hysteria."

"Such as…?" Sally said.

"The sonic attacks in Havana, Cuba, for example."

Ben frowned. "I thought that was due to some sort of Russian weapon?"

"Oh, right." Amanda smiled dubiously. "Microwave radiation that causes headaches, nausea, tinnitus, and hearing loss?"

Sally said, "Only US government officials and military personnel were affected. That seems pretty targeted to me."

"Those diplomats and soldiers were working in a country that has long been a foreign adversary to the United States. So you have a situation in which someone suffers a legitimate illness—food poisoning, maybe, or a tumor in the head—and they get paranoid. The longer the symptoms persist, the more paranoid they become. Their behavior makes those close to them paranoid too…friends, colleagues, family…until their psychological symptoms manifest themselves as physical conditions. They literally worry themselves sick. And there you go—a collective delusional outbreak spreading rapidly within a close-knit community. Mass hysteria."

Ben said, "I take it this hypothesis has never been proven?"

"Nor has one involving a secret Russian weapon," she responded. "Moreover, a report released by the FBI found no evidence of any kind of intentional sonic attack. And then there's the fact that more and more people reported having these identical symptoms in other places around the world, everywhere from China, Europe, and even Washington D.C. So you're telling me the Russians are somehow zapping people with microwave beams in the nation's capital?"

"Mass hysteria," Sally said, pondering that. "I never made that connection. In the 1600s, people put the blame for their unrealized fears on the devil and witchcraft. Today they put it on foreign bad actors and sinister technology."

"And clowns," Amanda said.

"Clowns?" Ben said. "Like Ronald McDonald?"

"More like Pennywise."

Sally said, "Are you talking about all those clown sightings a few years back?"

She nodded. "Rumors about creepy clowns in South Carolina trying to lure children into the woods go viral on social media and soon other rumors pop all over the country."

"But there actually were people dressing up in clown costumes."

"In some cases, yes. But those were hoaxes, people ginning up the fear that had already swept through the country. Almost all the 911 calls that the police received regarding killer clown sightings were never substantiated. And despite that, you had schools banning clown costumes and even clown-hunting riots. At Penn State University, hundreds of students turned into a vigilante flash mob after a clown was reportedly seen in the area. Same thing at Michigan State after a photo of a clown lurking outside a dormitory surfaced on social media —a photo, I should mention, that was later proven to have been Photoshopped. In Utah, the police actually made public announcements warning people not to shoot clowns."

Ben said, "And I thought all that was just some ingenious PR for the Stephen King movie that had just come out ..."

Amanda said, "More than likely it reflected growing social anxiety in the country. The election in 2016, clearly, had a lot of people worked up and on edge. But you also had a rise in mass shootings and violence, threats from international terrorism, racial tensions, all that."

"I don't even know why clowns are so scary," Sally said.

"They're scary for the same reason they're funny," Ben answered. "They're masked. They have exaggerated features. They're caricatured and grotesque. Also, they're tricksters, like the devil."

"I suppose I should point out," Sally told Amanda, "there was a case of mass hysteria in the town where Ben and I grew up in the eighties. It involved dancing, just like what's happening here."

"The town in Cape Cod?" Amanda asked, raising an eyebrow.

"Chatham, yes," Ben said, appearing impressed. "I didn't think anybody these days knew what happened there. Those events were the foundation for the book I mentioned I was writing. I found next to nothing online about the outbreak of dancing...and other stuff."

And other stuff, Sally thought, thankful he didn't elaborate.

"And what was your understanding of the cause of the dancing then?" Amanda asked.

Sally held her breath. Ben hesitated.

"In 1988 the country was in the midst of one of the worst droughts in its history," he said. "That might have contributed to the sort of social anxiety you're talking about. I can't say for certain. I was only twelve. But a few years earlier a serial killer had committed a number of murders in the town, and I know the adults were worked up about *that*. It's all they talked about for years."

"And about a week or two before the dancing began," Sally said, "a man was decapitated in a hotel room in Chatham."

"How fascinating!" Amanda said. "I didn't know about any of this. Perhaps I could interview you both on camera? I could definitely work Chatham into the Camp Verde story—"

"No thanks," Ben told her flatly. Then, "But back to Camp Verde. What's *your* take on what's causing the dancing now? There's no drought. No serial killer or decapitations. And most of the dancers, it seems, are just kids."

"We've just gone through two years of Covid," Amanda said matter-of-factly. "It was especially rough on kids, who couldn't go to school or see their friends. Plus, for the older folks, there's currently record-high inflation, making it hard for everyone to afford basic staples and gas. And in a lower socio-economic town like Camp Verde, those hardships are magnified." She shrugged. "But the spark that lit the proverbial powder keg was the disappearance of three people last month. They went camping in the desert and never came back. A fourth person was found, a teenage girl. She was—"

"Fucked two ways from Tuesday," Ralph said without

looking up from his phone, with which he was fiddling.

Amanda nodded. "And she was the first one in town to begin dancing—"

"Here they come again!" Ralph said, jumping to his feet and getting behind the camera.

On the street, a white ambulance was approaching the community center.

A rhinestone compact appeared in Amanda's hand. She checked her face in the little mirror, applied some powder, and stuffed the compact back into the pocket of her jumpsuit. "They've transported two teens here already this morning in that ambulance. With no stretcher in the back, there's plenty of room for them to keep on dancing without interruption." She picked up a microphone and went to stand before the camera, positioning herself so the ambulance and community center were also in the frame. "We good to go?"

"Rolling," Ralph said as he pressed one eye to the viewfinder.

Amanda began speaking in a professional, practiced cadence. Sally heard her peripherally; her attention was focused on the ambulance. Two paramedics emerged from the front cab, barely giving Amanda and the rest of them a glance. They opened the double doors at the back and disappeared inside the cabin. They reappeared with a middle-aged woman dressed in a pair of silk pajamas.

She was performing some kind of country hoedown, although her movements were slow and uncoordinated, almost drunken. The paramedics guided to the community center's front doors. One of them spoke a few words into a phone. A moment later a clean-cut man in a suit let them inside. The door clanked shut behind them.

Amanda concluded her monologue, saying, "It must be a heartbreaking experience for the families of those who've been affected by this dancing outbreak...both heartbreaking and frightening, frankly. And as you just saw, the outbreak is no longer confined to the younger population. It's just a terrible, terrible situation, what's going on here. Teenagers, adults, perhaps even young children—we just don't know given the lack of transparency by the town's officials. More and more people appear to be falling under the spell of this sociogenic illness. We pray their remarkable symptoms stop soon, and that nobody suffers anything more serious than a pair of sore feet."

CHAPTER 10

SCOOBY'S BIGGER PLAN

Lizzy's car was parked on the dirt road near Scooby's tree. Lizzy was sitting in the shade beneath the tree, on her phone.

"You left me, bitch!" he shouted as he approached her.

She looked at him. "You made it! I thought you were busted for sure."

"Nobody busts Scoob, you know what I'm sayin'?"

Lizzy got to her feet. "That guy was psycho! I mean, he woulda killed us if he caught us."

"Did you watch the video, yo?"

She nodded. "I'm reading the comments now."

"People are commenting? Lemme read that shit."

He snatched her phone from her.

"Seven thousand and ninety likes!" he exclaimed, hardly believing the number was correct.

Lizzy grinned. "And the video's only been posted for like half an hour. That number's gonna go way up."

"Damn, girl—we're gonna be rich!"

"Do you know how to make money from TikTok?"

"My boy Monster does. We'll hit him up for help getting all that shit done later. And damn—forty-one comments!" He scrolled through them. They ran the gamut from a simple "Funny..." to "What the hell is this?" (the prick clearly didn't read the post's title: "Girl with dancing bug can't stop dancing!!"), to some people questioning the ethics of filming a girl without her knowledge. One of the latter comments came from someone who apparently knew him. It read: "This is so not cool, Scoob. Like, I think it's actually illegal. How would you like it if somebody was filming you dancing if you had the bug? I hope she sues your skinny ass and you die in hell!"

"Who the fuck is MaryL23?" Scooby asked, reading the poster's username.

"Mary Limehouse?" Lizzy said.

He vaguely recalled a prissy blonde girl with whom he'd gone to elementary school. He typed a reply to her comment:

Blow me, bitch!

"What are you writing, Scoob?" Lizzy demanded, trying to swipe her phone back. "That's my account."

He batted her hand away. "Cool it, yo. I didn't write nothing."

"I saw you!" She went for the phone again and got it this time. "'*Blow me, bitch!*'" she said, scowling. "You wrote, 'Blow me, bitch!'? This is my account, Scoob! People are gonna think I wrote that!"

"Who cares what they think? What matters is we gotta get serious about getting rich. First thing first, you gotta change your username."

She was tapping furiously on her phone and didn't appear to hear him.

"You listening to me?"

"I'm telling everyone that was your comment, not mine."

"We need proper branding. It's all about branding."

She finished typing. "What's all about branding?"

"Getting more likes! We gotta ride this when it's hot, you know what I'm sayin'? Gimme a name of something popular on Netflix."

She shrugged. "Squid Games?"

"Squid Games," he repeated, nodding. "See, it's catchy? We need something like that for your new username. How 'bout Dancing Games?"

"Stupid."

"Then gimme another show. Something edgy."

She rolled her eyes. "Peaky Blinders?"

"Peaky what the fuck?"

"It's a show about gangsters a long time ago."

"Aight, cool. Peaky Blinders. I can roll with it. So how 'bout this. Peaky *Dancers*." He snapped his fingers. "Booyaka! Do it, change it."

She blinked at him. "You want me to change my username to *Peaky Dancers*?"

"Branding, bitch! It's perfect."

She shook her head vigorously. "No way, Scoob. There's no way I'm changing my profile name to Peaky Dancers. It sounds like I'm some sort of pervert peeking into people's houses."

"That's what we're doing! That's the genius, you know what I'm sayin'?"

"I'm not changing my profile name!"

Scooby scowled, but he let it go. He was a social media idiot; he didn't even own a smartphone. He needed to keep Lizzy on his side to get his new business off the ground. "You know what else we gotta do?" he said to her. "We gotta do more videos. That's how it works. Content. That's what you need. Content, and lots of it, 'cause anybody who watches one video is gonna want to watch more. Like a douchebag who scarfs down McDonald's every day, repeat customer, you know what I'm sayin'?"

Lizzy appeared skeptical. "You want to film more dancers?"

"What other hoes are dancing at home?"

"Kitty was the only one I knew about. Everyone else is at the community center."

"There's gotta be more dancers than just them. This thing spreads, right? We take a walk around town, I betcha we find some mo' fo's just dancing on their front lawn."

"Or we can just check the cops' Facebook group."

"Huh?"

"The cops made a special page for the dancers. They're encouraging people to post about anyone they know is dancing so they can check on them and make sure they're okay and not living at home alone without anybody to help them and stuff."

"And people have ratted out those mo' fo's?"

She brought up the Facebook page and showed her phone to him.

"Five tips so far," he said as he scrolled down to the bottom of the page. "Names and addresses, yo. But I don't recognize any of those names."

"'Cause they're probably older people who live alone."

"You think the fuzz would have checked on any of them yet?"

"I have no idea. But if they did, they'd probably take them to the community center with all the others."

"Then we gotta act fast," he said, and started toward Lizzy's car. A crazy plan was forming in Scooby's head, but it was a crazy plan that was going to make them rich. "Hustle that fine ass of yours, girl," he added over his shoulder. "I'll explain everything on the way to the hardware store."

∆∆∆

Twenty minutes later Lizzy rolled her shitbox to the south curb of a street near the center of town, and they peered out the windshield together.

"That it?" Scooby asked, looking at a small white house on a dirt lot.

"Mailbox says it's number sixteen."

"Then let's do this."

The latest entry on the cops' Facebook page (which had been posted while they'd been buying mousetraps at the Ace Hardware) had been by someone who'd reported he could see his neighbor dancing in her kitchen. He didn't know the woman's name but believed she was single with a young daughter.

That had been good enough for Scooby: a dancer *and* a cougar. Maybe after he made her famous, she'd become friendly-friendly with him. Invite him over for some afternoon shenanigans while her daughter sucked on a popsicle.

This TikTok gig is gonna be life-changing! he thought, getting out of the car and crossing the road with a spring in his step. He skipped up the steps of the front porch steps and knocked at the door. When nobody answered, he tried the doorknob. It was unlocked, so he stepped inside, calling out, "Anybody home, yo?"

The cougar was home, all right. A hot little thing in a white blouse and skin-tight blue jeans. She was about ten feet from him where the living room met the kitchen.

And unlike lame-ass Kitty Appleton, she was dancing up a storm: holding up the hems of an invisible dress, spinning this way and that, stomping the ground with her feet. She reminded Scooby of the way those crazy Greek bitches dance at weddings, only she wasn't smashing dishes.

"Hell, yes!" he exclaimed, stepping aside to let Lizzy inside. "Now we're talking. Get ready to film, girl."

Lizzy closed the door behind her. "You really gonna use the mousetraps?"

"I didn't dish out hard-earned cash on them for nothing. Now get filming!"

Lizzy obliged, and Scooby joined the woman dancing, mimicking her silly stomps and twirls and toe points, even getting a few ass grabs in as part of the show.

"Now for some fun, yo," he said to the camera after about thirty seconds of mock dancing. He shrugged off his backpack and produced one of the mousetraps he'd purchased. He tossed it on the floor near the woman's feet. Somehow she danced in a circle right around the fucking thing until, finally, one of her socked feet stepped on it, activating the spring coils. The jaws launched shut, biting (and bouncing off) her heel. She cried out—a high-pitched, girlish sound—but continued dancing.

Hooting with laughter, Scooby tossed the remaining three mousetraps around her feet. Almost immediately she stepped on another. Unlike the previous one, the spring-loaded metal jaws clamped onto her right big toe.

She leaped into the air...and landed awkwardly, her left ankle bending sideways in an unnatural, sickening way.

Unable to stand on that foot, she went down quickly. Her head smacked the edge of the Formica kitchen counter with a sharp clunk, and then she was lying on the carpeted floor, motionless.

The adjective *dead* also came to Scooby's mind before he quickly shooed it away.

He looked at Lizzy; the dumb bitch was still filming. "Turn that shit off!"

Lizzy lowered her phone. "Is she okay?"

"Does she look fucking okay?"

"Oh my God. Is that *blood*?"

Scooby glanced back at the woman. A pool of dark red blood was growing around her black hair like a macabre halo. His heart pounding, he sank to his knees next to her.

"Lady?" he said, shaking one of her delicate shoulders.

She didn't respond.

He used both hands to roll her over onto her back. The source of the blood was a savage gash in her forehead that resembled a messy bite out of a black cherry pie. But it was her slack expression and glazed eyes that turned Scooby's insides cold.

"Oh shit," he said.

CHAPTER 11

COMING HOME

While Gabriela walked home from school, she tried not to think about Katie and Helen and the other mean girls but what she liked about Camp Verde. She liked that the town was small enough she could walk anywhere she wanted, such as to the little museum, the library, or the farmers' market on Saturday mornings. She liked strolling along the bank of the river and watching the kayakers and rafters, or lounging in the shade beneath a tree and watching the horses and other farm animals in the nearby fields, which reminded her of the ranch back in Guadalajara. She liked spending a day at the Outpost Mall on weekends with her mother, wandering from shop to shop and admiring all the pretty clothing and packaged merchandise (it never struck her until then that much of the goods sold on the streets in Mexico were unpackaged). She also liked to simply hang out in the mall's food court and people-watch. It amazed her how much food Americans ate—and wasted.

Things will get better, she told herself. *And* Mami's *happy here. She likes her job at the high school cafeteria. We have a house and food. That's all that matters right now.*

A chain-link fence, the uprights leaning drunkenly in places, surrounded the house where Gabriela and her mother were living. Gabriela pushed the gate open, the rusty hinges groaning, and followed the cement pavers across the dirt yard. The house featured white clapboard siding and mauve trim. An awning that ran the length of one side offered shade from the sun. A few foldable chairs were clustered beneath it, as well as an old barbecue (which they hadn't used yet because there was no gas canister).

The house might not be fancy like the bigger ones on the land that straddled the perimeter of the town, but it had an air-conditioning unit in one window, working gas, and clean water—all luxuries, as far as Gabriela was concerned.

She was standing on the porch, fishing through her pockets for her key, when a bad feeling washed over her. She didn't know what caused it, only that something was not right. When she stepped inside, she recoiled in surprise.

Her mother lay on the floor, where the living area met the kitchen, a big pool of blood encircling her head.

"*Mami!*" she cried, squatting next to her. She shook her shoulders. "*Mami? Mami*, wake up! *Mami…?*"

But she knew her mother wasn't going to wake up. Her father was dead, and now her mother was dead too, and she was alone. The police would come and get her. A judge would send her to an immigration detention facility (*perreras*, or dog cages, as her mother had always called them), where she would probably be locked up for the rest of her life.

"Mom?" Gabriela tried one final time in English because that was what she was supposed to speak around the house.

Then she burst into tears.

CHAPTER 12

THE LITTLE GIRL AND THE SHERIFF

As they walked back to Camp Verde Suites, Ben mused, "Three people missing outside of town..."

Sally thought she knew what he was implying. Five people had died the night they had been held captive in Ryders Field. The gypsies had killed them and taken their bodies when they'd departed in the morning.

Does he believe the same gypsies—or in his mind, werewolves—are responsible for the disappearance of these three people as well?

She said, "You heard everything Amanda said about mass hysteria, Ben. It happens, and a lot. It's due to societal stresses and anxieties and fears. It has no connection to gypsies—or werewolves, for that matter."

"Mass hysteria doesn't, no," he agreed. "But I'm still not convinced mass hysteria is the cause of dancing plagues."

"I thought we talked through this," she said, picking her next words carefully so she didn't sound condescending. "A dozen schoolkids are dancing here, Ben. That just doesn't fit your theory about what happened in Chatham. Which means that's not what's happening here either."

"And the teenage girl Amanda mentioned who survived the camping trip, the one who was 'fucked two ways from Tuesday' and stuck in a mental institution—I know what can cause that kind of psychological trauma—"

"Anything could have caused her to snap. She could

have been raped, for Christ's sake. To make the leap to werewolves..." She shook her head. She'd had enough of this. "*If* the gypsies in Chatham had been werewolves, Ben. And *if* they were responsible for the dancing that happened there. And *if* they were now here doing the same thing...I mean, they were adults when we were kids. They'd be in the sixties by now. You think they're still terrorizing communities at that age?"

"I'm not saying it's necessarily the same werewolves, Sally. It could be a new generation. Or maybe it's a completely different pack. Who's to say only one pack exists? The country's a big place."

"Do you honestly—and I mean *honestly*, Ben—believe those kids in the community center are dancing so they don't turn into werewolves tomorrow night?"

He didn't answer her immediately, and they walked about a half block in silence before he replied. "Do you remember the first time you learned that Santa Claus wasn't real?"

The question caught her off guard. She shook her head. "Not really, no."

"I do. Chunk told me when we were seven, on Christmas Day, of all times. I was testing a Magic Carpet sled I'd gotten from Santa on the snowbanks that the snowplow had created out the front of my house. Chunk came by on a GT Snow Racer— you know, one of those fancy sleds with a steering wheel and skis? His parents always bought him the best stuff. Anyway, we weren't really friends then, but he lived right around the corner, so we saw enough of each other. He started making fun of my sled because it was just a piece of plastic. I asked him if he got his sled from Santa, and he told me Santa didn't exist. He told me to check the handwriting on the presents from Santa and the ones from my parents because they would be the same. I went inside and checked." He shook his head slowly. "Learning that Santa didn't exist—well, it sucked. It ruined that Christmas. The fun and magic sort of disappeared. But even though I was disappointed...I wasn't surprised. A part of me had already known Santa didn't exist, but I'd spent so many years believing he *did* exist, I simply couldn't imagine him not existing, even if I knew better." He went quiet for a bit before continuing. "And that's sort of how I feel now. I hear what you're saying. I'm a rational person, believe it or not. I know werewolves aren't real, can't be real, *shouldn't* be real. But I have memories of them, Sally. *Vivid memories.* I've had them for thirty goddamn years. And I'm…finding it tough to throw them all out the window." He gave her a tepid smile. "But don't worry about me. I just need a bit of time, I suppose, to process…things. If we get together in another thirty years from now, you watch, I'll be right as rain." He chuckled to himself. "That's what Chunk used to say. *Right as rain.* He got it from his dad. Jesus, I really do need to get my head out of the past—"

Sally touched Ben's arm. He saw what she was looking at: across the street a young girl in a yellow dress sat on the front steps of a run-down house, her arms and head resting on her bony knees.

"Is she crying?" Ben said.

"Let's find out," she said.

"I don't know if it's any of our business. I mean, kids cry."

"Look at her—sitting out on the front porch like that? She looks miserable."

"She's probably just got in trouble with her parents."

"I don't know about you, Ben, but my parents sent me to my room when I did something wrong."

"Mine made me sit on the staircase landing. You have stuff you can play with in your bedroom. There's nothing to do on the staircase—or on a porch, for that matter."

"I'm going to make sure." Sally crossed the street and stopped before the gate to the front yard. "Hello? Hi?"

The girl raised her head. Tears pooled in her dark eyes and streaked her cheeks. Her body stiffened as if she might bolt.

"It's okay," Sally said quickly. "I just wanted to see if everything is okay?"

She nodded her head, even as fresh tears spilled from her

eyes.

"Oh, honey, what's wrong? Aren't your parents home?"

She covered her face with her hands and began to sob, her small shoulders heaving.

Sally didn't see any bruises or other signs of physical abuse on the girl's arms or legs. She glanced at the house. She heard no shouting or arguing coming from inside. In fact, the place seemed too quiet.

"Where are your parents, sweetheart?" she asked in a gentle voice.

The girl didn't reply.

"Are they home?"

She peeked out from between her hands. "My...my... *mami*..." she stammered between sniffles. "She's... She's..."

"She's what?" Sally asked gently.

"*¡Está muerta!*" the girl blurted.

ΔΔΔ

Sally sat next to the rattled girl and pulled her into an embrace. Convulsions racked her little body as she sobbed into Sally's shoulder.

Ben pushed open the gate and came up the walkway.

"What's going on?" he demanded.

"I don't know," Sally said. "I think she said something about murder?"

"*Murder?*" Ben's eyes went to the house.

"Not murder!" the girl wailed. "Dead! My *mami's* dead!"

"Oh Jesus," Sally said, stroking the girl's head. "Ben, go check inside."

He was already moving past them up the porch steps.

Sally continued stroking and hushing the girl, telling her it was going to be okay.

When Ben returned, his face was grim. He held his phone in his hand.

"I'm going to call an ambulance," he said somberly.

"No!" The girl sprang apart from Sally, her eyes filled with fear.

"It's not your fault, sweetheart," Sally said. "You're not in trouble."

"No ambulance," she said. "No police. Please?"

"It looks like your mother fell over and hit her head," Ben said. "Is that what happened to her?"

The girl blinked. "No. Yes. I don't know. I just came home, and she was like that."

"So you see," Sally told her, "what happened isn't your fault. You weren't even home."

The girl rubbed tears from her eyes.

"Where's your father?" Ben asked.

"He's dead too."

"Dead?" Sally said, confused. She glanced at Ben. He shook his head as if to say his body wasn't inside the house.

The girl said, "He died at home."

Sally's confusion grew. "Isn't this your home?"

The girl didn't reply.

Ben asked her, "Do you have any other family in town?"

She remained silent.

"Any at all in the United States?"

She appeared as though she were about to burst into tears again, and Sally understood what Ben was driving at. The girl and her mother were undocumented immigrants. Her "home" was Mexico. That was why she didn't want Ben to call the ambulance or the police. Her mother had likely warned her to avoid the authorities at all costs.

What were they going to do? She knew they had to turn the girl over to the authorities…but with no other family members in the United States, she would either wind up in foster care or be deported.

Ben seemed to be thinking along the same lines, and he slipped his phone back into his pocket.

"Why don't we go inside?" he said.

△△△

The furnishings were of the sort you might find at a Salvation Army or some other charitable foundation: dated, worn-out, idiosyncratic. Two doors at the back of the house presumably led to bedrooms. The girl's mother lay on the floor near the kitchen. Ben had draped a sheet over her. Telling the girl not to look, Sally led her to a small den off the main living area. She sat her down on the ratty sofa, introduced herself, offered a few comforting words, and turned on the TV. She handed the girl the remote control and said, "Try to find a cartoon or something to watch. I'll be back shortly."

In the kitchen, out of view of the dead body, Ben stood before the open refrigerator, a carton of milk in his hand. He took a whiff of the folded spout and made a face.

"There's nothing to drink," he said.

"Are you that thirsty?" she asked.

"I'm looking for something for the girl."

Sally knew that, of course; she was trying to lighten the grim situation. "She told me her name is Gabriela. She said we can call her Gabby."

"Poor kid," he said simply.

"What are we going to do, Ben? You know that if we call the police, she's going to be sent to one of those awful detention facilities. Then what? Months in immigration court before more likely than not getting kicked back to Mexico with nothing but the shirt on her back?"

"Short of kidnapping her, or leaving her here on her own, what else can we do?"

"You checked her mother, right? I mean, to make sure she's… really dead?"

"I saw her, Sally."

She blinked. "You didn't check for a pulse?"

"She's dead. Trust me."

She did trust him, but she wanted to verify for herself that

Gabriela's mother was truly gone before getting the authorities involved.

"Gimme a sec."

"Sally..."

She went to the body, crouched next to it...and hesitated, her heart suddenly pounding inside her chest. The last dead body she had seen had been her daughter's. Seeing another one —even one belonging to a stranger—was not going to be easy.

She lifted the cover. Gabriela's mother—a pretty woman who couldn't have been any older than twenty-five—lay on her back. Her white blouse was saturated with blood spilled from a gash on her forehead, which also covered the champagne-colored carpet around her. Her open eyes stared blankly at the ceiling. One leg and one arm were bent, almost like the stereotypical chalk outlines of bodies at a crime scene.

Unfortunately Ben was right.

The woman was about as dead as you could get.

ΔΔΔ

The sheriff and two paramedics arrived within ten minutes. Gabriela stared fixedly at the TV (which was playing a cartoon about a child aardvark getting into shenanigans with his neighbors) and didn't give them a single glance. Either they scared her senseless, or she believed that by ignoring them, they might ignore her too. She didn't even look away from the TV when the paramedics lifted her mother's body onto a stretcher and rolled it out of the house.

Sally remained next to her on the sofa, holding her hand. When Ben finished speaking to the sheriff in the kitchen, he indicated for her to join them.

"You wait right here, sweetheart," she told Gabriela. "I won't be long."

The sheriff was Ben's height, though beefy and about ten years older. He had a sagging, unremarkable face that played second fiddle to a protruding, bulbous nose. Crafty eyes watched her approach.

"Howdy, ma'am," he said, removing his cowboy hat. Receding silver-white hair fell to his shoulders. "Sheriff Russell Walker. Terrible situation we got here."

"It's terrible for anybody to lose a loved one," she agreed. "That little girl over there is only eight years old, and she no longer has a mother."

"I was speaking about the town in general. We've suffered through serious droughts before. Floods on the Verde River. Two Cat 4 hurricanes in 2018. Last year we had five cases of the septicemic plague, one of them fatal. But we've never had a *dancing* plague. Shit, this lady's the fourth one we've lost so far."

Sally blinked in surprise. "You think she was dancing?"

"Her neighbor reported her on our Facebook page. It's something we set up to report anyone dancing around town. So we can get them looked after—before something like this happens. Only good news here is it don't look like she was one of us..."

Sally frowned. *One of us?* "You're referring to her immigration status?"

"I don't wanna jump the gun, but I doubt we're gonna find any documentation that proves she's *not* an illegal. You'd be surprised at how many we get here in Verde. Most don't stay too long. Just a stopover on their way to them big, immigrant-loving sanctuary cities. Makes me wonder though. Pretty lady like that, undocumented, why set down here? My guess? She found some sugar daddy online who's paying to keep her around, for company when the missus ain't home."

Sally kept her distaste for the man from her voice and said, "What's going to happen to her daughter?"

"If she turns out to be an unaccompanied alien minor?" He shrugged. "That would mean she got no lawful status in the country, wouldn't it? And if that's the case, she'll be sent to a Customs and Border Protection facility until they figure out whether she got any other adult guardians in the country. If she don't, then she'll be repatriated."

"She told us her father in Mexico is dead."

Sheriff Walker nodded. "Your friend here—Ben, ain't it?—already mentioned that. So if she wants to stay in the big, old US of A, she'll have to make a claim for asylum."

"She's only a child. She won't understand any of this."

"She'll have a government-appointed lawyer—on the taxpayer's dime, don't you worry your pretty head over that, ma'am."

"And then what happens?" she asked tightly.

"The Office of Refugee Resettlement, that's a department of HHS, will find her somewhere to live during her time in federal custody until a court settlement is reached."

"A detention center?"

"It ain't gonna be a Hilton, I'll tell you that."

"And if she's granted asylum?"

"They'll arrange a long-term solution."

"A foster-care center?"

"There's that. But the government got itself a national network of maybe two hundred state-licensed, independent shelters where she'll get free education, healthcare, legal services—all on the taxpayer's dime, 'course."

"What are the chances of that happening?"

"Getting asylum?" He smiled. "Not so good."

Sally wanted to slap the smugness off his face. If Gabriela was deported, and there was no family to take her in when she returned to Mexico, she would end up on the streets, where she would be a natural target for human traffickers and other scum that exploited young, destitute girls.

Ben was frowning, no doubt feeling as helpless as she did. He said, "I'm sure DHS will take everything into account, Sally. But it's going to be their call."

"What about in the short-term?" she asked Sheriff Walker. "What's going to happen to her tonight?"

"I'll place her on an immigration hold until the ICE man can come and get her."

"The Iceman?" she said, bizarrely thinking of Val Kilmer in *Top Gun.*

"An officer from ICE—Immigration and Customs Enforcement," he clarified.

"But what about *tonight*? Where will she sleep?"

"At the police station."

Sally was aghast. "You're going to lock her up in a *cell*? She just lost her mother! She's just a child!"

"Who broke the law."

"This is preposterous. Do you want to traumatize her more than she likely already is?"

"What do you suggest I do, ma'am?" he said acerbically. "Put her up in the spare bedroom at my house?"

"She can stay with me," she stated. "I have a room down the road at the Camp Verde Suites."

"Why would she want to do that? You're a total stranger. You only met her for the first time half an hour ago, ain't that right?"

"She'll have a proper bed and a friendly voice. Compared to the alternative that you're suggesting, I don't think it will be a hard decision for her to make."

The sheriff thought this over and nodded. "By all means, go and ask her then. She'll be one less headache for me—and God knows I got my share of fucking headaches at the moment."

CHAPTER 13

THE MOTEL

Sally turned off the bathtub taps and tested the temperature of the water with her hand: hot but not scalding. She returned to the main room. Gabriela was sitting on the bed, her back stiff against the headboard, watching television.

Sally said, "Bath's ready if you're ready, hon."

Gabriela's stomach grumbled loudly. Embarrassed, she clapped her hands over her belly.

Food had been second on Sally's to-do list, and she asked, "When was the last time you ate?"

"This morning," the girl said quietly. "I had Cheerios."

Sally recalled that the milk in her fridge had been off. "With milk?"

She shook her head. "Just Cheerios—and sugar."

"Why didn't you eat lunch?"

"There wasn't anything good left."

"Well, you can have whatever you want for dinner. How does that sound? What's your favorite food?"

"Pizza."

"Pizza it is then. Pepperoni okay?"

She nodded.

"Go have your bath. I'll order a couple of pizzas right now."

Gabriela slid off the bed and disappeared inside the bathroom, closing the door behind her. Sally performed a search on her phone and found a place called Crusty's

Pizza located about a mile away. She called the number, half-expecting nobody to pick up, given their experience at the steakhouse earlier. However, it was answered almost immediately. She ordered two large pepperoni pizzas, garlic bread, and a small antipasto salad (accepting the recommendation of homemade ranch sauce instead of traditional Italian dressing).

After she hung up she went outside and knocked on the door to Ben's room.

"Yeah?" he called.

"It's me," she said.

"Come in."

Sally entered. The room was empty.

"Ben?"

"I'm in the bath."

"Oh…"

"It's fine. I'm decent."

She wondered how one could be decent while taking a bath. Nevertheless, she went to the slightly ajar bathroom door and knocked lightly.

"Hey," he said.

She could have spoken to him from where she stood, but her curiosity got the better of her. She pushed open the door and looked inside. Ben was stretched out in the bathtub, his legs crossed at the ankles and propped up on the end lip. In his right hand was a green bottle of beer. The other held a sudsy facecloth over his private parts.

Sally blushed. "You look comfortable."

"I hate baths," he told her, "but the shower wasn't working."

"Room for two in there?"

"Unfortunately it might be a tad tight."

"Shame."

"Shame indeed," he said.

Sally assumed he was kidding around. Regardless, the flirtatious banter sent a tingle through her.

"You were always so modest as a kid, Ben."

"You're the one who poked her head into my bathroom."

"You invited me."

"You want a drink from the minibar? I'll dry off and be out in a sec."

"Ah, no…" she said. She definitely could have used a drink after what they'd witnessed at Gabriela's house, but she didn't want to leave the girl alone for too long. "I ordered a couple of pizzas. They'll be ready for pickup in about forty-five minutes. Do you mind driving over to get them?"

"Don't mind at all."

"It's called Crusty's."

"Got it."

"All right then."

They held each other's gaze for a moment of charged silence.

Sally felt herself blushing again. "I, uh, better get back to Gabriela."

ΔΔΔ

They were seated crossed-legged on the queen bed, Gabriela wearing a pair of unicorn-patterned pink pajamas she'd brought with her, Sally sipping on her second glass of red wine.

Sally had found a deck of Bicycle playing cards next to a brand-new looking Bible in the drawer of the night table. Gabriela had taught her how to play Manilla, a trick-taking game that used a forty-card deck. After several rounds of this, Sally had taught her Crazy Eights.

Now Gabriela slapped down a deuce of spades. "Pick up two!" she said, giggling.

"*Again?*" Sally said, feigning incredulity. She drew two cards from what remained of the deck. "You've gotten too good at this game."

"My turn?"

"Yup."

She studied the three cards fanned out in her hand. "What does *la Jota* do, I forget?"

"Show me?"

She flashed a Jack of spades. "It makes me miss a turn."

She set it down, followed by a three of spades. "Last card!"

"Oh, boy." Sally had five cards remaining. She played an eight of diamonds. "I change the suit to..." She had inadvertently glimpsed the girl's cards earlier (she wasn't very good at keeping them close to her chest, so to speak), and she knew she had an ace of hearts remaining. "...Hearts."

Gabriela's eyes lit up as she played her final card. "I win!"

Sally smiled. "You sure do."

"Can we play again?"

"Sure, sweetheart. But let's take a quick break so I can check on where our pizzas are, okay?"

"Can I watch TV?"

"Go for it."

Sally stepped outside the motel room with her phone. More stars than she'd ever seen above New York City glittered in the black sky, an impossible number that made her feel infinitely small. The air was cool, almost chilly, an amazing one-eighty from the sweltering heat of the day.

She checked her wristwatch. It was five minutes past eight o'clock. Ben had left to pick up the pizzas more than forty minutes ago, a trip that shouldn't have taken him any longer than fifteen minutes. Either he'd gone to the wrong place (even though she hadn't been able to find any other pizza restaurants in Camp Verde), there was a backlog of orders (hard to believe if most of the town was staying at home for fear of catching the dancing bug), or—the most likely scenario, in her mind—the restaurant had misplaced her order and had to make the pizzas from scratch upon his arrival.

If she'd had Ben's phone number, she would have called him to check in. But he'd never given it to her, so she dialed Crusty's Pizza instead.

After close to a dozen rings a woman answered. "Hi there —we're closed for the night," she said, sounding slightly annoyed.

"Closed?" Sally said, frowning. "I placed an order an hour and a half ago. Two—"

"Two pizzas, garlic bread, salad?"

"That's right."

"It's still here, and it's cold—but as I said, we're closed now."

"Nobody picked it up...?"

"There was somebody here for a bit, but he left."

"Did he have dark hair?"

"Dark hair, a bit lanky. Was wearing black."

"Yes, that's my friend! He just left?"

"I didn't see him leave," she said, her voice growing impatient, "but he was here before, and he's not here now, so, yes, he left. I don't know why. But I gotta finish closing up, all right? If you want, call back tomorrow, and we'll do your order again, on the house."

After they disconnected, Sally stared at her phone in confusion. Why would Ben leave the restaurant without their order? And where was he now?

She had no idea what was going on, but she didn't like it one bit.

A door closed loudly in the otherwise silent night. Sally was surprised to see the reporter for the Phoenix news station emerge from the room at the end of the motel.

She noticed Sally and waved. "Oh, hey! Didn't know you guys were staying here."

Sally didn't see the news van anywhere and assumed it was parked around the corner of the building. "It was either here or out by the interchange."

"Where's your friend?" she asked, lighting a cigarette.

"He went to get us pizzas..." She was about to leave it at that but decided she was too unnerved to keep her thoughts to herself. She walked over to the other woman—Amanda, she recalled—so they could stop shouting at one another. Dressed in yoga pants and an oversized sweater, the reporter somehow seemed as effortlessly fashionable as she had earlier in her pink jumpsuit. "I just called the restaurant," she continued.

"They said he was there—but he left without the pizzas. I don't understand it."

"Maybe he decided to get something different?"

"No, he wouldn't have done that. The pizzas were for...um, a girl we're looking after for the night."

Amanda took a drag on the cigarette. "Give him a call then."

"I don't know his number."

She raised her eyebrows. "For some reason I thought you two knew each other better... Didn't you say you grew up together?"

"We did. But we just got back in touch yesterday, and I never had any reason to ask him for his number. Anyway, I'm sure he'll turn up soon with a reasonable explanation. I should get going."

"If you guys are still interested in being interviewed about the dancing plague in Chatham, I'll be at the community center again tomorrow—"

Sally's phone chirruped.

Thank God, she thought, chiding herself for getting so worked up over Ben's odd behavior.

She opened the new message—and stared at it with a combination of dumb surprise and body-numbing dread.

"What is it?" Amanda asked her.

Sally couldn't take her eyes away from the photograph sent as an attachment.

"Oh my God..." she said in a barely breathed whisper.

PART 2
Return of the Gypsies

CHAPTER 14

MULLET MAN

Crusty's Pizza was sandwiched between a CVS/Pharmacy and the entrance to the garish brick-and-cement strip mall in which it was located. Like any good pizza parlor, the smells wafting from the stone oven were tantalizingly good: a trifecta of baking dough, melting cheese, and tangy sauce.

A stick-thin woman wearing a paisley kerchief over her auburn hair appeared from the kitchen. "Help ya?"

"I'm picking up an order for Sally Levine," Ben said.

"About another ten minutes. Something to drink?"

He declined and took a seat at one of the many empty tables. The restaurant had an old-school Italian feel, featuring wood booths upholstered in red and white and green, terracotta tiles on the floor, and frescos of the old country on the walls. A decorative cast-iron streetlamp stood next to the brick counter.

There was only one customer aside from Ben, a guy in his mid-twenties. He was leaning against a wall, looking at his phone while drinking a German beer. His blond-streaked hair was all business in the front and party in the back.

It wasn't just the guy's bold hairstyle that Ben found himself (strangely) admiring. The guy was unusually handsome. Ben couldn't recall the last time, if ever, he'd thought that about another man. But this guy with his tall frame and sharp, chiseled features certainly fit the bill.

Which made Ben wonder what Mullet Man was doing in an out-of-the-way place like Camp Verde. He should be in Miami or New York or Los Angeles, headlining a punk or glam band, dating runway models, and instigating affairs with the bored wives of the super-rich.

He looked up from his phone and caught Ben studying him. "How you doing tonight, my man?" he said.

"All right," Ben said.

"They got the best pizza in town here."

"Yeah?"

"Only pizza in town—but the best."

"Vlad?" the skinny woman said. She set half a dozen pizzas on the counter and returned with another half dozen a moment later.

The guy stuck a bill in the tip jar. "Thanks, Carla. I'm gonna miss your pies."

"You won't be back next month?"

"Think we'll be moving on shortly. You keep smiling, hear?" He stacked the pizza boxes into one precarious tower and scooped them into his arms. As he passed Ben on his way out, he said, "You keep on smiling too, my man."

"You've got some appetite."

He winked. "Must be the full moon."

△△△

Ben stared after the guy as he left the restaurant, stunned, uncertain, electrified. As soon as his cherry-red Mustang started away through the empty parking lot, the big V-8 rumbling, Ben dashed to the Camaro, got behind the wheel, and followed.

△△△

The Mustang sped north on State Highway 260, pushing 70 mph, fifteen over the limit. Ben kept pace, his thoughts and pulse racing, *"Must be the full moon"* on loop in his mind. Although it could have been an innocent reference to the imminent lunar phase, it could also be a cheeky, loaded comment a werewolf might say.

Moreover, Mullet Man had ordered a *dozen* pizzas. More than enough to feed a small group of people who might be looking to stuff themselves silly before their metabolisms went into overdrive and their bodies ate themselves from the inside out, transforming them into emancipated wretches.

"Jesus Christ," Ben mumbled to himself, unsure whether he was more terrified or excited. "Jesus fucking Christ, buddy."

The Mustang's brake lights flashed red.

Ben's immediate reaction was: *He recognized the Camaro! He knows I'm tailing him!* This was followed by: *No way. You have every right to be on the highway too.*

The Mustang angled to the gravel shoulder, its hazards flashing. Ben roared past moments later, noting a black-and-yellow traffic sign to mark the location. He couldn't brake. But he took his foot off the gas pedal.

The Mustang continued to recede in the rear-view mirror.

Come on, Mullet Man. Do it. What are you waiting for?

The car's headlights swung right—pioneering an off-road path into the desert.

ΔΔΔ

Ben made a U-turn, crossing over the grassy median onto the southbound lanes. He continued the way he had come until he saw the metallic backside of the road sign in his high beams. He checked that no cars were approaching from behind before braking and veering right into the desert. He bumped over the uneven ground for about thirty feet and parked behind a large bushy shrub. He killed the engine, got out, and hurried back to the highway. It was empty in both directions. He crossed the southbound lane, then the northbound one, and continued in the direction the Mustang had gone.

CHAPTER 15

MALENIA

Ten minutes later, just as he feared he had gotten himself turned around and lost in the darkness, he spotted several campfires in the distance at the base of a rocky knoll. The sight sent a shot of adrenaline to his heart. He redoubled his pace, thinking multiple thoughts at once. What was he going to find when he reached them? Boozing and pot-smoking and laughter, like he, Sally, and Chunk had observed in Ryders Field thirty-one years ago? The same group of characters, now geriatrics? He could only recall the gypsy woman with any clarity. Would she be there, in a rocking chair perhaps, wrinkled and shrunken? He had told Sally the werewolves in Camp Verde might be a different pack than the one that had been in Chatham, but he wasn't sure if he believed that. His gut told him that they were one and the same.

In the silvered light of the nearly full moon, he made out the shadowed shapes of three RVs, as well as nine or ten regular-sized vehicles. Voices raised in conversation—vociferous, boastful, inebriated—carried through the chilly night.

Ben altered his path to keep the parked vehicles between himself and the campfires. He wasn't planning on getting too close or sticking around for too long. Just a quick glimpse to satisfy his curiosity before hightailing it back to the Camaro. Tomorrow was a different matter. Tomorrow he would return prepared to capture their transformations from a safe, concealed distance—

He froze on the spot, hardly believing his eyes.

Parked on the far side of a large Winnebago were two derelict circus wagons, one red and the other yellow, their sides lined with black iron bars.

It's them! he thought. *The same ones!*

Ben's mind leaped back to the night in Ryders Field, Sally and Chunk and him locked up in the red wagon, Sheriff Sandberg and the deputy in the yellow one, the storm raging overhead, the werewolves prowling the night, all the blood and gore and death that ensued. His father…

He banished the memory but didn't take his eyes off the two wagons. Every instinct told him to go back, flee, never return. But he couldn't do any of that. The wagons didn't prove that the gypsies were werewolves, but they did prove that they were the gypsies that had been in Chatham in 1988 and that they had something to do with the dancing that had occurred then —and now.

Ben slipped his phone from his pocket, snapped a picture with both wagons in the frame, and sent it to Sally, feeling suddenly euphoric at the discovery—

He spotted movement in the shadows along the length of the Winnebago. He ducked low and turned to make a break back to the highway. Two men stood a dozen feet behind him.

Ben didn't know how they'd gotten so close without making any noise. But they had, and now his escape route was cut off.

A dozen options raced through his mind, none of them good.

"Who the fuck are you?" the man on the left said. Tattoos covered his forearms and neck all the way to his jawline.

"And what the fuck are you doing here?" the other one said. He had a lumberjack beard and was all muscle.

"He followed me from the pizza joint."

Ben spun around at the sound of the third voice.

Mullet Man stepped out of the shadows of the Winnebago.

"What I wanna know," he continued, "is why?"

△△△

Tattoos and Lumberjack gripped Ben by the biceps and steered him toward Mullet Man. He didn't fight. He knew it would be futile, just like attempting to run. All three men were in their twenties and looked as fit as professional athletes. Moreover, fighting or running would reveal that he had a reason to fear them, which didn't fit with the story he was quickly settling on.

"What the hell's going on?" he said when he reached Mullet Man, trying to sound indignant. "Is this how you treat a guest?"

"A guest?" Mullet Man said. "Is that what you are? I thought a guest needed to be invited to be welcome."

"If I'm not welcome, then let me go. I'll be on my way."

But Mullet Man had already started walking away.

Tattoos and Lumberjack frogmarched Ben after him. They passed through the collection of vehicles and approached three large campfires. The flames of each rose half a dozen feet into the night, crackling loudly and spitting sparks that twirled erratically on the warm updrafts. Ten men sat around the fires in camping chairs, all of them young, handsome, and in shape. Most were drinking beer from cans, though a couple held liquor bottles in their hands. The air was thick with the smell of marijuana.

"What did you fellas find lurking out in the desert?" one of them asked. He had his booted feet propped up on a cooler box and a cigarette in one hand. "Don't look like a coyote to me."

"Get Malenia," Mullet Man said simply.

"You go fucking get her. Do I look like I'm in the getting mood?"

"I'll get her, dipshits," a man with a buzzcut said, flicking his cigarette into the fire before him. He started through the night toward an RV with its windows lit up from within. Ben hadn't noticed it until now; it was parked at least a hundred yards away from all the other vehicles.

Tattoos and Lumberjack left Ben's side and reclaimed empty seats adjacent to one another. Clearly they knew he didn't have any chance of fleeing on foot.

Mullet Man went to a small table crowded with beer bottles. He picked up one that was half full and tipped it to his lips.

Ben said, "This isn't exactly the party I was expecting."

"Party?"

"Don't you want to hear why I'm here?"

"Save it for Malenia."

"Who's Malenia?"

Mullet Man ignored him and said, "Who has the fucking joint?"

A man wearing a denim vest over his bare chest held up his arm, a fat joint between his index finger and thumb. Mullet Man went over to him, pinched it, and took several quick puffs. Everyone resumed their conversations, most of which were rowdy, drunken banter laced with profanities, the kind of stuff you'd hear in a football locker room.

Given their general youthfulness—no one could have been older than thirty—they weren't the same gypsies from 1988. Ben suspected they could be the next generation, but if that was the case, where were the older ones? Did werewolves eat their weak and elderly? Or did they die young? After all, a wolf's life expectancy was much closer to that of a dog's than a human's, and if their genes were spliced with those of a canine...

Which brought Ben to the burning million-dollar question: were they werewolves or not? It was impossible to say for certain without witnessing a transformation. But it was evident they weren't, as Sally believed, raving mad cult members who dressed up as wolves...unless, that was, they kept their furs and headdresses stored away until the night of the full moon.

Maybe I'm *the mad one,* he wondered grimly. *No sane person could ask such a surreal question. So I'm either mad, or this is a dream. Go ahead, pinch yourself, Benny-boy. See if you wake up.*

Ben didn't pinch himself because he knew he wasn't dreaming. And he didn't think he was mad either. In his heart of hearts he believed what he'd always believed: werewolves existed. He'd encountered them as a child, and now he had made his way into their company again.

Only this time they weren't likely to show mercy on him. If they knew that he knew they were werewolves, he was dead meat—dead, *tasty* meat, more like it. Which meant his story for following Mullet Man had to be good. It had to be believable. And even then—even if he convinced them he was nothing but a foolish gay man looking for a good time—he was not so sure they would simply let him go. They might decide to lock him in one of the circus wagons until tomorrow night when he would be served up as a fresh and easy meal to fuel their transformation into blood-thirsty beasts.

Blood-thirsty beasts.

Giddiness bubbled inside Ben's chest, and he forced it away. If he began laughing right then, he didn't think he would be able to stop.

The man who had gone to the distant RV was returning to the campfires with Malenia. Her dark clothing blended with the night, making her all but undetectable except for the pale blur of her face. Ben watched them with growing apprehension, somehow certain this woman would decide his fate.

When she stepped into the warm orange hues of the campfires, he stared at her in bewildered awe.

Not only was Malenia the same gypsy woman from his childhood in Chatham, but in all the time between then and now it appeared as though she hadn't aged a day.

CHAPTER 15

THE INTERROGATION

Somehow Ben kept his composure, yet behind his cool façade, his mind was rioting.

It can't be the same gypsy woman! She looks all of twenty-five years old!

But it was her. He had never forgotten her face, and he never would.

It's her daughter, he realized with a burst of relief. *She's a spitting image of her mother, that's all.*

Even though this had to be the case, Ben couldn't help but fear she was going to recognize him. She would get inside his head with those telepathic powers of hers. She would read his thoughts as easily as a book. She would say something insouciant like, "Ben Graves, look at you now, all grown up."

None of this happened.

She simply stopped before him and said, "Who are you and what are you doing here?

Mullet Man said, "He followed me from the pizza joint."

She frowned. "Why did he do that?"

"Why don't you ask him?"

She looked at Ben, her dark eyes intense. "Well?"

He shrugged flippantly. "Look, I guess I read the situation wrong, okay?"

"What situation was that?"

He nodded at Mullet Man. "Your friend was checking me out

in the restaurant."

Everybody seated around the fires roared in laughter. Someone made a provocative catcall. Others propositioned Mullet Man.

Above the ruckus, Mullet Man fumed, "That's bullshit!"

"Like I mentioned," Ben said, "I read the situation wrong. He had a dozen pizzas. I figured, you know, there was some event, some party, going on. And I thought, you know, I might just show up. There's not exactly a huge gay population in Camp Verde. The more the merrier, as they say."

"My, what a nice cock you have, Vlad," one of the men ragged.

"Hey, man, you want some of my pizza?" another one added. "I got extra *sausage*."

This caused everyone to crack up again—except for Malenia, who remained unmoved and expressionless.

"Vlad is not gay," she said simply.

"No?" Ben looked past her to the others. "Then what's he doing hanging out with ten dudes in the desert?"

"Fuck you, motherfucker!" the man with the denim vest shouted. "Ain't none of us queer! Shee-*at*."

"Quiet Dennis," Malenia said without taking her eyes from Ben. She studied him silently for several long seconds. "What's your name?"

"Ben," he said.

"I might believe, Ben, that you found Vlad attractive. I myself find him quite attractive. And I might believe that you would be bold enough to follow him down the street in the hopes of discovering some like-minded company. What I'm finding hard to believe is that you would be bold enough to follow him for twenty miles into the desert."

"I'm here, aren't I?"

"Yes, you are."

Ben held her piercing gaze. He didn't know whether she believed him or not. But perhaps that didn't matter. She apparently couldn't read thoughts like her mother had been able to, and she had no reason to suspect he believed she was a werewolf. So unless she was planning to eat him tomorrow night, what reason would she have not to let him go?

"He took a picture of the wagons," Mullet Man said, exchanging the beer he'd been drinking with a full one from the table.

Ben said, "Not every day you see a couple of circus wagons like those two."

"Why are you in Camp Verde?" Malenia asked him.

"Got relatives here."

"May I see your phone?"

"My phone?"

Someone tossed a bottle onto a fire, where it shattered loudly. Someone else rifled through a cooler. Other than these sounds the night had gone ominously silent.

Shrugging, Ben slipped his phone from the back pocket of his jeans and handed it to her.

She opened his message app and then the message he'd sent to Sally. She said, "You sent the picture of the wagons to someone? Who?"

"My partner."

"He's in Camp Verde with you?"

Ben nodded.

"At your relatives?"

He nodded again.

She scrolled down several messages, then back to the top.

"1133 Broadway?" she said, reading the message his publicist had sent him yesterday. It was the address for Rizzoli's Bookstore. "I didn't know there was a Broadway in Camp Verde?"

"New York," he said easily. Fearing his story was about to collapse like a house of cards, he decided he had no choice but to inject it with as much truth as possible. "I had a book event there yesterday evening. I'm an author."

"You've only been in Camp Verde for the day?"

"That's right." He sighed in exasperation. "Look, I'm sorry

to have bothered you folks. I made a mistake. But what's the big deal? What's with all the questions? I'm not going to tell anybody you're squatting out here if that's what you're worried about."

"What's your surname?"

"Graves."

"Ben Graves?"

He nodded.

She typed it into Google. He saw a headshot of him appear in the search results.

"It's an old photo," he said.

"It's you."

"Who else would it be?"

She did another search, brought up his books on Amazon, and said, *The Dancing Plague.*" She arched an eyebrow at him. "Now that's interesting. There seems to be a 'dancing plague' happening in Camp Verde at the moment."

"My publicist mentioned the dancing plague to me yesterday. I thought I could generate some publicity by coming down here since I'd recently written a book on the subject."

"You said you were visiting relatives."

"No, I didn't. I said I *have* relatives here, and I'm staying with them."

She read the book's description out loud: "In the sixteenth-century hundreds of residents of Strasbourg in Alsace, now France, danced uncontrollably for days on end, many dropping dead from their exertions. Nearly four hundred years later the dancing plague has returned, this time afflicting the residents of an idyllic Cape Cod town. For three twelve-year-old friends, the inexplicable dancing mania is only the beginning of the horror to come..." She looked at Ben, her eyes unreadable. "Would that 'idyllic Cape Cod town' happen to be a place called Chatham?"

"How'd you know that?" he said, doing his best to appear surprised. When she didn't reply, he shrugged. "When I was researching dancing plagues for the book, I discovered there had been one in Chatham in 1988. Figured why not blend fiction with a little reality."

"Where are you from?"

"Boston," he said, knowing if she discovered the Wikipedia page written about him, which cited Chatham as his birthplace, he was busted.

"I wonder—what is the 'horror to come' you write about?"

"If I tell you that, I'd be spoiling the ending."

"Spoil away."

"Demon possession," he lied.

Malenia was silent for a long moment before turning her attention to the phone. She appeared to be scrolling through the reader reviews.

Initially Ben was bemused that she might be interested in whether the book was any good or not. Then he suspected what she might be looking for, and his blood turned cold.

She read a review, "I typically love Ben Graves's stories. But the ending of *The Dancing Plague* was just too much for me this time. Werewolves? Seriously? My teenage daughter could have come up with something more original than that!"

Although Ben never looked away from Malenia, he was acutely aware that the mood at the campsite had instantly changed. He could taste menace in the air.

"Werewolves?" Malenia said, her lips curling into a cryptic smile. "It seems, Ben, that you keep contradicting yourself. Why is that?"

"Demon possession, werewolves, vampires, I incorporate all that stuff—"

"You're a liar," she said bluntly. "You lied about why you came to Camp Verde. You lied about the content of your book. And I strongly suspect you're lying about why you followed Vlad here tonight. Tell me again, why did you take a photograph of the circus wagons?"

Ben swallowed tightly. He barely heard the question above the pounding of his heart, which seemed to be originating inside his head.

"They were a novelty," she answered for him. "I think you are lying to me about that also. Why do
they interest you?"

"They don't—"

"Lock him up, Vlad," she said tersely.

Mullet Man gripped Ben by the shoulders and shoved him toward the circus wagons.

"Wait!" he protested, struggling to break free. "What the hell are you doing? You can't lock me up! You can't do this!"

"You can't imagine what we can do, pal," Vlad told him threateningly. And Ben felt the warm, horrible lick of the man's tongue along the back of his neck. "Or maybe you can, huh?"

CHAPTER 16

THE SAFE HOUSE

Monster was at his computer, editing video from the Elden Ring stream he'd just completed, splicing together a collection of his best PVP invasions, when someone began pounding on his door.

Frowning, he got up from his desk and climbed the basement stairs, stopping on the landing where the door to the driveway was. He looked through the door's window. Scooby and Lizzy stood in the dark. It looked like they were high on something.

Shit, he thought, looking up at the door that led to the kitchen. It was closed and locked, but his parents would be up there somewhere. And when Scooby was high, he could get loud. The last time he had been over, he'd made enough noise that Monster's parents had resorted to banging on their floor (his ceiling) with the end of a broom to get Scooby to shut up.

Monster unlocked and opened the door a crack. "What's up, dude?"

"Fuck, bro. Fuck!" Scooby was pacing on the spot. "Fuck!"

"Shush, man! It's like ten o'clock. What's up?"

"Let us in."

"No, man, I'm working."

"You gotta let us in," he insisted, and before Monster could tell him no again, he whispered, "We *killed* someone, yo."

"*You* killed her," Lizzy hissed. "It was all your idea."

Monster was staring at them, telling himself this was a lame prank—and knowing it wasn't.

They're not high, he realized. *They're scared out of their minds.*

"Jesus, guys," he said, stepping back and opening the door wider. "Come in, but be quiet."

ΔΔΔ

The basement was a single large room. White acoustic ceiling tiles clashed with the black walls, which Monster had painted himself. But when the overhead lights were off and all his LED strip lights were on (as they were now, glacier blue), you didn't notice the ugly ceiling. Aside from the desk that held his gaming rig, there was a lumpy corduroy sofa that doubled as his bed, a beanbag chair, and a little console with an old flat-screen TV.

Lizzy had slumped down on the sofa, folding her arms across her chest, while Scooby paced from wall to wall.

Monster sat in his chair and said, "What's going on?"

Scooby recounted a story so bizarre it could only be a Scooby story.

"You threw *mousetraps* at her feet?" Monster said, shaking his head at his friend's stupidity.

Scooby shrugged. "To spice up the video, you know what I'm sayin'?"

"Is the video still online?" Monster wanted to watch it.

"Shit, no!" Scooby said. "You think we're idiots?"

"You did film yourself committing murder."

"*Scoob* murdered her," Lizzy said, scowling. "I didn't do nothing. I was just holding the phone."

"That's still accessory to murder," Monster pointed out. "Five to ten years, easy."

"No way," she said. "I ain't going to jail for this. It was all Scoob."

"Fuck you, bitch!" Scooby said. "You're balls deep in this with me."

"You ruined my life!"

"Cool your tits, girl. Let's think about this. We don't gotta go to jail. They gotta find us first."

"You gotta turn yourself in, man," Monster said. "The cops are gonna find you. Where are you gonna hide?"

"We're gonna go on the lam."

"I ain't going on the lam," Lizzy said. "You're retarded, Scoob."

"You wanna sit on your ass in a jail cell for the next ten years?"

"You gotta turn yourself in," Monster repeated.

"Fuck that, yo. We're going to Mexico. Nobody will find us down there."

"I'm not going to Mexico!" Lizzy said.

"Yeah, you are, bitch. I don't got a car."

"Oh, shit," Monster said. "Lizzy, your car's not parked in my driveway, is it?"

"No, bro," Scooby said. "We dumped it out at the monument until we're ready to split."

He was referring to Montezuma Castle National Monument, located outside of town, just past the Cliff Castle Casino. "You walked all the way here?"

"Once it got dark, so no mo' fo's would recognize us."

"How many people do you think saw the video?"

"Whoever was watching it live," Lizzy said. "Which is probably like a *lot*. The video of Kitty got like seven thousand views in the first half hour."

"Is that video still live?"

Scooby nodded. "It's got maybe thirty thousand views by now."

"You didn't delete it too?" Monster said, shocked.

"Why, yo? We didn't kill nobody on it. And it's got *thirty thousand* views. We're gonna need the cash from it when we're on the lam."

"What cash are you talking about?"

"From all our views, bro!"

"Have you joined the Creator Fund?"

"The what?"

"To make money on Tiktok, you gotta join that, but you gotta have ten thousand followers first."

"*What?*" Scooby looked at Lizzy. "How many followers do we have?"

Lizzy checked her phone. "Fifty-five," she said.

"*What!*"

"Lemme watch that video," Monster said, getting out of his chair and taking her phone. He tapped on the video and couldn't help but laugh when Scooby whipped off his wife beater and began swinging it in circles above his head while grinding against Kitty's leg.

Scooby, who'd stopped his pacing to watch the video over Monster's shoulder, laughed out loud too. "That's the shit, bro."

A man's voice sounded in the background, and the video ended a moment later.

"That was Kitty's dad?" Monster said.

"Crazy-ass mo' fo'. Girl, you should have kept filming. The look on that ape's face woulda been the best part of the video."

"Yeah, right," Lizzy said. "I know Kitty's dad. He's scary."

Monster read some of the comments posted below the video:

—I hope that other woman's okay. You guys are such pricks.

—Assault with a deadly mousetrap!!! Lolo

—I never saw the other video! Pls repost!

—Poor Kitty. Get better soon xx

—Who's filming this????

—The police are looking for Scooby. They've got a Facebook page up asking for information about him. If you know where he is, call 911!

Monster stopped reading after the last comment and looked at Scooby. "You gotta turn yourself in, man. The cops are already looking for you."

"I told you, bro, I ain't doing it."

"How do you know they're looking for us?" Lizzy asked.

"They've set up a Facebook page asking for information on

Scoob."

"Dammit!" She jumped up from the sofa and took her phone back.

"You can't stay here," Monster told Scooby. "I'll be aiding and abetting."

"Just for tonight, yo. Until we work out where we're going."

"You said you're going to Mexico."

"Yeah, bro, but we gotta plan shit first, you know what I'm sayin'?"

"I'm not going to Mexico!" Lizzy said. Then, "Oh my God... They *are* looking for us." She shoved her phone at Scooby.

He glanced briefly at the screen. "Dope."

"*Dope?*" Lizzy said.

"We're like Billy the Kid, yo. Outlaws. Wonder if they'll put a bounty on our heads?"

"You ruined my life!"

"Tell the cops it was just a joke," Monster said. "A joke gone wrong. They might let you off with a slap on your wrists."

"Bullshit they will," Scooby said. "We're eighteen. We're adults. We're going to jail for murder. That's why we're going to Mexico."

"I'm not going to Mexico!" Lizzy said. "Can't you get that through your stupid head?"

"Yeah, you are, bitch. And you're gonna need a new name too. Me, I already got mine. Kid Tree."

"Kid Tree?" Monster said.

"Because I look like Kid Rock, yo, but I got my tree. Gotta keep it real, you know what I'm sayin'?"

"Kid Tree?" Lizzy said. "Are you listening to yourself?"

"My new name got nothing to do with you, bitch! You're just driving the car!"

"I hate you! I hate you! I hate you! You ruined my life!"

Lizzy lunged at Scooby.

Monster slipped between the two of them before she could land any blows.

Banging on the ceiling: his parents with the broom.

"Guys," he hissed. "Quiet! You're pissing off my folks!"

Scooby, laughing, stepped back a couple of feet. Lizzy spat in his direction, then dropped onto the sofa and buried her head on her lap.

"Marinate, girl!" Scooby said.

"I'm gonna turn myself in," she mumbled.

"We can't!"

"Shhh!" Monster said.

"I can't go back to my parents' house," Lizzy said, sitting up, wiping tears from her eyes. "And I ain't going on the lam with someone who calls himself Kid Tree and has no money."

"We'll make money," Scooby said. "It's easy in Mexico. You can sell sunglasses on the beach, you know what I'm sayin'?"

"They got beaches in Mexico?" Lizzy said.

Monster might have said she was intrigued by the idea if she didn't look so crazy mad.

"Yeah, girl. Cancun. Spring Break hoes as far as you can see. Night clubs, cheap booze. Party central. Fuck yeah."

Lizzy screwed up her lips like she did when she was thinking.

Monster took advantage of the break in the fighting and said, "You guys want a bong hit or something while you figure this shit out?"

"Now you're talking!" Scooby said.

Lizzy, who never said no to drugs of any kind, nodded without hesitation.

Monster retrieved his bong from his desk, as well as the little wooden box in which he kept his pot and lighter.

"One hit each," he told them. "Then the two of you gotta scram. Deal?"

"Yeah, bro, whatever," Scooby said. "Pack that shit and let's get to it. Mexico ain't going to wait for us forever, you know what I'm sayin'?"

CHAPTER 17

PHONE GAMES

S ally swooned at the sight of the unreal photo on her phone.

Amanda gripped her shoulder. "Hey, take a deep breath."

The lightheadedness passed. Sally looked again at the photo. *How is that possible?* she thought, her terror turning to anger.

"Hey? Hello? Everything okay?"

Sally blinked at the reporter, her mind clearing. It might have been the concern she saw in the woman's face, or a need to talk through what she didn't understand, but whatever the reason she began telling her about the night in Ryders Field.

△△△

Sally concluded ten minutes later. "And that morning was the last I ever saw of Ben—until yesterday evening."

Amanda had said little during the rambling tale except to ask for clarification here or there. Now she was regarding Sally somberly.

"I don't care if you don't believe me," Sally told her, realizing she had never spoken at such length about Ryders Field to anyone except the shrink her parents had sent her to when she was a kid. "That's what happened. And these circus wagons"— she raised her phone, even though it was no longer displaying the photo—"were the same as the ones in Ryders Field. I'm positive of that."

"Okay, slow down," Amanda said in a placating tone. "I *do* believe you. I do. Why wouldn't I? I'm just trying to connect the dots. Because the odds of the gypsies showing up here, at another dancing plague how many years after the first, can't be random, can it?"

"No, it can't," Sally agreed.

"So they're...the catalyst behind the dancing?"

"Can you see how?"

Amanda smiled wryly. "Gypsy curses aside?"

"Curses, right." Sally chuckled without mirth. "That's actually more believable than what Ben has suggested."

"What has he suggested?"

"I'm not getting into it. You can ask him about it yourself when he gets back. But if you want my best guess as to what's going on? The gypsies heard about the dancing in Camp Verde and came here to check it out for themselves, just as I did."

"Because they'd experienced something similar before in Chatham in 1988."

Sally shrugged, "It's a reasonable explanation, isn't it? But I'm just as curious now about *how* Ben found those circus wagons." She navigated to the message app on her phone.

"What are you doing?" Amanda asked her.

"Finding out where Ben is."

"You're calling him?"

She frowned. "So?"

"I doubt he's brazenly walking around the gypsies' camp snapping photos. If you call him, you're going to blow his cover."

Sally checked her wristwatch. "It's been fifteen minutes since he sent the photo. You think he would still be hanging around their camp?"

"I doubt it. But it's better to be safe than sorry, right? So tell me."

"Tell you what?"

"Ben's theory as to what's going on." Amanda shot a Marlboro from her pack. She offered one to Sally, who shook her head—with reluctance. She had smoked heavily after Valerie's death until quitting this year (her New Year's resolution). "You clearly don't believe it."

"No."

Amanda lit up and took a drag. "He believes they're actual werewolves, doesn't he?"

Sally couldn't hide her surprise. "Why would you say that?"

"Because of the way you're acting." She turned her head aside to blow a jet of smoke into the wind. "Like what Ben believes has to be the craziest thing imaginable, and the craziest thing I can imagine is that these people who locked you up weren't just some cult members that *thought* they were werewolves but that they *were* werewolves."

Sally didn't respond.

"I'm right, aren't I?" Amanda pressed. "But I still don't get it. What do werewolves have to do with dancing plagues?"

Sally sighed. "That's the *really* crazy part—" Her phone bleeped. "That's got to be him!" she said, opening the new message.

Where are you?

She frowned. "Where am I? Where does he think I am?" She began typing a reply.

"Wait!" said Amanda, who had crowded close to read the message. "How do you know it's Ben?"

"It's the same number that sent the picture of the circus wagons."

"What I mean is... I covered a story last year about a man who murdered his girlfriend while they were traveling across the country. He knew some of her social media passwords and kept up those accounts for weeks so nobody would know she was dead."

Sally was aghast. "You think Ben is *dead?*"

"Well...no. God no. But they might be holding him against his will. If they caught him nosing around, they might want to know why he's sending a picture of their circus wagons to somebody, and if so, they'd probably like to know who that somebody is."

Sally stared at the phone. *Could Ben be in trouble? Could his life be in jeopardy?* "What should I do?" she asked. "I have to do something."

"Call him," Amanda said. "If that message was indeed from him, then it stands to reason he's no longer sneaking around their camp. He's on his way back and wants to know whether you're still at the motel or out for a walk or whatever. But if the message wasn't from him...well, then he's already been caught and you won't be blowing his cover."

Taking a deep breath, Sally called Ben's number.

It rang and rang and rang.

CHAPTER 18

THE SLEEPOVER

"Y ou can't stay here."

Sally stared at the reporter. "You think they might be coming for *me*?"

"They want to know where you are."

"Maybe Ben didn't answer because he's driving."

"Maybe..."

Neither of them, Sally knew, believed that.

"But they don't know where I am," she said.

"Ben might have told them."

"I don't think he would have done that."

"How many hotels are in Camp Verde? Two? Three?"

Fear infiltrated Sally's bones, numbing her from the inside out.

How is this happening? This trip was supposed to be a joke. We weren't supposed to find anything. The gypsies can't have Ben! They can't be coming for me! This is absurd!

"I suggest you find a hotel in Phoenix," Amanda said, crushing her cigarette beneath her sneakered foot. "Somewhere central with a lot of people around."

"And leave Ben? What if they really do have him?"

"What else are you going to do? You have no idea where he is."

"He's around Camp Verde somewhere," she said. "And I couldn't leave town even if I wanted to. Ben has our car."

"I'll drive you—"

"I'm not going anywhere!" Sally clamped her jaw tight. She felt unacceptably vulnerable standing out front of the motel. But where was she going to go?

And not just you. Gabriela too—

That's it!

"There's a house down the street," she said. "The girl I'm looking after lives there. Her parents...they're gone. It's a long story, but we can stay there for the night."

Amanda nodded. "Then get going. But I'll need your phone number first. I'll stay up and keep an eye out here. If anybody suspicious comes by, I'll let you know."

△△△

"Grab your bag, hon," Sally told Gabriela when she entered the motel room. "This place has termites in the walls. We need to sleep somewhere else tonight."

Gabriela turned off the TV with the remote control. "Where?"

"How about your house?"

Her face fell. "I don't want to go back there."

"It's just for tonight, I promise." *Because tomorrow night you'll likely be in the custody of the Iceman. But at least you'll be safe with him. You won't have a murderous cult hunting you down.* "Now go on and get your bag," she added, doing her best to sound upbeat. "And don't forget your toothbrush. It's on the bathroom sink."

△△△

Sally held Gabriela's hand as they walked north along a road that ran parallel to Main Street (but was much less conspicuous). She wanted to run. If she'd been by herself, she would have. She was all but certain a car would appear behind them at any moment, its high beams illuminating them in a wall of light, its engine throttling as it prepared to chase them down.

But she didn't run. What would Gabriela think of that if they did? She was already spooked enough that they were returning to her house, where her mother's dead body had lain only hours before. The last thing she needed was to suspect they were being pursued.

"Are we still having pizza for dinner?" Gabriela asked, adding a small skip to her step.

"The pizza store closed, hon," Sally told her. "But I'm sure I'll be able to find something to cook up at your house."

"Do I have to sleep in my bed?"

"Where do you want to sleep?"

"In the TV room?" She hesitated a moment before adding, "With you?"

"Sure. That sounds fun. We'll have a sleepover, you and me. Maybe I'll find some popcorn in the cupboards."

"I don't think there is any. I already ate all the good food."

"I'll find something, I'm sure."

They cut through the empty, overgrown lot onto West Head Street. The houses they passed were rundown and not much larger than trailers. Most had dirt or gravel yards cluttered with junk and furniture meant to be indoors. The cars parked in the driveways were all discontinued models, the most recent probably at least a decade old. Lights shone in many windows. Competing with the sounds of crickets and cicadas were over-volumed TVs, a mother shrilly berating her child (or perhaps her husband), and general household chatter. Guns 'N Roses' "Paradise City" blared from a grungy brown house with a black Stingray Corvette sitting on cement blocks in the driveway.

The moon hung low and nearly full in the star-filled night sky, an ever-present reminder that a cult of lycanthropes had likely captured Ben and was coming for her.

A cult or true-to-God werewolves?

Right then—walking through the dark in an unfamiliar backwater town—Sally could almost believe it was the latter.

Almost.

A rare streetlamp, attached almost as an afterthought to a power pole, flickered on and off in front of Gabriela's house. Moths and other insects congregated around the pulsating bulb despite it being infested with spiderwebs (and no doubt very full and content spiders).

Sally pushed open the front door and followed Gabriela inside. "I have an idea," she said, flicking on the nearest light switch. "You go turn on the TV. I'll be there in a sec."

While Gabriela went to the den, Sally went to the girl's bedroom. The furnishings were bare bones, with little more than a twin bed, a dresser with an attached mirror, and a basket in a corner filled with stuffed animals, dolls, and other toys. Sally stripped the unicorn-patterned duvet and pink sheet from the bed, stuffed a pillow beneath each arm, and carried it all to the den. She then collected the four chairs from around the kitchen table and arranged them in a square in front of the TV set.

"What are those for?" Gabriela asked her.

"We're going to make a fort to sleep in. Give me a hand, will you?"

Together they draped the pink sheet over the chairs and pinned them in place with cushions from the sofa. Sally raised the section that faced the TV to make an entrance.

"There you go!" she said. "Easy peasy."

Gabriela looked impressed. "Can I go inside?"

"Of course. Take your pillows and cover and get comfortable. I'll go see what I can whip up to eat."

In the kitchen Sally found a bag of potatoes. She washed and sliced a few into shoestring strips and fried them in oil on the stove. When they were crispy, she served them on a plate with a gob of ketchup. Not exactly a gourmet meal, but Gabriela seemed pleased.

"Are you going to come in the fort and watch TV with me?" she asked.

"I'm going to make you something tasty for dessert first."

Back in the kitchen she scavenged the basics—flour, baking powder, baking soda, salt, sugar, butter—and went to work baking an eggless vanilla cake.

She and Gabriela ate most of it while watching a Muppets movie. Gabriela nodded off before it finished, and Sally slipped out of the fort without waking her. While searching for the ingredients to bake the cake, she'd discovered a pack of cigarettes and a lighter on the top shelf of the pantry. She broke her abstinence by lighting up one on the porch now. She was just about finished it when her phone rang.

She answered it quickly and said, "Amanda?"

"Two men are here," the reporter told her quietly. "They pulled up in a red sports car about ten minutes ago. They must have inquired about you in the front office—I couldn't see and didn't want to stick my head out—but a couple of minutes later I heard them knocking on what sounded like either your or Ben's room. Whose name was the rooms booked under?"

"Ben's," Sally said tightly.

"Well, they would likely know his name, wouldn't they? So they probably asked the manager which rooms Ben and his friend were staying in."

"Where are they now?"

"Sitting in their car in the parking lot. I think they suspect you're just out for a walk and are waiting for you to return. You're at the girl's house?"

"Yes."

"Then you're fine. Just stay put."

"Should I…I don't know…call the police?"

"I'll do that. I'll tell them two suspicious-looking men are loitering outside my motel room. That will scare them off, at least."

"But it won't help us find Ben."

"I've taken down the car's license plate number. I know somebody who can run it and get a name. And tomorrow morning we'll go into the police station together and report Ben missing."

"They don't act quickly on missing person reports."

"They will if we tell them the guys in the red sports car came back, beat up Ben, and threw him in their car. We'll mention the circus wagons too. Hopefully that will be enough for the cops to search all the RV parks around town or wherever else these guys might be holed up."

Sally felt overwhelmed but incredibly grateful for the reporter's help.

"Thank you, Amanda. I really mean that—"

"It's nothing. Get some rest tonight. Everything will be okay tomorrow."

Sally hung up but didn't go to sleep. She was so wired that she felt as though it would be impossible to sleep. Instead, she poured herself a glass of wine from a bottle on the kitchen counter and went outside to the porch, where she sat in an old chair and chain-smoked cigarettes while brooding about how unpredictable life could be.

At some point her phone began to ring. She snapped awake —she hadn't even realized she'd fallen asleep—and checked the number, expecting it to be Amanda with another update.

It was Ben's number.

Sally's heart surged.

She answered with, "Hello...?"

A woman said, "Did the Fort Verde Suites fail to meet your standards?"

"Who are you?"

"Who am I? Who are *you*, dear?" She had a faint Russian accent that reminded Sally of the gypsy woman from 1988, though she sounded too young to be the same person.

"Is my friend okay?"

"He is perfectly fine."

Sally closed her eyes in relief. When she opened them again a moment later, she said, "What do you want from us?"

"Want? I want nothing at all. I am simply curious—curious as to why Ben sent you the photo."

Hearing the woman speak Ben's name made Sally's skin

crawl. "I don't know why," she replied. "He never said—"

"You lie."

She swallowed hard.

"You know what?" the woman went on. "I do want something, after all. I would like to speak to you in person."

"Why in person?"

"I take my privacy seriously, and I'm stumped as to why Ben had been infringing on it. He has so far refused to enlighten me. You are so far refusing to enlighten me. But perhaps if we all meet tomorrow in the light of day, we can work out this potential misunderstanding."

The proposition stunned Sally because it sounded too good to be true. Did this woman really just want to talk? Would she really bring Ben with her and release him when...?

When what....?

When I tell her we witnessed her cult murder innocent people thirty-one years ago?

No, of course she wouldn't admit that. Sally would come up with some other reason to explain Ben's behavior.

"All right," she said. "But I choose the place. That's the deal."

"Fabulous, dear. I look forward to hearing from you in the morning."

The line went dead.

ΔΔΔ

Sally spent the next two hours smoking the last of the pack of cigarettes and thinking about the next day's meeting. Then at a little past midnight she got in touch with an old acquaintance.

CHAPTER 19

WOLFIE

Chuck Hamman grabbed his wife's ass beneath the bed covers.[1]

Earlier in their eleven-year relationship Kelly would have responded by rolling on top of him for a middle-of-the-night romp. Now she didn't react to his touch at all, which wasn't necessarily a bad thing. They might not be where they were when they first began dating, but at least they weren't at the point where she slapped his hand away, or chose to sleep in a separate bed.

The iPad that doubled as a clock on the bedside table indicated it was 12:11 a.m. A dream—he supposed you'd call it a nightmare—about robots taking over humanity had woken him. The robots hadn't been frightening because they were self-aware and much more intelligent than their human masters, or because they commanded *Matrix*-like armies of unstoppable war machines. They had been frightening because they were scheming to overthrow mankind stealthily, from the shadows (in an enigmatic dream-like way), and nobody (except Chuck) suspected a thing until it was too late.

Chuck often had nightmares like this after binge-watching scary stuff on Netflix before going to bed. Nevertheless, he couldn't help himself. Not only had he never been good at reigning in his impulses, but he was also a geek at heart. He liked sci-fi, the newer the movies the better. He liked horror, the older the movies the better. He read comic books like *Vampirella* and Japanese manga like *Tokyo Ghoul*. He collected vintage Star Wars and GI Joe figures. Kelly called his hobbies "cute" and often referred to him as "a big kid." She was being condescending. She would have preferred him to watch foreign films and read classic literature and collect vintage wine and modern artwork. Even so, she couldn't bully him into changing who he was. He was the one paying for the house they lived in, the Mercedes she drove, and just about everything in her bedroom-sized walk-in closet.

Chuck wasn't ashamed of their excessive, materialistic lifestyle. At the cocktail parties and gala community events they routinely attended, he often glibly paraphrased Mae West's observation that if a little is great, and a lot is better, then way too much is just about right.

And why should he be ashamed? He had worked hard to get to where he was. He was proud of his success, especially because everybody always had pegged him as a loser who wouldn't amount to anything. It was true that in elementary school he was the goofball who never opened a book outside of class and copied his homework from all the smarter kids. But could you blame him for his educational laxity? With all the pot his parents had smoked at home, he had been high through osmosis most days. Moreover, they had never encouraged ambition in him, preferring to preach the Epicurean motto to pleasure yourself in the moment because tomorrow you could be six feet under. His father's accounting business had gone bust when Chuck was in college, and he and Chuck's mother had been living in a trailer park in New Mexico ever since. How merry they were now was up for debate, but they were definitely still eating and drinking to excess—and, of course, smoking pot too much.

Anyway, Chuck had taken the off-ramp from the dead-end road he'd been traveling down when he was in high school. In his freshman year his report card had been a shitshow of F's and D's. He worked a bit harder in his sophomore year and earned mostly C's with one or two B's. That was when he realized he wasn't as dumb as he'd always believed. In fact, he was rather intelligent; after all, he'd gotten all those C's and B's simply by putting in the minimal effort instead of no effort. This encouraged him to try harder, and in his junior year he began taking notes in class, remaining in the library after school until he'd finished all his homework (something he could never do at home with his parents' mid-week parties and loud music), and studying for every quiz, test, and exam until he knew the subject matter inside-out. The effort paid off, earning him straight-As both that year and the next.

It wasn't that Chuck liked studying like a madman and all the other stuff that went along with being smart. Nevertheless, the way he'd seen it, he was never going to be the best-looking guy in the room; he was never going to be the tallest or fittest or most charming; but he could be the most successful, and that was something to shoot for.

He attended a prestigious college in a small town north of New York City because it had offered him a full-ride first-year scholarship with conditions to extend it if he kept up his grades. Initially he'd considered getting into politics, or law. However, he'd decided politicians weren't paid enough, and practicing law seemed like a drag. In the end he set his sights on medicine. He'd earned a 3.9 GPA and a 530 MCAT score, and had been a competitive applicant at all the medical schools he'd applied to. Even so, the snobs at Harvard passed him over, although he was accepted at John Hopkins School of Medicine. Not a bad consolation prize.

After completing residency training in pediatrics, earning a license to practice medicine, and becoming board certified, he began his career at a Boston inner-city hospital. That was where he met Kelly, a cardiac nurse at the time (although she hadn't stepped into her blue scrubs in over ten years now). A few years ago he was contacted about a position by a headhunter organization in Salt Lake City, and the salary had been tempting enough to pack up his life on the East coast (which included his two daughters, Zoe, five, and Emily, three) and move cross-country to Utah.

All in all he was happy with his life choices—including the woman he'd married, even if she had become something of a *Desperate Housewives* diva who was more into her shoe collection than her husband.

Chuck gave Kelly's ass a little squeeze before removing his hand and rolling onto his side so their backs were to each other. He closed his eyes, thought about anything except intelligent robots, and tried to fall back to sleep.

His phone whistled in imitation of R2D2.

Chuck grabbed it from the night table, fearing the sound might wake Kelly. He usually turned off the notifications at nighttime but must have forgotten earlier that evening. While holding down the button to decrease the volume, he saw that he'd received a message. He tapped the screen and squinted to read the small text without his eyeglasses on:

This is Sally Levine from Chatham. I need to talk to you.

Chuck had a momentary brain freeze before placing the name. He reread her message.

I need to talk to you.

What the hell did Sally Levine need to talk to him about after all these years? He wasn't under any illusion that she suddenly remembered what a good-looking and fun guy he'd been and wanted to cook up a long-distance romance. More than likely she'd messaged him by accident.

But why mention Chatham? That implied that the intended recipient was from there, and that they hadn't spoken in some time.

Chuck browsed Sally's recent posts. She wasn't very active online, sharing only one or two photos or updates a year. Nevertheless, he had to admit that in those rare photos she looked good. She'd always been a looker, and apparently that hadn't changed.

Another R2D2 whistle:

Are you free now?

Now? Chuck thought, frowning. Her profile information indicated that she lived in New York City, where the time zone was three hours ahead of Mountain. What could she possibly want to talk to him about at 3 a.m.?

A third message appeared.

No text. Just a photograph of two circus wagons.

He immediately recognized them, and he typed:

Is this a joke?

He sat up in bed quietly and glanced at his wife. He half-expected her to be lying there with one eye open, somehow knowing exactly what was going through his mind. She would demand to know what happened in Ryders Field when he was a kid, which he had never told her about. She'd call him a kook, pack a suitcase, and take the girls to her mother's. The next time he'd see any of them would be in family court, working out a divorce settlement...

Kelly was sleeping soundly, her breathing deep and regular.

Chuck's phone vibrated in his hand. Sally was calling him.

He slipped quietly out of bed and went downstairs. In the kitchen he flipped on the lights and glanced at his phone. Still ringing. His finger hovered over the video-answer button. He looked like a sleepy mess, which wasn't the first impression he wanted to make after thirty-whatever years. On the other hand, given the late hour, Sally very well could be in bed. She could be wearing something skimpy and sexy. Her phone's camera could accidentally stray from her face. Or she could be one of those people who got off on voyeuristic stuff and *let* her phone stray...

Chuck shook himself and pressed the answer button.

"Sally?" he said.

"Chuck?" she said.

He immediately recognized her voice. He hadn't heard it since he was twelve, but there it was, exactly as he remembered. Her kid-face suddenly crystallized in his mind, and his heart ached a little. Although he'd only hung out with her for a few days in the autumn of 1988, he'd developed a crush on her (though of course as a chubby, unpopular kid he'd never dared to admit as much) that had lingered far longer than was healthy.

"Hi…" He cleared his throat. "Long time."

"I know, and it's late, so I'm sorry for disturbing you. But this is an emergency. I'm in Arizona with Ben."

"*Graves?*" he said, struck by a tinge of jealously.

They were still friends? More than friends? *Were they fucking?*

"They're here, Chuck," she said, popping his self-absorbed bubble. "The gypsies from Chatham. They've got Ben, and I need your help."

∆∆∆

After they'd hung up Chuck remained in the kitchen for a long time, thinking about everything Sally had told him. Then he went upstairs, changed into a button-down shirt and wool dress pants, and packed a duffel bag with clothes and toiletries. He told Kelly he had to make an emergency house call to one of his patients. She mumbled a reply without fully waking. He didn't know what he would tell her tomorrow to explain his continued absence, but he was sure it wouldn't be cross-examined; Kelly would likely be happy to have the house to herself for a few days.

Chuck went back downstairs to his office. Originally it had featured exposed brick and warm woods, like the rest of the farmhouse-inspired residence (which Kelly had chosen despite his preference for something more modern). He'd had the room gutted and rebuilt with a sleek steel-gray and black aesthetic. It included typical man-cave idiosyncrasies such as a pool table, a pinball machine, and a home theatre. But there were his unique touches as well: two LED-lit glass display cabinets that held his Star Wars and GI Joe action figures (including a 1978 vinyl Cape Jawa, a 1980 rocket-firing Boba Fett, and perhaps rarest of all, a 1984 Storm Shadow

THE DANCING PLAGUE 2

in the original, unpunched packaging); a wall dedicated to the highest-graded comic books that he had mounted behind UV-resistant acrylic cases (including *Batman* #121, which introduced Mr. Freeze for the first time; *The Fantastic Four* #12, in which The Hulk meets The Thing for the first time; and *Teenage Mutant Ninja Turtles* #1, which had cost upward of five grand); and on a rotating pedestal beneath a spotlight, his labor of love, a 1:8 scale LEGO Bugatti Chiron that had taken him several months to construct.

Hidden in plain sight, thanks to all the other fan-boy paraphernalia, were the werewolves.

A sixteen-inch statue of Kessler Wolf from *An American Werewolf in London*. Framed film posters of *The Wolfman*, *The Howling*, and *Teen Wolf*. A Werewolf Xing road sign he had picked up at Comic-Con International in San Diego. An oil painting of a snarling half-man/half-beast he had commissioned from a local artist. And numerous other werewolf-themed collectibles he'd picked up here and there over the years.

After what Chuck had gone through at Ryders Field, you'd think that he would never want to hear the word "werewolf" again. Yet it was just the opposite. He became a *fan* of them. He'd seen them with his own eyes, and that made him special by association. Consequently, he'd blabbed about what had happened that night to anybody who would listen. He kept this up to such an extent that in high school his classmates began calling him "Wolfie." That came about after a supply teacher played the movie *Amadeus* in class, and someone shouted "It's Chunk!" during a scene in which the pudgy actor playing Wolfgang Mozart crawled around on his knees and barked like a wolf. Chuck didn't mind the new nickname. It was better than Chunk. And far from discouraging him, it encouraged his affinity with werewolves. When someone said "Hey Wolfie!" in the hallways, he would respond with a howl or a snarl. When a girl mock-flirted with him, he would sniff her as a canine might. Moreover, the geeks he found himself hanging out with more and more supported his antics. That was the thing with geeks, he'd learned. They weren't just nerds; they were eccentric nerds, and they preferred the company of other eccentrics. Which meant Chuck fit right in with the likes of Wally Pinker, who often wore his tracksuits on backward or inside out; and Mike Aung, who was a goth in every sense of the word except for the fact he dressed all in white instead of black; and Larry Glodan, who proudly donned oversized horn-rimmed eyeglasses with non-prescription lenses.

The doppelganger that was Wolfie, however, died the day Chuck set foot on the bustling college campus in upstate New York. He knew nobody there, and nobody knew him. He was no longer the fat kid Chunk or the weird kid Wolfie. He could remake his reputation and become whomever he wanted. He could, for the first time in his life, be taken seriously. It was an opportunity he wasn't going to screw up.

Nevertheless, even though he would never mention Ryders Field to anyone again, he found he couldn't divorce himself from what he'd experienced there. Werewolves were too entrenched in his psyche by then; they were too much a part of who he was. To simply try to forget or ignore that they existed was impossible. This might explain why, after renting and enjoying a 1957 movie called *I Was a Teenage Werewolf*, he went on a mission to find and purchase his own copy (which he ended up discovering in a bargain bin at an independent video rental store). From that point on he spent much of his free time tracking down old VHS cassette tapes such as *Werewolf in a Girl's Dormitory*, *Face of the Screaming Werewolf*, *The Curse of the Werewolf*, *Frankenstein's Bloody Terror*, *Curse of the Devil*, *The Beast Must Die*, and so forth. The comics came next, then the books, posters, figurines, and everything else.

If he wanted to psycho-analyze himself, he would characterize his obsessive collecting as a kind of self-therapy. Some people repress a traumatic experience in their subconscious; some talk through it with a psychiatrist or other specialist. Chuck, he supposed, was attempting to *conquer* his. By collecting anything and everything related to lycanthropy, he wasn't only metaphorically taking possession of the creatures he'd encountered; he was taking ownership of them. They were his, and he could do with them what he pleased. That was somehow comforting to him. It let him sleep peacefully at night.

At least, when he wasn't dreaming about mutinous robots.

Chuck removed the framed *Teen Wolf* film poster from the wall and set it aside, revealing the face of a steel safe. He entered 9-6-5-3-4-3 (WOLFIE) into the combination wheel lock, opened the hinged door, and withdrew a large-bore Colt Anaconda revolver and a Planters Peanuts tin that contained .44 Magnum cartridges.

Chuck had never expected to encounter a werewolf again. Still, just as doomsday preppers might build a kitted-out bunker in the off-chance the apocalypse was right around the corner, he had decided it might be a good idea to be prepared in case the shapeshifting impossibilities ever came a-knockin'.

He tucked the gleaming revolver and the can of grizzly-bear-stopping bullets into his duffel bag, closed the safe, and returned the poster to its place on the wall. He left the house as quietly as possible through the front door, got behind the wheel of his Lexus SUV parked in the driveway, and dumped the duffel bag onto the passenger seat beside him.

A short time later he was on Interstate 15, speeding south at eighty miles an hour to a future that had been three decades in the making.

CHAPTER 20

THE PLAN

After her conversation with Chunky, Sally had climbed into the makeshift fort and laid down next to Gabriela. She remained wide awake in the dark on the hard floor. Was she making a terrible mistake by taking Ben's fate into her own hands? Should she simply do as Amanda had suggested and involve the Camp Verde police department? God, she wished she could. She wished the solution to this mess could be so simple. But the problem was she had no proof to back up her claims that Ben was being held against his will (and suffering physical abuse, if they went with Amanda's tale). The sheriff wasn't likely to drop everything to search for Ben based on her word alone, especially when he already had his hands full with the dancing plague that had infiltrated the town.

That was why Sally had settled on this course of action. She wasn't stupid. She didn't believe the gypsy woman would hand Ben over, have a chat and a coffee, and then allow the two of them to walk merrily away. The woman had something else up her sleeve. Sally didn't know what, but whatever it was, she had to be prepared.

Which was where Chunky came in to play.

Chunky.

Chuck.

It had been surreal speaking to him. There was the Chunky she remembered from Chatham, the crude, brash, nerdy kid who had puked in her swimming pool, who had only seemed to care about food and sex, even though he had almost certainly never experienced the latter. Then there was the Chuck she had spoken to on the phone, a measured, calm doctor who had been respectful, open-minded, and empathetic, despite the crazy things she had told him.

In fact, Sally had to admit she was surprised that Chunky—Chuck—had taken her seriously. Unlike the sheriff, he would understand her concern; he had been right there in Ryders Field with her and Ben. Yet that had been a long time ago—a lifetime ago—and here she was now, asking him to come to Arizona because Ben had sent her a photograph of two circus wagons that looked remarkably similar to the ones from their childhood.

Only they're not "remarkably similar," she told herself. *They're identical. Absolutely identical. Chuck would have recognized that too. Otherwise he wouldn't be driving ten hours through the night to meet me.*

Now stop it. Stop thinking so much. You've made your decision. All there's left to do is wait.

Sally closed her eyes and hoped sleep would come quickly.

ΔΔΔ

She woke three hours later and went to the kitchen to make herself a coffee before remembering there was no milk. She stuck her head inside the fort.

"Sweetheart?" she said.

Gabriela opened her eyes and seemed momentarily confused as to where she was. "Oh…" she said finally.

"I'm going to walk to McDonald's to get us some breakfast. Is there anything special you'd like?"

The girl sat up quickly. "A milkshake?"

"You want a milkshake for breakfast?"

She nodded.

"Okay, but what about some actual food?"

"A hamburger?"

"I mean breakfast food…"

"Like what?"

Sally frowned. "You've never eaten breakfast at McDonald's before?"

She shook her head.

"Why don't you let me choose for you then?"

"Okay... But, um... Miss...?"

"Just Sally."

"I don't want you to leave me."

"I won't be gone for too long."

"But later...?"

Sally knew what she meant, and her heart ached for the girl. "We'll talk about that when I get back." She put on a phony smile. "Now about that milkshake. Do you want chocolate, vanilla, or strawberry...?"

△△△

It was a two-mile walk to the McDonald's that Sally and Ben had seen the day before at the interchange. Sally kept up a brisk pace in the clear, crisp morning, the exercise feeling good after a night spent sleeping on a thinly carpeted floor. Her route took her past a shopping center called Outpost Mall (where she saw the signage for Crusty's Pizza), a tire shop with stacks of tires lining the road, a drab-looking Christian school, a sprawling RV park, a giant dollar store, and a lot of undeveloped space. In fact, by the time she reached the north-south highway that led to the interchange, there was little to see but desert. Although few cars passed her at the early hour, she nevertheless kept a good distance to the right of the asphalt, on brown grass next to a barb-wire fence.

She reached the McDonald's about fifteen minutes later. There were only a few customers seated at tables and nobody in line.

Everybody's still staying at home, trying to avoid catching the dancing bug, she thought, realizing she had given the dancing epidemic little to no thought since learning that the Chatham gypsies were in town. *How quickly one's priorities change.*

She ordered a smorgasbord of artery-clogging food and returned the way she'd come along the highway. When she was about halfway back to Gabriela's house, she called Amanda.

"Sorry for ringing so early," she said. "I hope I didn't wake you."

"I've been up since the crack of dawn," the reporter told her. "In fact, I was just about to call you."

"What happened last night? Did you call the police?"

"I did. Two cops arrived. They had a talk with the men in the sports car. I don't know what was said, but everybody departed afterward. The car never returned."

"They called me," Sally said.

"The police?" Amanda said.

"The gypsies."

"Oh my God! What did they say?"

"It was a woman. She wants to meet me this morning. She said she's going to bring Ben."

"Bring Ben...? *Where?*"

"I haven't decided yet. But it's up to me where we meet."

"Jeez, Sally. I don't like the sound of this."

"If there's a chance she's playing it straight, and she's going to have Ben with her, I have to meet her."

"She's held him against his will overnight, confiscated his phone, pretended to *be* him, and when that didn't work, she sent a couple of thugs to abduct you...and now all of a sudden she's going to play it straight? What does she get out of doing that?"

"She wants to know why Ben was interested in the circus wagons."

"And what are you going to tell her? That you know she belongs to a psycho cult? That's not going to go over well."

"Actually..." Sally said, and she explained.

ΔΔΔ

Back at Gabriela's house Sally set out breakfast on the kitchen table: Egg McMuffins, hashbrowns, pancakes with maple syrup, a deep-fried apple pie, and one large chocolate milkshake. Sally had an Egg McMuffin and left the rest for Gabriela to gobble up. After she finished eating, she went to the front door to watch for Amanda, who had agreed to come by at eight o'clock. The reporter appeared right on time. However, instead of approaching Gabriela's house, she went to the one directly across the road.

She was halfway up the walk before Sally opened the door and called to her.

"Oh, hey!" Amanda waved, crossed the street, and came up the porch steps. "Didn't you say it was the house with the blue truck out front…?"

"A slight misdirection," Sally admitted. "I wanted to make sure you were by yourself."

Amanda looked hurt. "You thought I would double-cross you?"

"No, of course not. I wanted to be sure nobody was following you. I couldn't be sure those thugs weren't watching the motel." She opened the door. "Come inside."

Gabriela had finished eating at the kitchen table and was now sucking on her milkshake, her cheeks dimpled with the effort.

"Hello," Amanda said. "You must be Sally's new friend? What's your name?"

"Gabriela," the girl said in a shy voice.

"It's nice to meet you, Gabriela. I'm Amanda."

"Gabby," Sally said, "I have to go somewhere this morning. I've asked Amanda to stay here with you until I return. Is that okay with you?"

"You're coming back?"

"Of course I am. Hopefully I won't be very long either."

"Okay."

"Good. Now why don't you go watch TV? I need to talk to Amanda for a little."

After Gabriela went to the den, Sally said, "Got any cigarettes on you?"

"I didn't think you smoked?"

"Seems like I started again last night."

Outside on the porch Amanda produced a folded map from her handbag. "Here's what you asked me to bring. It looks like one of those Disneyland maps, but it was the only one in the motel's reception."

Sally unfolded and flattened the map on a wobbly metal table. It was a cartoony 3-D rendering of Camp Verde. "Okay, we're right about here." She placed a finger over their location.

"If you're asking me," Amanda said, "I would want to meet this woman in the most populated spot possible. So...what about there?" She tapped a spot marked with drawings of a giraffe, tiger, and rhinoceros. Ash from her cigarette fell onto the map. She brushed it aside.

"Out of Africa Wildlife Park," Sally said, reading the small text.

"If they haven't temporarily closed, I'm sure there will still be some people there today. Or how about the visitor center? It looks like it's just down the street from here."

"I'd rather meet her somewhere *not* populated so I know she's alone. What about that?" She pointed to a place on the outskirts of town called Montezuma Castle National Monument. "Is it an actual castle?"

"Not really. You know the ancient ruins in Jordan that are carved into a cliff face? Montezuma is kind of like that, only on a smaller scale. Most importantly, there's only one way in and out. You'd have a clear view for miles of anybody approaching."

"That sounds a bit *too* isolated..."

"The ruins are Camp Verde's main tourist attraction. There's a park, a little museum. Surely there will be other people there."

Sally flicked her spent cigarette into the dirt yard. "You've been, I take it?"

Amanda did the same with hers. "My boyfriend took me

there last year—ex-boyfriend. He was always trying to find romantic things to do."

"Sounds like a good guy. What happened?"

"The trying part. He was always trying so hard to make me happy. You might think that sounds endearing, and it was. But it also drove me up the wall. You shouldn't have to *try* to make the person you're with happy. Sometimes, sure, like on a birthday, Valentine's Day, or whatever. You put in special effort. But not *all* the time. If the two of you are compatible, you should just be happy in neutral, if you know what I mean?"

"An overly affectionate boyfriend," Sally said lightly. "Gosh, you have it tough. Want to swap problems?"

Amanda didn't appear amused. "Ben's situation is my problem too. I'm sticking with you until we get him back. Now, what's your verdict on Montezuma Castle? Is that where you want to meet the woman?"

Sally studied the monument's location for several more seconds.

Finally she nodded. "I think it's as good as we're going to get."

CHAPTER 21

HELLO, STRANGER

Chuck had fallen a good hour behind schedule after stopping to fill up the Lexus's tank at a Shell gas station. He'd purchased a sandwich and two Red Bulls from the convenience store. After eating the sandwich in the SUV, he'd decided to rest his eyes for ten minutes or so before getting back on the highway. That had been at a little past four in the morning. When he opened his eyes again, it was nearly five-thirty.

Nevertheless, he'd made back nearly all that lost time with aggressive driving that paid little heed to the posted speed limits. Now he was cruising through northern Camp Verde, surprised by how few people were out and about on a Saturday morning. He hadn't expected the small desert town to be a hive of activity, but it almost felt like an abandoned outpost in a post-apocalyptic world...

A woman in an empty Walgreens parking lot on his right was pirouetting on the spot like a music-box ballerina.

Chuck braked, buzzed down the passenger-side window, and watched her for a few moments before calling out, "Hello? You okay over there?"

The woman went right on dancing.

Sally had told Chuck about the mass hysteria affecting many residents of Camp Verde, and so he wasn't—or, at least, he shouldn't have been—surprised to see a person dancing in a trance-like state. Nevertheless, the sight of the woman was a nostalgic punch to his gut, bringing up old memories from Chatham. The teacher dancing in the window across the street from Justin Gee's place. The woman dancing to no music on the night Ben beat up the Beast at the beach. Ben's own mother dancing in her living room.

Sheriff Sandberg tearing out his deputy's throat with his teeth…
The werewolves ripping Ben's dad apart limb by limb…

Chuck gripped the steering wheel tightly as familiar black dizziness waved over him. As a kid he had done an admittedly impressive job of coping with the horrors he had experienced in Ryders Field. But of course he had been affected by them, and deeply. He had created an alter-ego named Wolfie, for God's sake. And while his wolf-like antics might have appeared light-hearted and foolish on the surface, there had been a whole lot of darkness churning below that surface, darkness that had manifested itself in irrational panic attacks in his adult years. These were typically caused by unexpected noises. A rustle of something in a dark alleyway. A loud slam in an underground parking lot. It didn't matter that the source of the sound was a cat sniffing around in a dumpster bin, or somebody getting into their car. Once Chuck's panic was triggered, reason ceased to exist. His body would simply melt down, leaving him nauseous, trembling, and struggling to breathe while he waited for the attack to peter out. Sometimes that happened within minutes, though often it would take much longer.

Thankfully today it was the former.

Chuck opened his eyes and took a series of deep breaths. He released the steering wheel and wiped his sweaty palms on his thighs. Then he took the little bottle of Xanax he always kept on him from the inside pocket of his blazer, shook out three pills, and dry-swallowed them.

When he looked back at the Walgreens parking lot, the woman was no longer there.

Pull yourself together, buddy, he thought, accelerating away from the pharmacy. *What happened in Chatham might have been a Saturday night Creature Feature come to life, but it's usually the sequels when the shit* really *hits the fan. You gotta be ready for that.*

Chuck glanced at the vehicle's GPS.

Three minutes to his destination.

△△△

When he pulled up to the address Sally had given him, he found two women on the front porch, one of them smoking a cigarette, the other drinking coffee from a paper McDonald's cup. The smoker was a blonde bombshell dressed in plain gray jeans and a white-and-gray V-neck sweater. The coffee drinker was Sally Levine. Despite her shoulder-length chestnut hair appearing unbrushed and her blue dress slept-in, she was the more attractive of the two, as far as Chuck was concerned. She had the same girl-next-door prettiness that had turned heads when she was a kid.

He killed the engine and got out of the SUV. The Xanax had already started to kick in and he felt relaxed and a little floaty —though his legs and butt ached from sitting in the same position for so long.

"Chuck!" Sally said, smiling as she hurried down the porch steps. Upon reaching him she seemed undecided on whether to shake hands or hug.

He opened his arms. "Sally," he said as he embraced her briefly.

When they stepped apart, she said, "Wow, you look great."

"I've been driving all night with no sleep, so I doubt that's true, but thank you anyway," he said, though he was admittedly pleased by the compliment. He wasn't Fabio, but he was no longer obese. He'd lost most of his excess weight while in med school. "But you," he added, "*you* look great."

"Are you two just going to stand there all day complimenting one another?" the blonde said, coming down the steps. She crushed out her cigarette beneath her sneaker.

"We haven't seen each other in thirty years," Sally said. "It's trippy."

"Thirty-one years," Chuck corrected. He extended his hand. "I'm Chuck Hamman."

The woman shook. "I'm Amanda. I've known Sally all of one day, but what a day it's been."

"You're from around here?" he asked her.

"I'm a reporter in Phoenix. I'm here to cover the dancing pandemic."

"I saw a lady dancing in a Walgreens parking lot by the shopping center. I don't know if Sally's told you, but we experienced a dancing pandemic where we grew up. And while it was a bizarre experience when you're twelve years old, it's even more bizarre when you're forty-three. In any event, what's happening with Ben? Has his situation changed?"

"No," Sally said, concern filling her brown eyes. "We were just deciding where to meet the gypsy woman. I was waiting until you arrived before telling her the location. I want to be there first to be sure we're not walking into an ambush. You're still...cool with everything?"

"I've been second-guessing myself for the last ten hours. But, yes, I'm committed."

"And you brought a gun?"

Chuck opened the Lexus and withdrew the Colt Anaconda from his duffel bag on the passenger seat, along with the Planters Peanuts tin.

He hefted the heavy revolver in his hand. The brushed stainless finish appeared bluish as it reflected the bright morning sky.

"Jesus, that's huge," Amanda said.

"And it weighs a shitload," he said proudly, "which actually helps with the recoil."

"You've fired it before?" Sally asked.

"Sure. At least a thousand rounds over the years at a gun range. It's about as much gun as most folks can handle, to be honest, but I've grown comfortable with it. Now check these out." He handed Sally the peanut tin.

She shook it. "I'm guessing those aren't peanuts inside?"

"Go ahead and have a look."

She removed the lid and said, "Bullets."

".44 Magnums," he said. "Take a closer look at them."

She held one of the bullets in front of her. "What am I looking for?"

"Aren't cartridges usually made of brass?" Amanda said.

Chuck nodded. "Brass, copper, lead. But these..."

"*What!*" Sally said as her eyes widened. "Are they *silver*?"

"Yup!" he said happily. "I had them cast from a silver ingot at a gun shop in Salt Lake City. I don't know whether werewolves are actually allergic to silver, or whether that's just folklore. But I figured it couldn't hurt to jacket some ammunition in it to be safe."

Sally and Amanda exchanged what appeared to be uneasy glances.

Chuck frowned. "What's wrong? They still pack the same punch as regular bullets."

Sally shook her head, searching for words. "I don't...I don't want to get into a debate about this, okay? But I think...before we go ahead with the meeting with the gypsy woman...I think we need to be on the same page."

"I have no idea what you're talking about, Sally."

"The gypsies in Chatham and the gypsies that now have Ben...they're *people*, Chuck, not *werewolves*."

"You mean before they transform...?"

"*Werewolves don't exist!*"

"Don't exist?" he said, confounded. "Are you nuts?"

"No, Chuck, I'm not. I've already been through this with Ben, and I'm not getting into an argument with you too. Not now. We don't have the time. I just thought that had to be said. Werewolves don't exist. The end. Okay?"

"No, it's fucking not okay!" he shot back, his anger surging. "You were right there in Ryders Field with me, Sally, for God's sake! How can you say those gypsies were *people*? You *saw* them. You saw what I saw—"

"We were kids, Chuck. And kids are magical thinkers. They explain events to themselves through magic, fantasy, the supernatural—"

"Don't give me that child developmental bullshit! I know what I saw. I know exactly what I saw. I have a photographic memory. That's right, a grade-A visual memory. You want to know what kind of cake I had on my twelfth birthday? I can tell you that—peanut butter brownie ice cream cake. When I see something, I don't ever forget it. And something like what happened in Ryders Field? Jesus, I can recount what happened that night minute by minute. But I'm not going to. I try not to think about it at all because whenever I peek into that little box in my mind where I keep those memories I wig out. But I know what's in that box. I know exactly what's in that box. Magical thinking, my ass!"

Chuck glared at Sally, and the shock on her face made him immediately regret the outburst. But sometimes he couldn't help himself. He had a short temper. Kelly would often tell him the best remedy for that short temper was a long walk, and he usually took her up on the suggestion—slamming the door behind him on his way out.

He exhaled loudly. "I'm sorry for getting so worked up... I'm just feeling a bit...played...right now..."

"Played?" Sally said. "How am I playing you, Chuck?"

"You call me up in the middle of the night, you say the werewolves—or in your words, our old 'tormentors'—are back, and they've abducted Ben. You say you need my help and I need to come to Arizona right away. And now that I'm here, you're saying what we went through in Ryders Field never happened? I don't get it."

"I'm not saying it never happened. It did. Just not the way you think it did."

"Not the way I think? The sheriff—Sheriff Sandberg. He was right across from us all night in the other wagon. He was literally ten feet away from us. You don't recall his pointy ears, his snout? I mean, he had fur over every inch of his body!"

"He was dressed up. They were all dressed up."

Chuck was stunned into silence. *"Dressed up as werewolves?"* he said finally. "Why the fuck would a bunch of grown adults *dress up like werewolves*, Sally?"

She shrugged. "They were likely in some sort of cult—"

Chuck held up his hands dismissively; he couldn't listen to any more of this nonsense. It was as ridiculous as someone telling him the sun no longer existed because they couldn't see it behind a bank of storm clouds.

Sally was still speaking, but he cut her off. "You mentioned you've had this argument already with Ben. What's his opinion on whether the gypsies were werewolves or not?"

She shook her head. "It doesn't matter..."

"Of course it matters! He was there with us! He's the only other witness to what we saw."

"He thinks the gypsies were werewolves."

"There you go!" Chuck said. "That's a majority opinion." He raised his hands again before she could interject. "But enough of this. It doesn't matter what you believe or what I believe. Whether gypsies have captured Ben or whether werewolves have, it doesn't change anything, does it? So give the she-wolf you spoke to on the phone a call, and let's get this show on the road."

CHAPTER 22
THE ETHICS OF MURDER

As Sally drove Chuck's Lexus through the mostly empty streets of Camp Verde, she tried to concentrate on the upcoming meeting with the gypsy woman, but her thoughts kept shifting to Chuck, who sat in the passenger seat next to her. She was so confused. Ben believing in werewolves was one thing. He was a writer with a turbocharged imagination. Anyone who could come up with something like The Sack Man and make the existence of the bogeyman seem reasonable certainly had the capability to spin his own memories and convince himself that werewolves existed. But Chuck believing in werewolves too? She felt outnumbered, and she was. So was it possible she was wrong and they were correct? She wasn't a supercilious person who always had to be right. She enjoyed debate and discussion and broadmindedness. She would be the first to admit when she didn't know something, or when she was wrong.

But this wasn't a matter of being right or wrong, was it? It was a matter of being sane or insane. Because sane people didn't believe in vampires or zombies or werewolves.

So what are you saying? Ben is insane? Chuck is insane? You don't believe that.

No, she didn't. But she didn't believe she was insane either.

"Do you really have a photographic memory?" she asked Chuck without taking her eyes away from the road. Her hands were gripping the steering wheel too tightly, and she loosened them.

"How do you think I got through med school?" he said.

"I'm being serious."

"I am too. I'm on the spectrum."

Sally glanced at him. "You're autistic?"

"I haven't been officially diagnosed by a psychologist, but I'm well aware I have certain behavioral symptoms associated with high-functioning autism."

"Such as a photographic memory?"

"That's one of them. However, you might have noticed my tendency to say whatever's on my mind. Neurotypical people such as yourself think I have a big mouth. But the truth is I can't help myself. I've always been this way. What I'm thinking just comes out, unfiltered."

"You did say some pretty outlandish stuff as a kid," she said lightly.

"I still do. All the time. Just ask my wife. I'm also a stickler for routine and details and numbers. All that *Rain Man* stuff but without some of the more obvious social or communication issues." He shrugged. "But it is what it is, and I am who I am. Make a right here."

Sally veered right onto a two-lane road that passed between an ACE Hardware and Circle K gas station. She said, "How good is your memory, really?"

"Do you remember what you were wearing the day we met?"

"You mean when you and Ben were sneaking through my backyard?"

He nodded. "You were about to have a cigarette. By the way, what kind of thirteen-year-old kid smokes by themselves in their backyard?"

"I was bored and my parents were away. It seemed like a fun thing to do. What was I wearing?" She shook her head. "I have no idea."

"A GUESS tee-shirt, kind of hanging off one shoulder. You had a leopard leotard beneath, and red shorts—really short red shorts."

Sally thought back. She couldn't say for sure whether she

had been wearing those clothes or not, but she knew she had owned them. She'd bought the tee from a GUESS shop during a weekend trip to Boston with her parents. And the leotard had been a birthday gift from one of her girlfriends. She used to wear it while dancing around in her bedroom with a Madonna cassette playing on her boombox.

"The fact you remembered that," she said, "would be creepy if you didn't have a photographic memory."

"I can tell you what Ben was wearing too if you want..."

"Do you remember when Ben and I made you guess the flavors of all those donuts at my house?"

"You guys didn't *make* me guess the flavors. I wanted to do it."

"What were they?"

"The flavors?" He shrugged. "Whatever I tell you won't prove anything if you can't remember them yourself."

"You can't tell me, can you?" she challenged.

Chuck hesitated only a moment before saying, "Chocolate glazed, maple, double chocolate, glazed, cinnamon, apple fritter, vanilla glazed with sprinkles, a Long John, and a sugar-powered one with custard filling. That's also the order in which I tasted them, if you're wondering."

She knew he was telling the truth.

And if he could accurately remember details like that...

Sally felt suddenly sick to her stomach. She swerved to the shoulder and put the SUV in park. She closed her eyes, but the darkness made her feel more nauseous. She shoved open her door but couldn't get out. The damn seatbelt! She jabbed the release button on the buckle and stumbled outside, doubling over, dry heaving. She stuck two fingers into the back of her mouth to get it over with.

Vomit shot up her throat and out her mouth, striking the sidewalk near her feet, some of it splashing her shoes. She at least had the presence of mind to hold her hair out of her face.

At some point she realized Chuck stood next to her, his hand on her back.

She wiped her hand across her eyes, then her mouth.

Although the nausea had passed, the fear that prompted it remained, a cold, firm fist squeezing her insides.

"They're real," she said softly, looking at Chuck and seeing the boy he had been, not the man he had grown into. "They're real, Chunky, aren't they? Werewolves are real."

ΔΔΔ

The world rolling past the windows as they resumed the drive to Montezuma Castle National Monument felt surreal, almost as if it were one gigantic soundstage, and Sally and Chuck were characters playing the roles of Sally Levine and Chuck Hamman. The slow, underwater sense of unreality extended to Sally's thoughts as well. The lyrics to "Follow the Yellow Brick Road" played in her mind, only the wizard she was imagining was the gypsy woman with the exotic accent she had spoken to on the phone, and the puppeteer pulling the strings behind the curtain wasn't a cornfed, dried-up old man; it was an emaciated, salivating werewolf. Sally almost felt like singing along to a variation of the song—*You're off to see the Werewolf, the terrible Werewolf of Oz, you'll find she is a beast of a Beast, if ever a Beast there was!*—and she wondered if she might be on the brink of a nervous breakdown.

Out of the blue Chuck said, "Nobody calls me Chunk anymore—or Chunky, for that matter. It's Dr. Hamman, or Chuck, or maybe Chucky to close friends. So drop the Chunky, all right?"

This was the first either of them had spoken since getting back into the SUV. Sally had been too preoccupied to speak. Her concept of nature, and biology, had been flipped on its head in a matter of minutes, the implausible suddenly plausible, the fantastical, existent.

She had figured Chuck had been holding his tongue to let her get her head around all of this. Yet she now realized his silence was due to anger that she had called him by his loathed childhood nickname; the sharp, reproachful tone of his voice made that perfectly clear.

"Sorry, Chuck," Sally said, deciding that she might have been premature in her judgment earlier. The impressive Dr. Chuck Hamman might not be so different from the petulant Chunky she remembered from Chatham, after all. "I've just had a bit of a mind-bending day, and I wasn't thinking too clearly."

"Make sure it doesn't happen again."

Yes, sir, Chunky, sir! she felt like saying. But what she said was, "You know the gypsy woman is going to have something up her sleeve, right?"

"Which is why I'm here with you."

"I know. And I've been thinking about our plan... What if she brings a gun too?"

"Then I'll shoot her."

Sally started. "Shoot her? That's not why I asked you to bring the gun, Chuck. It's to scare her if she tries anything."

"Don't worry about me. I'll put a round right through her heart if need be."

"No, you will not!"

"Why the hell not?"

"First of all, you've only ever shot at paper targets. That's not the same as shooting at a living person."

"That's not true," he said. "I shot Sheriff Sandberg when he was changing into a werewolf with Ben's dad's gun. It was easy."

"If I recall correctly, you missed him by a mile."

"The point is, I shot *at* him. I have no problem shooting a person—or a werewolf, I should say."

"Let's set the ethics of the matter aside. I don't think you're grasping the legal consequences of shooting her. You'd be committing murder."

"I doubt killing a werewolf would be classified as murder. At most, it'd be a felony animal cruelty charge."

Sally glanced at Chuck. His voice had been matter-of-fact, and his face was expressionless—before it broke into a grin.

"This isn't something to joke about, Chuck!" she said. "This is…it's just crazy. It's crazy stuff. But if it's real, it's not something to kid about."

"So what do you want me to do if she whips out a gun?"

"I don't know. Maybe you could shoot her in the leg?"

"That's idiotic."

"Why is it idiotic? It wouldn't be committing murder."

"Why do you think cops are trained to shoot criminals in the chest? It's the easiest spot to hit. If I try for her leg and miss, she's probably going to put a round in *my* chest."

Sally considered this and said, "I suppose if she has a gun, and you shot her, it would be self-defense…"

"Now you're thinking."

"But what if…?" She had to force out the rest of the question: "What if she has special werewolf…powers? What if you can't stop her with a bullet?"

"No chance of anything like that when she's human. And the moon won't be full until tonight."

"Thanks for reminding me."

"We'll be long gone by then. So the question you should be asking is, what if she doesn't have Ben with her? What's the plan then?"

"I won't get out of the car. I'll drive away."

"And if she follows us?"

"I'll go to the police station and let them deal with her."

Chuck was nodding. "Shit—that would be something."

"What would be?"

"Imagine the gypsy woman was arrested and thrown in a jail cell. She'd transform right in front of everybody's eyes tonight. Better yet, imagine *we* captured a werewolf—even a dead one? If we could isolate and analyze the virus in its blood? *If we proved werewolves existed?* We're talking *Time* Person of the Year stuff here."

Sally didn't like the fanatic edge that had crept into Chuck's voice. It made her wonder if he was having a spur-of-the-moment realization or sharing something he'd previously thought about. "We're not out here to capture a werewolf, Chuck," she said sternly. "Our mission is to get Ben back, that's all. Then we're gone, and I'm on the first plane back to New York for a long session with my shrink."

"You're the one who said we can shoot the gypsy woman in self-defense."

"Right. Self-defense. If she has a gun and it looks like she's going to try to shoot us."

"All right, I hear you. But why not just shoot her anyway and toss her body into the trunk?"

"Are you listening to yourself?"

"What's the problem, Sally? We save Ben and get famous at the same time."

"What if she's *not* a werewolf, Chuck? Then you're going to be spending the next twenty years in prison."

"You know she is."

"No, I don't!" she exploded. "I don't! I don't know what I think!" She forced herself to take a deep breath. "I only know we're not going to go around shooting people if we don't have to."

"Werewolves aren't people."

"Chuck, enough!" If she hadn't been driving, she might have whacked him on the head to knock some sense into his thick skull. "You know the plan. You're here only in case the gypsy woman tries something funny. If she doesn't, you're not going to shoot her." Suddenly it felt as though the weight of the world was on her shoulders. Tears warmed her eyes, and she feared she was going to lose it.

I can't do this, she thought, second-guessing everything. *This is a nightmare. We have to turn back—*

"Check it out," Chuck said, pointing ahead to an empty parking lot. "Looks like we're here."

Sally frowned. "Where is everybody?"

"Tourists, you mean?"

She nodded. "I figured there would be at least some people here today..." She slowed to read an A-frame sign on the edge of the road:

MONTEZUMA CASTLE CLOSED FOR REPAIRS.

"Great," she said, her stomach sinking.

"What's wrong?" Chuck asked.

"We're alone out here. There aren't going to be any witnesses around to stop the gypsy woman from pulling some sort of shenanigan."

"Like what?"

"Like, I don't know…pulling a gun on us?"

"Relax," he told her. "Whatever gun she might have, mine's a hell of a lot bigger."

CHAPTER 23

A TENSE EXCHANGE

Sally pressed the pair of binoculars Chuck had brought with him against her eyes and watched as a red sports car (presumably the same one Amanda had seen at the Verde Suites the night before) followed the winding road through the foothills toward the Montezuma Castle parking lot. It disappeared and appeared like a phantom as it passed through shimmering thermal currents. "Ben's in the car," she said, relief washing over her.

"Who's driving?" Chuck asked. He had moved to the back seat of the SUV, where he could hide.

"A young woman. I presume she's the person I've been speaking with." Sally had last communicated with the woman half an hour ago, telling her the location of the meeting spot and to come alone.

"Anybody else with them?"

"Hold on..." Sally waited until the road swung west and she had a side view of the car. "Nobody," she added. "It's empty."

"Someone could be out of sight."

"Ben would know that. He would warn me as soon as they get here. It must be just him and the woman." Her chest was a knot of anxiety. She shook her hands as if to expel the nervous energy out of her body through her fingertips, then took a deep breath.

"Stay calm," Chuck told her. "This is going to work out fine."

"I know, I know. But...something doesn't feel right."

"What doesn't?"

"I don't know!"

"It's just your nerves, Sally," he said dismissively. "Now get your shit together. They're going to be here any minute."

△△△

Sally was standing next to the SUV when the red sports car entered the parking lot. She kept her hands balled into fists to stop them from shaking and swallowed to lubricate her bone-dry mouth. She had never been so afraid in her life, not even when she was locked up in the circus wagon in 1988, an admittedly much more perilous situation than what she currently faced. However, she was only thirteen years old then. Fear, like all emotions, matures with age. Its full potential can only be unleashed when a person has developed the self-awareness to understand they are mortal, their time is finite, and there will be an end to their life just as there was a beginning. Because what fear feeds on most, what fuels its black appetite, is an individual's intimate understanding not that death exists in the world but that it can happen to *them*.

And Sally, as a forty-four-year-old adult, was fully cognizant of her mortality and the grim possibility that it could be taken away from her at any moment.

Her gut instinct that something was not right was stronger than ever, and her mistrustful mind continued to conjure different ways the gypsy woman might outsmart her...and in every scenario she was left lying on the hot pavement in a pool of her blood with the midday sun beating down on her dying body.

Quit it! she told herself angrily. *It's just your nerves.*

The sports car rolled slowly toward her. Sally gave Ben a small wave. He didn't appear to respond, though she couldn't be certain as the white ball of the sun reflecting off the windshield made it hard to see inside the vehicle.

The car turned right and stopped in a parking spot ten up

from where Sally had parked. The engine shut off, and the driver's door opened. The woman who emerged was in her twenties, lithe, beautiful, with pale skin and long black hair. She wore a blue chiffon tee-shirt, knotted at the front, and a pair of faded and torn denim jeans. "Hello, dear," she said in her exotic accent while shading her eyes with her hand and looking around. "An interesting location you have chosen."

"Ben?" Sally called, looking past the woman. "Are you all right?"

He didn't answer.

"Let him out of the car!"

"Calm yourself, dear, and I'll fetch him for you. My name's Malenia. And you are?"

"Sally," she said. "Now let him out."

The gypsy woman went to the passenger-side door and opened it. Ben got out, his head and shoulders appearing above the roof of the vehicle. It wasn't until the woman had led him around the hood that Sally realized his hands were bound behind his back.

"What's going on, Sally?" he demanded, his terseness surprising her. "What deal have you made with this woman?"

"Our deal," Malenia said, "is your freedom in exchange for the information that you failed to provide me."

Sally frowned in puzzlement. If you'd asked her an hour ago what the gypsy woman from Chatham had looked like, she wouldn't have been able to tell you. But if you asked her now, she would say she looked identical to the woman standing next to Ben.

Of course that couldn't be the case. She would be in her fifties or sixties now.

"Get back in your car, Sally," Ben said, "and drive away."

"I'm not going anywhere without you."

"As soon as you tell her what she wants to know, she'll kill us. I don't care what she's promised you, she's not letting us walk away."

"Kill you?" Malenia appeared amused. "Little old me?"

Ben glanced over his shoulder, then back at Sally. "Some of her goons have probably followed us. They could be here any minute. Get out of here, Sally. Now."

A chill shot down Sally's spine. What if what Ben was saying was true and others were on the way? There was only one route in or out of the parking lot. They would be trapped.

She scanned the foothills and the road leading up to the parking lot and saw no other vehicles approaching.

Yet.

"All right then," she said, trying to project confidence. "I'm going, but you're coming with me, Ben. She can't stop you."

"Oh no?" Malenia stuck a hand behind her back. In the next instant she was pointing a pistol at Ben. The weapon, as Chuck had predicted, wasn't anywhere near as big as his revolver, but a gun was a gun. "You sadden me, dear. I thought we had a deal. Does nobody keep their word these days?"

"Sally, go!" Ben said.

Malenia aimed the barrel at her. "You're not going anywhere."

Sally had never had a gun pointed at her before. The urge to run and seek cover, she discovered, was nearly overwhelming.

The gypsy woman shifted the barrel a little to Sally's left. "Please open the back door of your car for me. I'm curious as to why that window is down."

"Because we're in the desert, and it's baking hot. I put all the windows down while waiting for you."

"Understandable. But I'd still like to see inside for myself."

Sally opened the back door, revealing the empty interior. "Happy?"

"I'll be happy when you tell me how you know of us."

She started. "Know of you?"

"I believe you understand what I mean."

Sally swallowed. Although she had told Chuck she had come around to believe that werewolves existed, it wasn't until this very terrifying moment that she really, truly believed it.

The gypsy woman had just admitted as much.

"As Ben mentioned," she said, fighting to keep her voice from wavering, "if I tell you, you'll shoot us."

"I can shoot you regardless of whether you keep your side of the deal or not, can't I? So you have a choice to make. Go back on your word and die today, in this parking lot, where you will be food for the vultures before anybody discovers your body. Or keep your word and tell me what I've asked. As a woman of *my* word, I will let you go if you do so, as I have promised."

"Don't do it," Ben said.

"What if she's telling the truth?"

"She's not."

"She'll kill us anyway."

"If she does, then her secret is out. Everybody will know."

"Excuse me?" Malenia said.

"Do you think I would sneak into a camp of werewolves," he told her, "without some insurance against my safety."

"Ah, so you *do* know. You are in a rather small club, Ben Graves. Tell me about this purported insurance you have."

"Before coming to Camp Verde, I instructed a friend to release all the information I've gathered about you and your pack if I went missing."

Something shifted in Malenia's dark eyes. Skepticism? Or was it concern? "Why are you only mentioning this now?"

"Because before now you haven't threatened to kill me."

"I don't believe you."

"And I don't believe you'll let us go."

A charged silence followed the exchange. Sally had been so swept up in the encounter with the gypsy woman that she hadn't given much thought to Chuck, except in a vague back-of-the-mind way, hoping that he would reveal himself at any moment and end the standoff.

But that moment should have come already; it should have come as soon as Malenia produced her pistol.

What the hell are you doing, Chunky? she thought. *What are you waiting for?*

Sally had to resist the urge to drop to her knees and peek

beneath the SUV where Chuck was lying in wait. He'd decided at the last moment (correctly) that the gypsy woman might want to search the SUV to make sure Sally was alone.

Has he lost his nerve? Is he chickening out because Malenia has a gun?

"I'll tell you what you want to know," Sally said to buy time while raising her voice so Chuck would hear her. "But only under two conditions. One, you let Ben stand over here with me. And two, you put down your gun."

"So the both of you can hop in your car and drive away?"

"There's no way we could get in the car, let alone get it started before you picked up the gun again. There's also no way I'm telling you anything with a gun pointed at me. So this is where we are. A reset, a show of trust."

The gypsy woman considered that then said, "Go ahead, Ben Graves, join your friend."

Ben hesitated momentarily, then crossed the dozen feet to Sally.

"I hope you know what you're doing," he mumbled under his breath.

"Put down the gun," she said loudly.

Malenia placed the pistol on the asphalt. She rose and opened her hands to show she was unarmed. "Now tell me how you know about us."

"Sally..." Ben warned.

She barely heard him. Her thoughts were screaming for Chuck to reveal himself and shoot the gypsy woman. She might have been against this earlier, but that was before she had a gun pointed at her.

Come on, Chunky! Get off your ass and shoot the bitch!

But he didn't appear, and Sally knew the only way to buy more time was by confessing the truth. She said, "We've met members of your pack before."

"Oh?" Malenia said. "When was that?"

"A long time ago. Thirty-one years to be exact."

"You would have been a child."

"I was."

"Where did this encounter happen?"

"Chatham, Massachusetts, in a forested area of the town called Ryders Field."

Malenia's eyes narrowed. They flicked to Ben, then back to Sally. Then a knowing smile crept across her face. "Yes...I see now." Her smile broadened. "Yes, I remember you both very well."

"You remember *us*?" Ben said. "I doubt you were even born then."

"Ah, but don't you recognize *me*, Ben Graves? It was I who locked you up that night—for your safety, I might add. And it was I who released you in the morning. And as I recall, there were three of you. Where is that third Musketeer today—?"

"Right here, motherfucker!"

And the deafening report of a gunshot ripped through the air.

CHAPTER 24

SHENANIGANS

The gypsy woman was lifted off her feet and landed flat on her back. Her left arm and leg twitched several times, and then her body went still. Blood bloomed beneath her blue tee shirt, forming a spreading dark stain on her upper chest. Her right foot was bare; the white tennis shoe she had been wearing was six feet away, from where she had previously stood.

Her ears ringing, Sally spun around to see Chuck on the other side of the Lexus, his elbows locked, the huge revolver pointed skyward. Like a gunslinger in an old Western movie, he blew at the smoke drifting up from the barrel.

That didn't work out like it did in the TV tropes. Some of the smoke, or perhaps burnt gunpowder, swirled into his eyes, causing him to turn his head away and cry out.

"Jesus motherfucking Christ!" he said, dragging his forearm across his face. "It stings!"

Ben, Sally noticed, was staring at Chuck in utter shock as she untied the thick rope that bound his wrists.

"Chunk...?" he said, in an unsure way.

"It's Chuck, pal! Chuck! I just saved your fucking life, so show some respect!"

Ben threw his head back and laughed. "Chunk, buddy! It *is* you."

He went over and embraced his old friend, who patted him a few times on his back with the hand still holding the revolver.

Sally joined the reunion, wrinkling her nose at the acrid stench of propellant in the air. "Maybe I should take this?" She carefully removed the Dirty Harry-sized revolver from Chuck's grip, amazed by the weight of it.

Ben and Chuck stepped apart. Ben looked at the gypsy woman, who remained unmoving on the ground. "I think you killed her."

"Fucking-A I did! I just bagged myself a werewolf—"

The loud clap of a gunshot cut him off, and for a moment Sally feared she had accidentally discharged the revolver. But the gunshot had originated in the distance. Then Ben's hand was on her shoulder, shoving her into a crouch.

"Stay down!" he said, scanning the foothills surrounding them.

"Someone help me get the werewolf's body!" said Chuck, also squatting.

"Forget it!" Sally said. "We have to get out of here!" She reached up to open the passenger-side door of the Lexus a moment before the door's window exploded. She shrieked and covered her head with her arms as hundreds of gummy shards of glass rained down on her.

She heard Ben shout "Chunk, don't!" and forced open her eyes. Chuck was scrambling on all fours toward the gypsy woman. He only made it halfway to her when a second gunshot boomed. Chuck stopped, turned around, and scampered back to the SUV, disappearing around the hood.

"Come on!" Ben said, taking Sally's hand and leading her to where Chuck had taken shelter on the other side of the vehicle.

"We can't stay here!" she said. "We're sitting ducks!"

Ben said, "Where are the car keys—"

A third gunshot, followed by a *pshhhh!* sound of air leaving a punctured tire.

"Fuckers are shooting the tires!" Chuck said.

Sally gasped. "Chuck, are you all right?" The upper left shoulder of his white dress shirt had turned crimson.

Frowning, he stuck his hand beneath the fabric. When he

removed it, his fingers were slick with blood.

"Dammit," Ben said. "You've been shot."

"I don't feel anything..." Chuck grunted when he tried to raise his left arm. "Spoke too soon."

Sally said, "We need to get you to a hospital."

"We need to get out of this parking lot first!"

Ben said, "Call 9-1-1."

"There's no reception out here," Sally told him. "I couldn't get a single bar while waiting for the gypsy woman to arrive."

"Then we have to make a run for it."

"*Run?*" Chuck said. "Where are we going to run to? We're in the middle of the fucking desert!"

"There's no way we're driving out of here—"

The sharp report of another gunshot caused them all to flinch. Sally heard liquid gushing and peered beneath the SUV's chassis. Gasoline was pooling on the ground on the far side of it.

"They punctured the gas tank!"

Ben said to Chuck, "Can you run?"

"They'll pick us off."

"We just have to get to the visitor center, then we'll be out of their line of sight."

They looked toward the midcentury structure. It was maybe thirty feet away.

Chuck said, "They'll come after us."

Ben said, "Which is why staying where we are isn't an option! *Now can you run?*"

"Yeah, yeah, I was shot in my arm, not my leg."

"Then you go first after they take the next shot. Sally, you follow him. I'll be right behind you both—"

Another gunshot. Another explosion of glass.

"Go! Go! Go!"

Chuck took off, hunched low, his arms shielding his head.

Saying a silent prayer, Sally followed him.

PART 3

Montezuma Castle

CHAPTER 25

BEACHES AND PALM TREES

Scooby was on a deserted beach, climbing the smooth, narrow trunks of palm trees and cutting bunches of ripe coconuts loose with a machete. Things had been going great, life was sweet...until Lizzy, the dumb bitch, wandered beneath the tree he was in. A huge hairy brown coconut dropped on her head with the weight of a bowling ball. When he scampered down the tree, he found her lying on the sand with a big ring of blood around her head. Only it wasn't Lizzy anymore. It was the dancing cougar, and she was as dead as she'd been in her shitty house. In the distance he heard police sirens. Somehow they'd tracked him down. He considered escaping into the jungle, but he figured they'd probably have dogs that could follow his scent. He ran to the ocean instead and dived below the surf so he was invisible to anybody on land. He was able to hold his breath indefinitely, he realized, and while swimming along the sandy bottom amongst the corals and fish, he'd never felt so free—

A hand plucked him from the water. No, the hand was shaking him. He wasn't in the ocean; he was lying on a hard floor, his head on a beanbag chair.

Monster stood next to him, his black-rimmed eyeglasses tilting drunkenly on the bridge of his nose. "It's late, man. Time to get going."

Scooby sat up. He felt stiff and groggy. Lizzy was next to him, still asleep, her hair spread around her head like black spiderwebs. "What time is it?"

"Past noon, man. I gotta start my streaming soon. So you guys gotta split."

Everything from the previous day came back to him. He was a fugitive. The cops were looking for him. He was facing a decade behind bars.

Suddenly all he wanted to do was sit in his tree, and the fact he couldn't saddened him tremendously.

"I'm still tired, yo."

"I don't care, man. You were supposed to leave last night. The cops are gonna figure out you're here sooner or later, and then I'm gonna get in trouble."

Lizzy sat up and rubbed her eyes with her fists. She yawned and said, "What time is it?"

"Late," Monster said. "And you guys gotta go."

"I gotta piss," Scooby said. He got up and went to the basement's little bathroom. It was unfinished, all wood studs and plyboard and visible pipes and wiring.

When he returned to the main room, Monster was at his computer, and Lizzy was on the sofa, staring at her phone.

She looked up at him and said, "My parents disowned me."

"They *what*?"

"They disowned me! They said I can never come home, and if I do, they're calling the cops. They said I'm a criminal and belong in prison."

"They know you killed that bitch?"

"*You* killed her! But they know I was filming. Everybody does. Because it was my TikTok account we posted the video to."

Scooby shrugged. "Who cares what they say?"

"*Who cares?* I care! They *disowned* me!"

"I haven't spoken to my folks in years. Who needs 'em? Besides, we're going to Mexico, girl."

"You ruined my life, Scoob! I hate you! I hate you so much!"

"That's real shitty, Lizzy," Monster said. "But I gotta start my stream soon. You guys gotta jet."

"We can't go yet, bro," Scooby said. "It's light out. We gotta wait until dark."

"Then you shoulda left last night!"

"You kept packing bowls."

"Come on, guys!"

"Look, bro, you do your thing. You won't even know we're here."

"You're gonna start fighting. You always fight."

"Nah, we're cool. We'll just be planning our trip to Mexico."

Monster sighed. "Either of you makes any noise while I'm streaming, *I'm* gonna call the cops on you." He turned back to his computer.

"I ain't going to Mexico, Scoob," Lizzy said.

"You're gonna love it, girl," he replied, unperturbed by her stubbornness. He knew her too well. She always went along with him in the end, and this would be no different. "Beaches and palm trees and piña coladas, you know what I'm sayin'?"

She glared at him.

Scooby put his arm around her shoulder and walked her to the far side of the basement. He stuck his hand in the pocket of his shorts and took out two colorfully decorated tabs of acid.

Lizzy stared at them, and he could almost feel her icy anger melting away. She whispered, "Where'd you get them?"

"Scoob always has the goods," he told her. "So we gonna get high?"

Grinning, she nodded.

"Who do you love, bitch?"

"I hate you."

"Tell me you love me."

"I hate you."

"You wanna get high?"

"Yeah."

"You wanna go on a trip?"

"Yeah."

"Then tonight, after this trip, we go on *another* trip."

Lizzy hesitated.

"Beaches and palm trees, surf and sun. It's gonna be wild.

You and me, babe."

Her grin returned. "Did you call me babe?"

"Yeah, bitch."

"I like it better when you call me babe."

He shrugged. "I can call you babe."

"All the time?"

"24/7, starting now." He stuck one of the blotters in his mouth, then raised the other. Lizzy opened her mouth obediently, and he placed the small square of absorbent paper soaked with LSD on her tongue. "To Mexico, babe."

CHAPTER 26

CAUGHT BETWEEN A ROCK AND A HARD PLACE

They reached the visitor center without anyone else getting shot and ran down the breezeway, past the entrance and a gift shop. When they emerged on a paved pathway shaded by a grove of sycamores, they kept running. A short distance later Montezuma Castle appeared on their right. It didn't feature towers or battlements or other accruements of a medieval castle as its name might suggest. Rather it was a bland mud-and-river rock architectural anachronism several stories tall, built seamlessly and almost two-dimensionally into the face of the limestone cliff in which it was located.

A series of three tall ladders led up to the ancient structure.

Ben glanced behind them to make sure they weren't being followed and then came to a stop on the path. Sally and Chunk did the same. All three of them were already out of breath.

He pointed to the monument. "I think that's our best bet."

"Now's really not the time to sightsee, Ben," Sally said, wiping sweat from her brow.

"I can't keep...running," Chunk said, panting heavily. His face was so white and tight that it almost seemed he was wearing a mask. His brown eyes stood out in stark contrast to it, wide, intense, almost feverish.

"There's only one way up or down," Ben said. "Once we're up there, we can defend it and prevent anyone else from coming up."

"Or...any*thing*," Chunk agreed.

"We'll be trapped!" Sally said.

"You'd prefer to wander around the desert at night with werewolves hunting you?"

"We can make it to town well before dark. The casino can't be more than a couple of miles from here."

"Do I look like I'm in any condition to hike two miles? I'm about to pass out. But fuck it, you go. Gimme back my gun first."

He reached for it. Sally backed away.

"Give it to me!" he snapped. "It's my gun!"

Sally looked at Ben.

"Chunk's right," he told her.

"It's Chuck!"

"He's right," Ben repeated. "He won't make it to the casino. And we're not splitting up. That monument is our best bet. We can hold it until morning."

"And then what?" she challenged. "We'll still be trapped in there—"

Chunk abruptly started away from them in the direction of Montezuma Castle.

"Sally," Ben said quietly but sternly, "we don't have a choice here. Chunk's losing a lot of blood. We need to get him patched up. We can't do that out in the open. There's no doubt the shooter is already coming for us, most likely with others."

She glanced past him the way they had come, then to the monument. "If we try to hide in there, they're going to get us, and we're going to die."

"If we're lucky, they might not even check there."

"Wishful thinking, Ben, and you know that."

"We can't split up, Sally. I'm not letting you go off on your own, and I can't leave Chunk on his own either. Please...we're running out of time."

She shook her head furiously as tears filled her eyes.

"We're going to die," she repeated and then hurried to catch up to Chunk.

ΔΔΔ

Chunk climbed the ladder at the base of the monument first. Sally went next, repeatedly telling Chunk to hurry up despite he only had the use of one arm. Ben went last, looking over his shoulder every few rungs to make sure the shooter or shooters hadn't caught up with them. When they reached a narrow rocky ledge, they followed it right to the second ladder, which unlike the previous one was nearly vertical. The final ladder, also nearly vertical, was ten feet to their left along another narrow ledge. While waiting for Sally to ascend it, Ben glanced down at the ground far below them, which caused a dizzying surge of vertigo. The monument hadn't seemed nearly so high when standing at the bottom of it and looking up.

Sally was now halfway up the third ladder. Ben steeled his nerves and began to climb after her, though much more slowly than before. His fear of heights had kicked in, a nearly immobilizing mind game that had turned something as mundane as ascending a ladder into a Herculean feat. Consequently, he was no longer capable of simply gripping the uprights and scampering up; instead, he was hugging each rung as he took one baby step after another.

"Made it!" Chunk bellowed from above him.

Ben kept his gaze fixed on the rock directly in front of his face.

"Ben, are you okay?" Sally called down.

"Fine!" he said.

"Are you climbing the ladder or fucking it, dude?" Chunk said. The jibe was followed by his obnoxious, honking laughter that had changed little over the years.

"Hurry, Ben!" It was Sally again, although her voice had risen several glassy octaves. "They're here!"

Here? he thought. He couldn't muster the nerve to turn his head and scan the ground below. *Where was here?*

"Climb, motherfucker!" Chunk shouted.

A gunshot rang out. Ben heard the bullet *zing!* off the cliff somewhere to his right.

"Faster, Ben!" Sally cried.

He began moving faster, his fear of being shot trumping his fear of heights.

A second gunshot followed the first. This time the bullet ricocheted off the limestone so close to his head it produced a cloud of dust that he could taste.

Sally and Chuck continued to urge him on, although they sounded like they were on the other side of a thick slab of glass. Ben knew he had to be nearing the top of the ladder. He also knew—he was fatalistically certain—that a bullet would punch through his back at any moment, and he would plummet a hundred feet to his death.

He continued to entertain these morbid thoughts even as hands gripped his shoulders and arms and pulled him off the ladder. It was only a few moments later after he'd stumbled into a dark room on jellied legs that he realized he was no longer in immediate danger. He collapsed to his knees and then flopped onto his back in a spread-eagle position.

The solid ground had never felt so reassuring.

CHAPTER 27
TRUE COLORS

"**Y**ou had me worried there, buddy," Chunk said, looking down at Ben. He had taken off his blazer and was pressing it against his shoulder wound. "What the hell was wrong with you?"

"I don't like heights," he said simply, pushing himself up onto his elbows. The monument's room was built on a naturally occurring limestone alcove, which had then been sealed off with masonry walls and a low ceiling.

"You can't climb a ladder?"

"Acrophobia, ever hear of it? It's a mental thing. I have no control over how my body reacts to heights."

"So the great Ben Graves ain't so great, after all."

Frowning, he said, "The great Ben Graves?"

"You were always so great at everything. It's nice to know you're not perfect."

"I was hardly great at everything."

"Soccer, handball, basketball. You were usually picked first."

Ben couldn't tell whether Chunk was serious or not and said, "Those were recess games."

Chunk said, "It wasn't just sports. I seem to recall all our teachers always holding up your stuff during art class as a model of how whatever we were doing was supposed to be done."

"I was a good artist, so what?"

"And girls? You always had all the girls chasing after you."

Ben laughed; this was ridiculous. "Bullshit."

"No?" Chunk held out his hand and counted on his fingers. "Mary-Lynn Cherepinsky in grade seven. Heather Russell in grade eight. You even 'married' Bayley Buchannan in grade six."

"That was all just stupid kid stuff. Mary-Lynn, I walked home with her a few times. Heather, we touched our knees at a party. And Bayley...someone started a rumor she liked me and suddenly we were married. I don't think I'd ever said more than a few words to her. I certainly never had girls chasing after me."

"What do you think, Sally?" Chunk said. "You were drooling all over Ben as a kid. Was that just stupid kid stuff, or did you want to jump his bones? I bet you still want to jump his bones now, don't you?"

Sally appeared either mortified or bemused or perhaps a combination of the two. "I think you're acting like a buffoon, Chuck," she said. "You have a bullet stuck in your shoulder, and all you care about is how popular Ben was in elementary school?"

"I don't give a shit about how popular he was or not. I'm just saying it's nice to know the big-time famous author here ain't perfect."

Ben said, "Where the hell's this coming from, Chunk?"

"Chuck!" he bellowed. "Jesus fucking Christ! Do I look like that stupid shit I used to be? I'm no longer *fat*, and I'm no longer *Chunk*. Got it?"

"Yeah, yeah," Ben said, and although he would start calling him Chuck, he knew he wouldn't be able to think of him as that. Although his old friend didn't much resemble the chubby kid he had gone to school with—especially dressed importantly in pleated slacks, an Oxford button-down shirt with monogrammed cuffs, a gold necklace, and a stainless-steel Rolex—he was still Chunk to him and always would be. "Chuck, I got it. So just...chill."

"Chill? I'm chilled, pal. I'm chilled. You know, I sent you a

Facebook friend request like ten years ago. You never accepted it."

Ben nearly laughed again but didn't; Chuck had always been volatile and unpredictable, but all this, from a grown man... Ben didn't know what to make of it and didn't want to upset him further. Instead he said simply, "I don't use Facebook."

"I don't care if you use Facebook or not. You have an account. You saw the invite."

"I do have an account, and I did see your request," he admitted. "But I only started the account because I'd sold my first book and my publisher wanted me to promote it on social media. I wasn't planning on using Facebook for personal stuff."

"You and Sally are friends."

"What?"

"People can see who your friends are, dipshit. I checked while I was on my way down here to help save your ass. You've got ten friends, and Sally is one of them."

Sally exhaled in exasperation. "We've never even messaged each other, Chuck."

"He still accepted your friend request, or you accepted his."

Ben shook his head. "This is crazy, Chuck. Are we really discussing this?"

"Yeah, we are, pal. Because we used to be best friends. Then you took off and I never heard from you again. I'm just seeing where I stand now."

"You're my friend," he said. "You're still my friend. We just... grew up. Our lives took us in different directions."

"You could have kept in touch."

And you could have kept your mouth shut in Ryders Field instead of luring the werewolves to my dad. But what he said was, "Yeah, I guess I should have. But, look—I'm proud of you. A doctor. That's impressive."

Chuck's eyes narrowed. "How d'you know I'm a doctor?"

"For one, you blurted it out earlier when Sally called you... your old nickname. Also, she told me yesterday." Deciding the best way to diffuse Chuck's temper would be to stroke his ego, he added, "She said that you've been successful...and that you have a smoking hot wife."

Chuck cocked an eyebrow at Sally. "You told Ben that?"

She shrugged. "That you're a doctor? Yes. That you have an attractive wife? Yes. I've seen the pictures you post of her online."

Chuck contemplated that and said, "The wife *is* smoking hot —a real bitch, sure, but smoking hot. I'd take that trade-off any day."

Ben grinned. "I know you would, buddy. And I'm glad some things haven't changed."

"I ain't fat anymore. That's changed."

"But you're still *you*."

"I guess I'll take that as a compliment." He removed his blazer from his shoulder, examined the wound, then reapplied pressure to it. Grimacing, he said, "Good news is there's not much external bleeding."

"And the bad news?" Sally asked.

"Don't know if there's any internal bleeding or nerve damage."

"Is there anything else we can do?"

"Got any disinfectants?"

"Well...no..."

"Surgical equipment?"

"No..."

"Then what are you planning on doing, Sally?"

She scowled at him. "I was offering moral support."

"I don't need moral support. I need proper medical attention."

Ben said, "Should we...I don't know...try to get the bullet out?"

"Maybe if this was a scene in one of your books, we might," Chuck said. "But bullets are only dangerous because of their speed. Now that it's in there, it's not doing any harm—unlike having an amateur poking around in unsanitary conditions."

"Jeez, you've got great bedside manners for a doctor," Sally said.

"Currently, I'm both doctor and patient, so I can be as goddamn crabby as I want to be."

Ben said, "Maybe you should sit down and rest."

He removed the blazer from the wound again and said, "Can you check the inside pocket for me?"

Ben produced an orange pill bottle.

Chuck pressed the blazer back against his wound and said, "Tap a few into my mouth, will you?"

"What are they?"

"Benzos." He opened his mouth.

Ben removed the white cap and fed Chuck two. He dry-swallowed them, then said, "Couple more."

"You sure?"

"Yeah, I'm sure."

Ben gave him two more, then returned the bottle to the blazer pocket. "Must be nice to be able to write your prescriptions."

"I get panic attacks."

"So the great Chuck Hamman ain't so great, after all," Sally said, doing her best to imitate Chuck's voice.

He snorted. "People like you are the reason I'm on meds."

"Hilarious, Chuck."

"Go play hide and go fuck yourself."

She checked her phone, then looked at Ben. "Still no reception. I'm going to go up to the roof to see if I can get a signal there. Do you want to join me?"

"Good idea," he said, nodding. "Chuck, you'll be okay here by yourself? We shouldn't be too long."

"Yeah, pal. I'll be fine." To Sally he said, "Leave me the Colt."

She hesitated.

"Someone's gotta guard the entrance, don't they?"

She passed him the revolver, which had been tucked into the waistband of her jeans. "Don't shoot yourself. Someone, somewhere, might miss you."

"Kiss my ass."

"Which one?"

"Oh, bravo, Sally, so witty vitriol. Started menopause a little early, have we?"

CHAPTER 28
THE ROOFTOP

"**H**e's despicable," Sally fumed.

"He's Chunk," Ben said.

They were passing through another dark, musty room one level up from where they'd left Chuck. Daylight filtered through a porthole-sized window, allowing them to see where they stepped. At some point park service workers had propped up the wooden sycamore beams that supported the low ceiling with a network of steel poles. Everything appeared to be structurally sound...but you never knew in a millennia-old adobe building.

Sally remained focused on Chuck. "Don't people grow out of making childish insults? 'Started menopause a little early, have we?' I mean, what a *jerk*."

"He's always just sort of said stuff, without a filter."

"He blames that on his autism."

Ben was surprised. "Chunk's autistic?"

She shrugged. "Says he is. Says he can't help what he says. But I think that's BS. He's just an asshole. He was an asshole as a kid, and he hasn't changed."

The next room they entered was smaller than the last one and windowless, yet Ben could make out a ladder leading up to a hatch in the ceiling. The ladder wasn't made by the indigenous Native Americans who had constructed the castle, but like the steel poles, it wasn't a recent addition either.

Sally climbed the ladder first, and Ben followed. They emerged in a room where smoke had blackened the rock walls. Part of the ceiling was missing. The cross-section revealed that twigs and reeds had been placed on top of the wood beams to create thatching, which had then been covered with a thick layer of mud. There were two doors on the exterior wall. One opened to a wide balcony, the other to outer space.

Sally peeked out the latter. "You wouldn't want to take the wrong door when you wake up in the middle of the night to pee. It's a sheer drop. Take a look."

"I'm fine over here," Ben said.

"Is your fear of heights that bad?"

"You saw me earlier."

"You were fine on the airplane."

"That's different."

"You were thirty thousand feet in the air."

"It's just different." He crouched and studied what appeared to be fingers- and handprints in the plaster of the southeast-facing wall. "Check this out."

Sally came over. "Small hands."

"People back then would have been much smaller in stature than we are now."

"Or perhaps the females built this place while the men were out fishing?"

"What the fuck were they doing outside of the kitchen?"

Sally stared at him in surprise.

He grinned sheepishly. "I was trying to channel Chunk. Sorry."

They exited through the doorway that led to the balcony. No railing guarded the edge, so Ben made sure to stick as close as possible to the cliff face. At the far end they entered through a door about half the height of a contemporary one, forcing him to crouch nearly to his knees to get through. A few peepholes in the new room let in enough light to reveal squiggly lines and geometric shapes carved into the walls.

"Petroglyphs!" Sally said, running her hand along one

elaborate design.

"Funny that we think of abstract art as 'modern' when it's been around for thousands of years. Watch your feet," he added as he stepped over the broken rubble of a collapsed false wall.

"It's amazing how much rockwork they did. All these walls, built way up here on narrow ledges. There must be at least a dozen or so rooms in this place."

"I'd guess a lot more than that. It's gotta be four or five stories high."

"Their lifestyle was almost romantic if you think about it. Waking up to a million-dollar view every morning. No taxes or bills to pay, no nine-to-five grind. Just living day to day, at one with nature."

"And sleeping five people to a tiny room," he pointed out. "Battling bloodthirsty neighbors. Losing all your crops to unpredictable floods or storms. High infant and maternal mortality. Constant disease."

"Sheesh. You're optimistic."

"Pragmatic."

They climbed another ladder and progressed through more soot-covered rooms. While all were empty shells (albeit modified to include rock features such as benches and storage niches), in Ben's mind's eye he saw life as it would have been a thousand years ago: the elderly and sick huddled before a hearth on a cold, wet day. A woman working a loom to weave cotton clothing and blankets. A man starting a fire with a friction drill. Other villagers milling corn, weaving baskets, or creating clay pottery. Children plowing the fields and proud hunters returning from a hunt with wild game.

On the next level up much of the floor had collapsed. It had been replaced with steel stanchions and wide wooden planks, creating a kind of permanent scaffolding.

In a very small room they came upon a gruesome discovery: the skeletal remains of dozens of small rodents.

"What happened here?" Sally said, concerned.

Ben said, "I've never heard of rats committing mass suicide."

"Rats, no. Lemmings, yes."

"Lemmings live in Alaska, not Arizona."

"I don't like this…"

"Some bird of prey probably made its nest up here. They were dinner."

"Do you see a nest anywhere? Or feathers, for that matter?"

"Rat poison?"

"In a structure uninhabited by people?"

"I don't know what killed them, Sally, but they've clearly been dead for a long time. It's nothing to worry about."

They climbed a final ladder in the adjacent room and emerged on the top floor of Montezuma Castle. There was a little barrier made from river cobbles and mud mortar, which ran from one side of the cave to the other. This area was the only part of the monument that could be described as a "cave," as it had a natural stone roof overhead.

The view of the desert was breathtaking, even for someone prone to acrophobia. The trees and shrubs far below looked as though they were part of a miniature scale model. In the distance foothills rose against the blue sky.

Ben said, "This must have been their lookout spot."

Sally said, "I don't see the shooter anywhere."

He scanned the path they'd followed to the monument—a tiny, snaking line—until where it curved out of sight behind the cliffs to their left. It was indeed deserted.

"Maybe he left?" Ben said hopefully. "I'm pretty sure the woman Chunk killed, Malenia, was the leader of their pack, or whatever the collective noun for werewolves is. So maybe he was rattled and returned to their camp? Maybe they're all going to say to hell with us and take off to wherever they want to go next?"

"Where's their camp?" Sally asked.

"North of Camp Verde. Off the highway, in the desert, next to a rocky knoll."

"How did you ever find them there? You were supposed to be

getting pizza."

"I was in the pizza joint, and there was this guy. He'd ordered a dozen pizzas. On his way out I remarked that he must be hungry, and he told me it must be the full moon."

Sally raised an eyebrow. "And?"

"And I got in the car and followed him."

"Because he made a crack about the full moon?"

Ben shrugged. "You had to be there, I guess. It was the way he said it. It sounded—as crazy as this may seem—it sounded like something a werewolf would say to an unsuspecting human. He even winked."

"He winked at you?"

"He winked and said, 'Must be the full moon.'"

"Sounds like a villain in a daytime soap opera. So you followed him out of town into the desert?"

Ben nodded, explaining how he was ambushed when he reached the camp, interrogated by Malenia, and then locked in one of the circus wagons.

"You were locked up in one of them—*again*?" She appeared horrified. "I think if that happened to me, I might have lost my mind."

"It was a pretty shitty sense of déjà vu," he admitted.

"You must have been terrified."

"That's an understatement." Ben shuddered as he recalled the nihilistic state of mind he had been in the night before. "I knew they were going to kill me. It's one thing to say something like that. But to *know* it..." He shook his head. "To be locked in a cage with that knowledge, helpless to change the outcome...you can't put into words how that feels. If I could have...if I'd had something to kill myself with...I probably would have done it. I've never contemplated that before. But I knew they weren't simply going to kill me. They were keeping me for the full moon. They were going to...eat me."

Sally surprised him by kissing him on the cheek. "Well, they didn't, did they?" she said softly. "You're here now."

"Thanks to you."

"Well, I couldn't let them *eat* you." She wiped her eyes with the back of her hand and said, "Better check if we have reception." She took her phone from her pocket. "Dammit, nothing."

Ben hadn't believed ascending a few floors would make a difference to the strength of the phone's signal, but it had been worth a shot.

"Should we go back down?" he asked her.

"We have a better view of anybody approaching from up here."

"Until it gets dark," he pointed out.

"Even then, it's a full moon tonight. Hey, I just had an idea. Maybe we should toss Chunky off the cliff. A sacrifice to the werewolves. Maybe they would leave us alone then."

"It's 'Chuck' when you're around him, remember. Don't press his buttons."

"He sounded so different last night on the phone. You know, like a real adult..."

"So what happened? What's he even doing here? You called him out of the blue and told him the werewolves from Chatham were in Camp Verde?"

She explained about the suspicious text message she'd received, the stakeout at the motel, the phone call with Malenia, and the agreement to meet the following morning. "Chuck was the only person I could think of who might believe me. So I sent him the photo of the circus wagon that you sent me. Then we talked. He was just like you. One hundred percent believed in the werewolves. Said he could be here by noon the next day."

"Lucky he had that revolver."

"If he didn't, I would have bought something from the gun shop we passed on Main Street. It was right next to the restaurant where we had lunch."

"It was a hell of a risk you took, Sally," he said and gripped her hand in his. "Thank you."

She blushed. "Will you stop thanking me? I'm a bit of an

emotional mess right now, and you're going to make me cry again."

They looked out over the desert for several silent minutes.

Eventually Sally said, "Amanda knows we're out here."

Ben blinked. "The reporter?"

She nodded. "I'm worried she will come looking for me when I don't return to town."

He understood her concern. "Because if the werewolves are down there somewhere..."

"She's a dead woman walking."

CHAPTER 29

TO THE RESCUE

Amanda had been waiting impatiently for ten minutes in the reception area of the Yavapai County Detention Center in Camp Verde before the duty officer escorted her to the sheriff's office. The sheriff sat behind a small desk, speaking on the phone. He scratched his large nose—it was almost a pick—and indicated for her to sit in a chair opposite him. On the surface of the desk was a gooseneck lamp, a photograph of which she could only see the back, an in/out box, a computer, and three yellow pencils standing upright in a white cup. Miniature Arizona and US flags, each attached to black plastic sticks with gold spear toppers, bookended a brass nameplate that read: RUSSELL WALKER.

The sheriff was doing more listening than talking on the phone before saying, "Hopefully this is the beginning of the end of this goddamn freak show. Keep me posted." He hung up and squinted at Amanda. "What do you want?"

"Have some of the dancers stopped dancing?" she asked.

"Half the girls at the community center, but other dancers keep popping up all over town. I was told you're not here to talk about any of that?"

"No, I'm not. I'm here to report a kidnapping."

"Another one?" He ran a hand through his shoulder-length, greasy hair. "The other day a guy filled up his pickup truck at the pump at the Quick Country Store in Verde Village, went into the store to pay. When he came out his truck was gone —along with his three-year-old daughter who had been in the back seat. We found the truck in the middle of the road on State Route 260 at the Out of Africa parkway, engine still running. A witness saw a man in a sports coat, no shirt, and pajama pants fleeing the scene. We've yet to find him. So you gonna tell me your kidnapping includes a man in pajama bottoms?"

"No, Sheriff," she said, and explained everything, from Ben Graves' abduction the previous evening to Sally Levine and her friend Chuck going to Montezuma Castle National Monument several hours earlier to get him back—and never returning.

"Let me get this straight," Sheriff Walker said when she finished. "These folks witnessed these—*gypsies*, you called them?"

"Gypsies, vagabonds, call them what you want."

"So these folks witnessed these gypsies kill police officers in 1988, they recognized them here in Verde more than three decades later, and this Ben Gates—"

"Graves."

"He gets himself kidnapped, and when his friends go to pay the ransom, they go missing too?"

Amanda nodded. She'd added the ransom embellishment to make the farfetched story more believable.

Sheriff Walker barked a laugh. "Are you fucking bullshitting me, ma'am?"

"No, Sheriff, I'm not. And I'm worried they're all in very serious trouble. They should have been back at least an hour ago."

"More than three decades. You're saying these folks recognized the cop killers after more than *three decades*. Hell, I can barely remember what the wife looks like until she wakes up in the morning."

"They have two circus wagons in their caravan. They're the same ones they had back in 1988. I saw the photograph that Mr. Graves took of them and sent Miss Levine. Look, Sheriff Walker, I know how this sounds—"

"It sounds like the craziest shit I've ever heard," he interrupted, shifting his weight in his chair. Then he exhaled in what sounded like frustration. "Which is why I haven't already kicked you out of here for wasting my time. I can't imagine why you'd make something like this up. Where'd you say those cops were killed?"

"Chatham. In Cape Cod, Massachusetts."

He slipped on a pair of eyeglasses and typed on the computer's keyboard. He clicked a button on the mouse a few times. Then he went silent for about a minute while he read what he'd brought up on the monitor. His face visibly hardened in anger.

"Six cops," he said, without taking his eyes away from the screen, "including Chatham's sheriff, never heard from again."

Amanda nodded.

He finally looked at her. "And you say the assholes responsible for their disappearance are in my town?"

She nodded again.

"Jesus bloody Christ," he mumbled, slapping his Stetson on his head and standing abruptly. "Never a dull moment this week."

△△△

Amanda sat in the passenger seat while Ralph drove the Channel 7 broadcast van through the desert toward the Montezuma Castle National Monument.

"You think the sheriff is gonna be mad when we show up uninvited?" her cameraman asked.

"He never told me *not* to come," she said. "And if these gypsies are still at the monument, this story could be huge." She imagined the headline and said, "Cop Killers Captured After Thirty-One Years on Lam."

"If they killed six cops thirty-one years ago, what's to say they're not going to simply kill these hick cops too?"

"My God, now *that* would be a twist!"

Ralph glanced sidelong at her.

"I'm kidding, Raf," she said. "It wouldn't happen. The

gypsies have to be pensioners by now."

"Pensioners can still fire weapons."

"Do you want to keep covering silly community news for the rest of your career? This story could be the break we need. If we cover it right, and it turns out to be as juicy as it sounds, Tony might finally let us cover the big issues that people care about." Tony Rogers was the assignment editor at Channel 7, a sexist prick who had once told her she didn't have the right "look" for real reporting, which explained why the majority of the garbage he assigned to her was frivolous events such as car accidents and restaurant openings and lost pets that had been reunited with their owners. The gender-biased glass ceiling was infuriating. When Amanda had graduated from Arizona State University with a degree in journalism, she'd imagined herself one day in the not-too-distant future reporting feature stories on breaking news events. That had been eight years ago, and look at her now. Covering a dancing epidemic in a dustbowl town. She was the laughingstock at the station, the pretty blonde nobody took seriously.

She turned in her seat and asked Gabriela, "How are you doing back there?"

"Okay," the girl replied quietly. She was seated in the floor-bolted swivel chair at the transmission control desk that occupied most of the vehicle's cargo area. Amanda had tried to persuade her to remain behind at the police station. The effort proved futile, and Amanda had reluctantly allowed her to come with them.

"We're here," Ralph said. "And we're not alone."

Amanda turned back around. More than a dozen vehicles, including a trio of impressively large RVs, were parked at the far end of an otherwise empty parking lot. "They're here!" she exclaimed.

"The sheriff's SUV is here too, but where is he? And everyone else, for that matter—"

The windshield exploded.

"Shit!" Amanda cried as the van lurched to the right.

Ralph, she saw, was slumped in the driver's seat, blood leaking down his slack, wide-eyed face from a perfectly round bullet hole in his forehead. His foot must have still been heavy on the accelerator because they were careening toward a six-foot-tall stone wall that lined the north side of the parking lot, where it cut into the side of a large hill.

Amanda grabbed the steering wheel and tugged it to the left. She was too slow.

There was a huge explosion of sound and force as the van went from forty miles per hour to zero in less than a second. She watched in a kind of time-warp as the dashboard pushed toward her. She didn't notice the airbag deploy, but her face struck what felt like a soft pillow. The next thing she knew, she was staring through yellowish smoke and the shattered windshield at the too-close stone wall. Her sunglasses, which had been perched on the bridge of her nose, were now sitting neatly on the dashboard, unbroken.

Amanda's first thought was that she'd just been in a car accident and might be injured. Her second was that she had to get out of the van, run, hide.

From her right and somewhere above her she heard a male voice say, "Looks like more *hors d'oeuvres* have arrived. And one of them looks *tasty*."

The passenger door shrieked open, and then rough hands were on her, releasing her seatbelt and yanking her out of the vehicle into the blazing hot afternoon sun.

CHAPTER 30

THE BAD MEN

Gabriela struck her head against something hard when the van crashed into the wall. When she opened her eyes, she found herself sprawled on the floor and could taste blood in her mouth. She tried to get up, but pain zapped through her back, keeping her face down on her tummy. She was about to start crying when she heard a man talking. Then one of the front doors opened and the pretty blonde-haired woman began screaming. Gabriela couldn't understand what she was saying; she sounded more like a wild animal than a person. A man was laughing, and then both their voices got smaller as they moved away from the van.

Gabriela knew the Bad Man was going to come back, and when he did, he might shoot her with his gun. She had to hide. She tried getting up again, and this time she gritted her teeth and pushed through the pain. The desk with all the electronic equipment and TV monitors (she had never seen so many buttons and switches in one place in her life, and she couldn't imagine why somebody would ever need so many or know what they all did) was L-shaped, running along the length of the van's wall and bending so it continued behind the two front seats. Those seats could swivel around so the people in them could use the equipment on the desk. She knew this because the driver's seat had swung far enough around during the crash that Gabriela could see the driver. He remained strapped by the seatbelt. Blood dripped down his face, some of it staining his tee shirt. He wasn't moving, and Gabriela was certain he was dead. She had seen dead animals back on the family ranch in Guadalajara, but—aside from her recently deceased mother—she had never seen a dead person before. She thought the sight should frighten her, but strangely it didn't; the man was in Heaven, where her father and mother were, and Heaven was a good place, better than Earth. Gabriela had sometimes reflected that she wouldn't mind terribly if she died (especially on the days she was teased at school by Helen Appleford and Katie Weiss and the other girls). Nevertheless, she never seriously considered jumping off a bridge or stepping in front of a bus because she knew how sad (and mad) it would make her mom. But now that her mom was dead just like her dad, what was stopping her from joining them in Heaven? Perhaps the best thing to do would be to let the Bad Man catch her and—

No! she thought, surprised by how loud that single word sounded inside her head. But she agreed with it. She would be reunited with her parents at some point in the future, but not now, not today. She wanted to grow up and become a doctor or an astronaut and get married and buy a house and a car and do everything else that her mom said she could do in America.

She wanted to live.

Gabriela glanced around the inside of the van. The only place to hide, she decided, was beneath the desk. But even then the Bad Man would be able to see her...

Unless...

Gabriela crawled on her hands and knees under the desk, trying to ignore the pain in her head and back. She pulled a plastic container away from the wall (for a moment she'd feared it would be too heavy to move) and squeezed in behind it. She knew it would be protruding a little from beneath the desk, but there was nothing she could do about that.

She had only been concealed for a few seconds when she heard voices approaching. The side door of the van rattled open. Bright sunlight spilled inside.

"Who the fuck would have contacted the media?" a man said.

"It was parked at the motel last night where the woman was supposed to be," another man said. "They must all know each other."

"I say we split, dude. There're still a few hours until the party. We could be in New Mexico by then."

"And leave those fucks up in the cliff? They know who we are. Worse, the writer knows what our vehicles look like. If he's allowed to talk, everybody in the fucking country is going to be on the lookout for us. We have to get rid of them. Mal will be furious if we don't. Beyond furious."

"Fuck, I just don't like it, Buzz. We've been through this before. When the cops don't return, more are going to come out here looking for them."

"And like before, we'll take care of them too. Then we're gone, by first light, right? No witnesses. That's what Mal always says. No witnesses. Not one. Ever. No one else is here, so let's go take care of those fucks on the cliff."

When the men had left, Gabriela released the breath that she had been holding. Then she wiggled to get a little more comfortable.

She was going to have a long night ahead of her.

CHAPTER 31

THE FOUNTAIN OF YOUTH

C huck stood by the entrance to the monument, peering down at the scorched desert below. He had yet to see any sign of the asshole who'd shot him, and he hoped the prick hadn't tucked his tail between his legs and run away. Because if that were the case he—and whomever he was with —would inevitably take Malenia's body with them, robbing Chuck of his prize.

He clenched his jaw in frustration. When Sally had called him and told him about the gypsies, he'd driven through the night to get to Camp Verde ASAP partly because Ben was in trouble, but mostly because he'd seen it as a real opportunity to capture a werewolf. If successful, his face would dominate the front page of every newspaper across the country. He'd be a guest on all the late-night talk shows. Producers at CNN, FOX, NBC, ABC, and other TV networks would be clamoring to book interviews with him. He'd be more famous than any rock star on the planet.

But now his ambition was much greater.

The fountain of youth, baby. The fountain of motherfucking youth.

It was real, it was within his grasp. He'd seen Malenia in that second or two before pulling the Colt's trigger and putting her ass on an express train to hell: she was the same woman he had encountered as a kid, and she hadn't aged a day.

Besides, she had *admitted* as much, he thought. While he'd

been hiding out of sight behind the Lexus, he'd experienced one of his panic attacks. For what had seemed like ages the world had swum in and out of darkness as he struggled to control himself. But control himself he did, and just in time to hear the woman confess that it had been she who had locked him and Ben and Sally in the circus wagon in Ryders Field, and it had been she who'd released them in the morning.

Now, Chuck was by no means an expert on aging—or in the scientific parlance, senescence—but it had come up often enough during medical school that he knew a good deal about the condition. People grow old because DNA damage builds up in their cells over time, causing mutations and genomic instability. This weakens the body, making it more susceptible to disease. Sooner or later the person's health fails and it's lights out.

The fact that Malenia's cells weren't tiring out and declining in function but were continuing to heal damaged tissue and keep her young—well, that wasn't just a game-changer. That was *the* game-changer.

And it underscored just how important it was that he get himself a werewolf, dead or alive, so that he could put it under a microscope and learn all about its biological magic.

Chuck heard Ben and Sally approaching and turned away from the little doorway.

"Get a signal?" he asked them.

Sally shook her head. "Unfortunately, no."

Chuck was privately relieved. He might have a bullet in his shoulder, but he wasn't going to die. And had the police been summoned, they most likely would have scared away the shooter, ruining his plan.

"We didn't see the guy who shot at us either," Ben said.

"He's probably cleaning up Malenia's corpse."

"Cleaning it up?"

"Dragging it to his vehicle. Burying it in the desert. I don't know. But you don't leave a werewolf lying in a parking lot for anybody to find."

"I don't get that woman," Sally said. "I understand that she lured me here to kill me so I wouldn't talk about her. But why'd she confess to locking us up?"

Chuck shrugged. "Why not? She was about to waste the both of you."

"Exactly. So why would she lie about something like that?"

"Lie?" he said, surprised. "Why the hell d'ya think she was lying?"

"She was no older than twenty-five," Ben told him. "Ryders Field happened before she was born."

"You *saw* her, dude," he said, perplexed. "It was *her.* How else do you explain that she was the spitting image of the gypsy woman from Ryders Field?"

"She was her daughter."

Chuck stared at Ben incredulously. "Right, her daughter. Come on, pal! She even *said* she was there."

"She was screwing with us."

"That's horseshit."

"It's not horseshit, Chuck," Sally said. "It's reality. Care to check in?"

Ignoring her, he said, "Come on, Ben. You're acting like a blind man looking for a hat that doesn't exist and finding it!"

"You paraphrase dead mystery authors these days? You never used to be much of a reader."

"He has a photographic memory," Sally said.

"Fuckin-A I do," Chuck said. "Which is why I know what I saw, and I know I'm not wrong."

"You have a photographic memory?" Ben said skeptically.

"Test me."

"For real?"

"Do it, Ponch."

"Ponch, right. I forgot about that nickname. All right, fine..." He squared his jaw in thought. "What movie poster was on the ceiling above my bed?"

"*Nightmare on Elm Street 3: The Dream Warriors.* Easy."

"What movie did we watch on the night we snuck out to the

beach and met Sally?"

"*Trick or Treat*. You wanted to watch *Forbidden World*, and my first pick was *Chopping Mall*, but you said it looked too cheesy, so we settled on *Trick or Treat*."

Ben laughed. "Jesus Christ, Chuck! You do have a photographic memory! Who would have guessed? But I suppose that's why you were always so good at remembering movie lines." To Sally he added, "After we watched a movie, he'd go around quoting all the good bits for days."

"So Chuck has a good memory, so what?" she said. "That doesn't mean the gypsy woman didn't age. What are we supposed to believe? That she's immortal?"

"I never said she's immortal," Chuck snapped. "She simply didn't age, or aged very slowly."

"Is that so?" she said sarcastically. "That explanation's so obvious I wonder why I never thought of it."

"Because you're a moron, that's why."

"Says the genius who believes werewolves are immortal."

"I never said *immortal*. Blow a werewolf's head off, and its days are over. Acute trauma will kill an organism without aging it. So there's a big difference between immortality and someone showing no sign of senescence. Pay attention, will you, Sally? You're not hot enough to be this stupid."

She rolled her eyes at him.

Ben said, "Explain to us then, Chuck. Why hasn't the gypsy woman aged in thirty-one years?"

"For one night each month her body undergoes a rapid transformation into something that resembles a wolf almost as much as it does a human. We agree on that, right? Well, the only biological way for that to happen is for her to grow new stem cells that divide into the differentiated cells—bones, tissue, nerves, and other organs—that, in turn, create the creature. And we also agree that the changes revert themselves by morning, right? Well, for something like *that* to happen, she would once again have to grow new stem cells to regenerate the old cell types of her human body. Now here's my point.

Why would she grow stem cells with faulty and damaged DNA, which is what happens to the DNA in all our cells over time as we age? If you ask me, she wouldn't, and didn't. They grow the way they were in their original state when she was first infected with lycanthropy—hence her ageless appearance."

"You're saying her body rejuvenates itself after each transformation?"

He nodded. "Exactamundo, pal. Sort of the same way certain jellyfish rejuvenate themselves, giving them, if they're not eaten or diseased, infinite lives."

"That's the stupidest thing I've ever heard!" Sally blurted. "Werewolves aren't jellyfish! You're comparing apples and oranges."

"She's right, Chuck," Ben said, folding his arms across his chest. "Jellyfish are completely different organisms to werewolves. They don't have stomachs or hearts. I don't think they even have brains."

"Which is exactly why capturing a werewolf is so important! Werewolves are like *us*, pal. They're pretty much one hundred percent human before they change. This means if we can capture one and study it in a lab to learn how its cells rejuvenate themselves every month, we're on the doorstep to discovering the fountain of youth! Can you dig that, man? You and me, two kids from Chatham, Massachusetts, discover the cure for aging! We'll be fucking trillionaires!"

"Two kids from Chatham, huh?" Sally said. "Am I invisible?"

He grinned at her. "So you suddenly want aboard the Chuck train, do ya?"

"I would never, ever, get aboard any Chuck train, boat, plane, or car. I think you're absolutely bonkers—"

A gunshot in the distance cut her off.

CHAPTER 32
A MORAL DILEMMA

A second gunshot rang out immediately after the first. "Who are they shooting at now?" Ben wondered out loud.

"Chuck," Sally said, "go check."

He frowned. "Why me?"

"You have the gun!"

Grumbling, he went to the monument's entrance and stuck his head outside. "I don't see anyone anywhere."

"It's Amanda," Sally stated suddenly and joined him at the door. "It has to be her. She came, after all—and she's in trouble."

Ben followed on her heels. There was nobody down on the ground. At least, nobody he could see. Whoever was firing the gun—and whoever was being fired at—were in the parking lot, out of sight.

Sally stepped away from the door and said, "We have to go down there."

"Are you mad?" Chuck said. "They'll shoot us too."

"Amanda came here looking for us. We have to help her."

"Help her? If that was Amanda they were shooting at, she's dead."

"You don't know that."

"The two gunshots sounded identical," he said. "That means they were the same caliber and likely from the same gun."

Sally looked at Ben, her eyes troubled.

"Chuck's right," he said with a helpless shrug. "It didn't sound like a shootout. And nobody's still shooting..."

"Give me the gun, Chuck," she said stubbornly. "I'll go by myself."

"I don't think so," he replied. "We'll be unarmed up here."

"Give it to me!" She lunged at him.

He backed away. "Cool it!"

Ben stepped between them. "Guys, stop!"

Eyes fierce, Sally stalked off to the connecting room.

When she was out of sight and earshot, Ben said, "Try to be a little more understanding, will you?"

Chuck scoffed. "The reporter's brains are frying on the asphalt. Hers would be too if she went down there. She's not thinking straight."

"She's stressed. We all are."

"Someone needs to smack some sense into her."

Ben frowned. "What's the deal with you two? Where's all this animosity suddenly coming from?"

"Suddenly? Maybe you were too blinded by the crush you had on her back in Chatham, pal, but she and I have never been on each other's Christmas card list. I don't know why that would change just because some time has passed."

"Three decades, Chuck. People grow up."

"She rubs me the wrong way."

"Just cut her some slack. We just need to get through the night. Together."

"Get through the night. Right. That's what you keep saying, get through the night and everything will be better. But we don't know that for sure, do we, Ben? We don't know that the gypsies are just going to pack up and leave in the morning. They might try to starve us out."

Ben shook his head. "The monument is undergoing renovations. Workers will likely be back on Monday."

"Who's to say the gypsies won't shoot the workers?"

"The workers have families. They'd wonder why they didn't return home. The police will come out to investigate."

"And might get shot themselves."

"Might. But then state troopers will investigate. And if they get shot, the FBI will come and whoever else has jurisdiction in these types of things. You really think the gypsies, whose existence is based on anonymity, are going to go down that path just to try to silence three people who know they're werewolves, a claim that nobody of sound mind would ever take seriously—"

A third gunshot erupted from somewhere in the desert.

It was followed by a screech of tires and a *pop!* of metal.

"What the hell...?" Chuck said.

Ben scanned the ground. He still couldn't see anybody.

Sally returned, looking concerned. "What was *that*?"

"The police?" Ben suggested. "Maybe the gypsies didn't shoot at Amanda earlier. Could be they shot at the police, and they took cover and called for backup—which just arrived."

"And crashed and burned," Chuck said.

"You don't know that," Sally said.

"I know I just heard what sounded like a car crashing into something."

"We need to find out what's happening,"

"It's suicidal," Chuck told her. "But go for it, by all means."

"I will," she retorted. "Give me the gun."

"Don't think so."

Ben held out his hand. "Give it to me, Chuck," he said. "Sally's right. We need to find out what's happening."

Chuck backed away from him and raised the revolver slightly. Not pointing it at him...but no longer pointing it directly at the ground. "I'm not giving you or Sally the fucking gun! I'll be a sitting duck up here!"

"If it's the police down there, the gypsies will be distracted. I'll be able to sneak up on them. If there are only two or three of them, I'll engage. The police and I will have them flanked. If there're more than that, I'll come back. Then at least we'll know what we're up against."

Chuck shook his head, backing farther away. "Sorry, Ponch.

It's my gun, I'm keeping it, and that's all there is to it."

CHAPTER 33

DOUBLE AMBUSH

Chuck went to the far corner of the dark room, the second of five on the monument's first level. Tucking the revolver temporarily away against the small of his back, he unzipped his trousers. While a stream of urine trickled against the stone wall, loud in the otherwise silence, he thought to himself: I'm running out of time.

Ben was most likely right that the gypsies would hit the road by tomorrow morning. They'd killed some cops today, so it was too risky for them to stick around for much longer. In fact, if it wasn't for the full moon in a couple of hours, they probably would have already skedaddled.

This should be good news...and it was, on one level. Ben, Sally, and Chuck were going to be all right. Chuck would be in a bright, clean, sterile hospital tomorrow getting his shoulder patched up. He'd be back in Salt Lake City shortly after that, with the wife and his two girls. Back at his practice, performing annual checkups and sports physicals on his young patients, ordering x-rays and blood tests and urine samples, diagnosing strep throat and pinkeye and bronchitis, reassuring paranoid parents that their child's growth spurt was coming, be patient.

And all of that was fine and good, all of that was normal... only "normal" no longer seemed acceptable.

Chuck had bigger aspirations in his life now, much bigger aspirations.

Trillion-dollar aspirations.

But first he had to bag another werewolf. That meant descending the ladders. Not now, not in the daylight. As he'd told Ben and Sally, that would be suicidal. They were almost certainly outnumbered and outgunned.

Nighttime, however, would be a different story.

Because werewolves didn't fire guns, did they? They were mindless beasts, nothing more than that. They had sharp teeth and claws, yes, but they were no match for his Colt Anaconda. All he had to do was descend to the first ledge and wait under the cover of darkness for one of them to come sniffing around. When it did, he'd blow its head off, hide the corpse, and then wait things out until morning. After the gypsies left, and he was back in Utah, he would rent a fully equipped laboratory facility to begin his research. Of course, he'd need to bring experts on board to uncover the remarkable secrets: geneticists, chemists, biologists, and other medical specialists. Nevertheless, if they wanted to work with him, if they wanted to make history with him, he would force them to sign contracts that gave him the patents and exclusivity to any discoveries they made.

This was going to be his show, and his alone.

Within a year, his name would be known around the world.

Chuck Hamman.

The man who cured aging.

He finished urinating and turned away from the corner and zipped up. He took the Colt from where he'd tucked it against the small of his back and was about to return to the first room —but froze before taking a single step.

A head rose stealthily from a hole in the floor in the center of the room. Chuck had peered into the hole earlier. It led to a tiny room filled with light, likely an ancillary entrance to the monument.

Now Chuck watched with bemused amazement as a man with a blond mullet extracted himself from the hole, cat-quiet. He unstrapped a rifle hanging off his shoulder, pointed it in front of him, and started for the room where Ben and Sally were guarding the main entrance.

Chuck aimed the barrel of the Colt squarely between the man's shoulders.

"Hey asshole," he said.

The man spun around. Surprise and alarm flashed in his eyes.

Chuck squeezed the trigger.

Without the earplugs and earmuffs that he used at the shooting range, the discharge of the .357 Magnum was deafening. When his vision recovered from the muzzle flash, he saw that the man was sprawled on the ground, unmoving.

Ben and Sally burst into the room. They were asking questions, but Chuck couldn't hear them due to the ringing in his ears.

He simply pointed at the hole in the floor and said, "He came through there. Must have monkeyed up the side of the goddamn monument."

They all crowded close to the body for a better look. Sally groaned, apparently grossed out by the bloody wound, and looked away.

Ben said, "He's the guy from Crusty's Pizza. The guy I followed to the gypsy's camp. They called him Vlad. I got the feeling he was number two in charge, after Malenia."

"What should we do with him?" Sally asked.

"He's the property of yours truly now," Chuck said. "Him and all the secrets that his biology holds. I shot him, I killed him, so he's mine, so don't either of you think about fucking touching him. Got that?"

CHAPTER 34

THE HORS D'OEUVRE

T he man who'd pulled Amanda out of the Channel 7 news van was barrel-chested with a full, thick beard and muscular arms. He'd thrown her over his broad shoulder and carried her, still weak and woozy, past the parked RVs and other vehicles, past the lifeless bodies of the sheriff and his deputy, to where a large number of young men were sitting in chairs in a rough circle, drinking like it was the Fourth of July.

"Pretty, ain't she?" the large man carrying Amanda said above the chorus of catcalls and hoots and hollers.

"Let me go..." Amanda said, mustering what little strength she had to squirm from his grip.

"Sure thing, love."

He stopped in the center of the circle, bent over, and let her body slip off his shoulder. She landed on her feet, wobbled, and glanced with frightened eyes at the men surrounding her. She recognized two of them; they had been in the red sports car back at the Verde Valley Suites. One had tattoos on every visible part of his body except his face; the other had long silver-blond hair tied in a ponytail and Versace sunglasses. Silver chains hung around his neck, and flashy jewel-encrusted rings adorned most of his fingers. The rest of the men in the circle were clad in similar jewelry and sunglasses. And all of them wore rock star clothing: a denim vest over bare flesh; belts with outrageous buckles; silk scarfs wrapped around necks or dangling from torn jeans; zippered or buckled leather boots; brimmed hats, trucker caps, bandanas.

Leering and laughing at Amanda, they cracked sexist remarks:

"Nice legs, sweetheart!"

"Liked it better when you were bent over, babe!"

"If you can dance, I got a pole!"

It was sensory overload, a wall of crass sound. She was terrified and baffled at the same time. Frantic thoughts raced through her mind, demanding answers:

Where are Sally and her friend, and the friend they'd come to rescue?

Where's the woman Sally had been talking to on the phone?

Why'd these men shoot the sheriff and deputy?

Why'd they shoot poor Ralph?

That last thought almost made her burst into tears, but she held them back, fearful of showing weakness. She stepped toward the widest space between two of the chairs encircling her. The man in the chair on the right—wiry frame, no shirt, ripped abs, leather pants—snapped to his feet. He made a disapproving *cluck, cluck, cluck* sound while shaking his head and pushing his sunglasses up his forehead. The steel Amanda saw in his eyes froze her on the spot. He went to a nearby pickup truck, hopped up on the running board, reached through the open driver-side window, and started the ignition. Def Leppard blared from the stereo. He took two beers from a battered Eskimo cooler next to the truck and approached her. His skin had a deep tan, his dark hair coiffed and gelled. He grinned at her, showing bone-white, straight teeth. "Cold one, sweetheart?" he said, offering her one of the beers.

Amanda only stared at the bottle.

These men were killers, and she was a prisoner.

Wasn't she?

"Party's just starting, mama," he added. "And you look like you could use something to help you relax."

"Please let me go," she said.

"Let you go?" He chuckled. "And where is it you think you'd like to go?"

"Please," she said, balling her hands into fists to prevent them from shaking.

"'Fraid we can't do that."

"At least not until supper," the burly man with the beard said from his chair. He took a swig from a nearly empty bottle of vodka.

"That's right," the shirtless man said. "We'll let you go then. We like working for our food."

The conversation was surreal, something from a bad horror movie. Yet Amanda had never been more afraid in her life.

They're talking about eating me, she thought with cold terror. *Sally said they dressed up like werewolves and ate people, and now they're talking about eating* me.

Tears finally flowed from her eyes. She clamped her jaw tight, but she couldn't stop the sobs from escaping her mouth. Her entire body trembled.

"Ah, love, don't do that," the shirtless man said. "I'm a softie at heart, and I hate to see a woman cry, 'specially one as pretty as yourself."

Amanda didn't stop. Couldn't.

"Here," he said, offering her the beer again.

She shook her head.

"You just holler if you change your mind," he said and returned to his chair, settling into it with a deep sigh and twisting the cap off one of the beers.

Amanda remained standing in the center of the circle, eyes downcast, listening numbly to the chatter, the laughter and macho bravado, the disgusting jokes, the crude talk, most of it still directed at her. She felt eyes undressing her, vulnerable, naked. Her vision was so blurred with tears that she could hardly see. Her thoughts were so muddied with fear that she could no longer think straight. She heard the assignment editor at Channel 7, Tony Rogers, say: *What's that silly girl gone and gotten herself into now? I always told her she didn't have what it took to be a real reporter, and look what she's gone and gotten herself into. Nobody to blame but herself, if you ask me.*

Eventually the world seemed to fade around her: the men, the heat, the vehicles. At some point she realized she was seated on the hot tarmac. She didn't remember sitting down, but there she was, her knees pressed to her chest, her arms around them, her head resting on them, her eyes squeezed closed, trying to be invisible.

Later—five minutes, an hour, she didn't know—she tried to focus her thoughts on escape. This seemed impossible, surrounded by men clearly younger and fitter than she was.

When she opened her eyes, it was still light out but less bright. The sun's heat no longer felt like a dragon breathing down on her. The music was just as loud as before, maybe louder. Same with the boisterous conversation swirling around her.

Party's in full swing, she thought dimly.

Thankfully she no longer felt like the center of attention. In fact, the men seemed to have forgotten about her. She studied the ones in her field of view, but never for long, and barely raising her head. She didn't want to meet any of their eyes and remind them she was there.

Looks like more hors d'oeuvres have arrived. And one of them looks tasty.

We'll let you go then. We like working for our food.

Amanda shuddered. But the more she fixated on the possibility she was on tonight's menu, the more she told herself it wasn't true. Sally was wrong. They weren't a cult of lycanthropes. They didn't dress up as werewolves and eat people. They might have joked about eating her, but that was all it was: black humor. *They're not going to eat me.* She continued to tell herself this, and she finally convinced herself of it. Not that she felt she was out of the frying pan, so to speak. She remained their prisoner and was an attractive young woman. They were frat-like young men with no regard for the law, clearly evidenced by the two dead cops less than a hundred yards away. Which meant they would have no moral qualms raping her one after the other, passing her around their circle just like the joints they kept passing around. And when they were done, they'd more likely than not slit her throat and toss her in the bushes where, ironically, she would be eaten after all, not by them, but by the coyotes and other predators that roamed the night.

Raped then *eaten*, she thought bleakly...and her tears, which had stopped long ago, sprang forth again. She pressed her knees even tighter to her chest and tried to be as small as possible.

The laughter and conversations eddied around her, flowing and ebbing with a discordant rhythm.

The music blared, just noise.

A bottle shattered.

Vaguely she heard what might have been a gunshot, but she wasn't sure. It sounded far away, a world away.

She was sinking back into her protective bubble where her senses were dulled and her thoughts were minimalized...when she realized the music and conversations had stopped.

Amanda opened her eyes. It was darker now, twilight. Two men who hadn't been part of the circle earlier, with rifles slung over their shoulders, were speaking to the man with the beard. Their backs were to her. They were facing the tourist center, sometimes nodding or shaking their heads, sometimes pointing to the limestone cliffs that were now draped in purple-black shadows.

Amanda glanced around the circle of men—and was shocked to see they were all naked and passed out. Then she noticed the tourniquets and small glass vials. Some had nodded off with the needles they had used to inject themselves still protruding from the veins in their arms.

Her head cleared in an instant. She rose silently to her feet. She turned around to flee—and her heart dropped.

The man who'd worn the denim vest—though he was now naked too—sat in his chair behind her, the only one in the circle not yet high. He raised a syringe in his hand and said, "Morphine, baby. To numb the pain."

To numb the pain?

What pain?

She didn't ask. She didn't care. She didn't even care why her captors had taken off their clothes. For the first time since she'd been yanked from the wreckage of the Channel 7 news van, she felt hope. Because her captors were drug addicts, they were off in Happyland...and hopefully the four who were still conscious would join them there soon.

And then she'd be free.

Amanda sat back down on the asphalt.

Above her in the darkening sky the first of the night's stars had revealed themselves.

Far on the eastern horizon a huge full moon, draped in bloody orange-red hues, was on the rise.

CHAPTER 35

ORIGIN STORY

Clutching Vlad's rifle with both hands, Ben got up from where he was sitting with his back to a wall and looked out Montezuma Castle's main entrance. The distant rock music had stopped a while ago. Twilight had descended, an effervescent veil that gave the still, silent Mohave desert a shimmering illusion of unreality. His high-octane imagination half expected to see the dozen or so gypsies rushing toward Montezuma Castle in one final attempt to breach the monument before the sun went down. However, what he saw was what he'd seen every time he'd peeked his head out the low doorway over the last two hours: nothing. No gypsies. No animals. Aside from the occasional bird, nothing.

Suddenly, from the direction of the parking lot, the music started again—"Dreamer" by Ozzy Osbourne—and Ben returned to where he'd been sitting.

The music freaked him out. It suggested the gypsies weren't merely psychotic; they were depraved. They'd tried murdering Ben, Sally, and Chuck earlier. They'd likely shot some cops earlier. Maybe the reporter too. And now they were kicking back, partying, like it was just another day as usual?

And perhaps it is, he thought. After all, they were werewolves. They turned into blood-thirsty animals once a month. What did the death of a man, woman, or even a child matter to them?

Sally shifted her body a little where she was seated across the room from him. Her eyes were closed. Hopefully she was getting some rest. They hadn't said more than a few words to each other over the last hour. He couldn't speak for her, but he had little appetite for conversation. He was sick with worry about the approaching night, and the monsters it would give birth to. The ball of greasy dread in his stomach was ever-present and had nearly made him vomit two or three times already.

He told himself they were safe. Werewolves couldn't climb ladders. They couldn't scale vertical walls as Vlad had. Those actions required intelligence (at least climbing a ladder did), and from what he'd witnessed as a kid in Ryders Field, werewolves were mindless brutes incapable of any cognitive ability aside from the most primitive instincts involved in hunting and feeding.

This was what he told himself.

Did he really believe it?

He didn't know. He was talking about werewolves, for God's sake, creatures from myth and lore. He didn't know anything about them for certain. Maybe they retained some glimmer of their human intelligence and cunning. Maybe they *could* climb ladders and scale vertical walls. Maybe they could even fire rifles...although he thought that was giving them a little too much credit.

The point was, he could tell himself all he wanted that they were going to be safe, that retreating high into Montezuma Castle had been the right decision, but you could also tell yourself a tropical lagoon was a safe place to take a dip on a sweltering afternoon...and be mauled by a crocodile the moment you got in.

In other words, tonight anything was possible.

This was why after some debate they had agreed to take two-hour shifts guarding the two entrances to the monument. Chuck was currently watching the secondary entrance that Vlad had the misfortune of climbing through, while Ben was watching the main entrance. When this first shift finished— in approximately twenty minutes—Sally would take Chuck's spot, Chuck would take Ben's spot, and Ben would have two hours to rest before he began his next two consecutive shifts. They would cycle through this rotation until dawn.

But Jesus, that seemed like a long time from now.

"Dreamer" ended and some heartland rock song began playing.

At least they have decent taste in music, he thought.

Werewolves had decent taste in music.

Ben rubbed his forehead. He'd had a ghost of a headache for the last hour, and now it was solidifying into something real, a steady, dull whumping behind his eyes. His tired mind drifted, went on tangents, but kept returning to the partying gypsies, their eternal youth, their accents, their origin.

The word "werewolf," he knew, came from the Old English *wer* meaning "man" and *wulf* meaning wolf. It was related to the Anglo-Norman *garwalf*, the Middle Dutch *weerwulf*, the Old Frankish *wariwulf*, and the Old High German *werwolf*. Clearly the beasts had roamed and been known across Europe. Indeed, beginning in the late Middle Ages there had been eyewitness reports of werewolves everywhere from Romania to Poland to the Netherlands, although according to the historical record, most had been in the Baltic region.

Before today's encounter with Malenia, Ben had always believed she was of Russian descent. This was because, as a kid who'd never stepped outside the borders of Chatham, he hadn't known better. She'd sounded like the Russian villains in the movies he'd watched at sleepovers with Chuck, and so she must be Russian. That belief hadn't changed over the years; he'd had no reason to connect her to five-hundred-year-old werewolf sightings in Europe. Nevertheless, given Chuck's theory that she didn't age, or at least aged very slowly, he found himself wondering if her accent was not Russian but rather Estonian or Latvian, and if she and the gypsies might have inhabited those lands as far back in time as the Middle Ages.

Of the dozens of werewolf encounters that Ben had read

about in Europe between the 12th and 17th centuries, only one had involved a female werewolf, or shewolf, as they were sometimes called. It occurred in the sixteenth century, outside the small city of Offenburg, Germany. One night in May a family of six people witnessed several men and one woman shapeshift into supernatural beasts. After an official investigation discovered the remains of the family's two cattle, as well as more than a dozen slaughtered wild animals scattered in the fields and forests around the farmhouse (including badgers, deer, boars, and foxes), the police and a band of local hunters joined forces to track down the shapeshifters.

Suspicion eventually fell on a group of travelers staying at a large inn in Offenburg. When confronted, however, all the travelers managed to escape except for one eighteen-year-old man, who would later become known as The Werewolf of Offenburg. During his court trial he confessed that he'd been a werewolf for the better part of two years. He claimed that during his periods of transformation, which occurred on each full moon, he was unable to speak but maintained a basic animal-like consciousness. He also claimed that he'd received his power to shapeshift from a person he would only describe as "a woman in black." The authorities interpreted the woman in black to be Satan in disguise, and therefore concluded that The Werewolf of Offenburg was no werewolf at all but rather a witch. They found him guilty of sorcery, and he was burned at the stake.

The werewolves that had escaped the inn were neither seen nor heard from again, yet the fear they'd wrought on the city persisted for months afterward.

Interestingly, all this occurred right around the time a woman began to dance fervently and uncontrollably in the streets of the neighboring city of Strasbourg, which eventually led to hundreds of people dancing for weeks on end in what would become the largest case of a dancing mania in history.

Ben had always known The Werewolf of Offenburg and the

Dancing Plague of 1518 had been connected in some way, though he could never say exactly how. Until yesterday, he had believed wholeheartedly in his theory which he had written about in *The Dancing Plague*: a powerful werewolf such as Malenia had the psychic power to induce a trance-like state of dance in individuals infected with the disease of lycanthropy which, in turn, would prevent them from transforming into werewolves on a full moon. And while this theory had seemed feasible to explain what had happened in Chatham, he had been aware it could not explain the much larger scale mania that had occurred in Strasbourg (which was why he had conveniently omitted any mention of the Dancing Plague of 1518 from his last book).

But now the mystery, it seemed, was cracked.

The missing link between The Werewolf of Offenburg and the Dancing Plague of 1518 was mass hysteria and all that mumbo jumbo Amanda had been talking about yesterday, the phenomenon of one person wigging out and causing dozens or hundreds or even thousands of others to do so as well. The woman who began the dancing in the streets of Strasbourg might have had a friend or relation in Offenburg and heard about the werewolf trial that way, or perhaps she simply learned about it through general gossip, given the two cities were only a stone's throw away from each other. Either way, the idea of bloodthirsty creatures stalking the countryside caused her to wig out and dance, creating a domino effect that caused all the other four hundred or so people in Strasbourg to wig out and dance.

In his research into werewolves over the years, Ben hadn't uncovered any other possible links between sightings of the beasts and cases of dancing manias, but he wouldn't be surprised to find out there were in fact more.

Because don't forget that werewolf sightings in Europe petered out around the same time that dancing plagues did.

He hadn't forgotten about that, of course. And it very well could be a coincidence. But then again... What if, for instance,

Malenia and the gypsies had been the werewolves that had terrorized Offenburg in 1518? What if they had been the only werewolves to have existed in Europe? What if they had decided to sail across the Atlantic as the New World colonists did? Such a trip in the 1700s would have taken roughly six weeks. That meant they would have been on board for one full moon during which they would have shapeshifted into werewolves. Ben could imagine their three- or four-masted ship drifting into a Boston or Virginia harbor, its captain and crew missing, most of its passengers missing...except perhaps ten or eleven, who would claim they had been the only survivors of a deadly disease. Or perhaps they waited a little longer and hitched a ride on one of the first steamliners, which could do the transatlantic voyage in as little as fourteen days. Either way, they would have had all North America to roam and hunt, a continent twice the size of Europe with a fraction of the human population at the time, which could explain the lack of werewolf sightings there—as well as the lack of dancing plagues (until Chatham, that was).

I'm becoming a conspiracy kook, Ben thought, still knuckling his forehead. *I'm going crazy—only I'm not because there's a pack of werewolves partying under the full moon not five hundred yards away from me.*

What bad luck to run into them twice in his life.

Well, that wasn't true, was it? It wasn't bad luck. The first time was, granted. But not this time.

Ben glanced across the dark room at Sally and felt foolish and frustrated that he'd agreed to let her come to Camp Verde with him. Now here she was, her life in jeopardy. Again. Because of him.

His heart ached for her. She'd had a rough life. An unfair life. Losing a child? Her only child? He couldn't imagine what that would feel like, the pain, the loss, perhaps the unfounded guilt that she hadn't been able to save her daughter.

As a kid Sally had always been intelligent, fun, happy. She was still intelligent and fun, clearly, but happy? She put on an upbeat front, but he saw the truth in her eyes, the sadness and the hardness...

Ben was becoming depressed, so he switched his train of thought, recalling when Sally entered his bathroom at the Verde Camp Suites. That made him smile. The way she'd blushed, the flirtatious banter.

Room for two in there?

Unfortunately it might be a tad tight.

Shame.

Shame indeed.

His smile grew at the memory of when he'd spotted her at Rizzoli's Bookstore in New York. His first thought was incredulity that she was the Sally Levine from Chatham, his childhood crush. Yet right on the heels of that was how damn good she'd looked. He'd been instantly enamored. And that feeling hadn't changed. In fact, it had only grown during the rollercoaster ride of the last two days.

He was, if he was being honest with himself, falling for her all over again, thirty-one years later.

And that frightened him. Because if they survived until morning, if they escaped this nightmare alive, what was he going to do? Tell her how he felt? She'd been in a failed marriage. She might want nothing more to do with men. And Ben? Could two people who'd been through the shit he and Sally had been through together—not once but twice—become romantically involved? Would their baggage make their relationship stronger? Or would it sink it?

Abruptly Sally opened her eyes and saw him watching her.

He kept his smile. She smiled back.

They didn't say anything, just looked at each other for what felt like a long time.

Ben was about to finally say something when from the other room Chuck shouted, "Almost time!"

Ben stood and stretched, groaning at the pain in his butt, back, and joints. He looked out the main entrance. The full moon hung suspended in the black, star-filled sky. It had shed its fiery cloak of dusk and now gleamed as white as a luminescent pearl. On the ground it was difficult to make out anything in the dark except the twisted shapes of the sycamores and other trees at the base of the monument.

He saw no movement anywhere and turned to Sally.

"Get any rest?" he asked her.

"No," she said, yawning. "Maybe. I don't know if I was dozing or just thinking. But whatever I was doing, it wasn't resting."

"I don't mind taking your shift if you—"

"No," she said, shaking her head and getting to her feet. She came over to him. "I'd rather be doing something anyway."

"Better take this then."

As he handed her the rifle, their hands brushed. A zap of electricity ran through him, and he told himself, *Screw it, do it, you may never get another opportunity*. He leaned forward and kissed her on the lips. She returned the kiss after a brief hesitation. Nostalgic memories flooded through him. They were accompanied by a rush of feelings, powerful and euphoric, which he hadn't experienced since his youth when he'd kissed her while dancing to "Stairway to Heaven" in her living room.

"Yo, Ben!" Chuck shouted. "Come in here for a bit, will you?"

Ben and Sally broke apart. He felt himself blushing hotly...or maybe that was just the adrenaline from the kiss.

Sally whispered, "Chunky has always had a knack for breaking the moment between us."

Ben said, "I better go see what he wants."

He stepped away from her, his fingers feathering her palm, reluctant to let go. She smiled at him again. It was her first real smile since they'd reunited at Rizzoli's, and it made him smile too.

Please, Lord, he thought as he walked away. *Let us get through this night.*

CHAPTER 36
THE UNRELIABLE NARRATOR

The room was as dark as the previous one, with everything draped in black shadows. Chuck was seated cross-legged next to the hole in the floor, the revolver resting on his lap. Vlad's body was sprawled on the ground to his left, just as dead as before.

Ben said, "What's going on?"

Chuck shrugged. "I'm bored."

I stopped kissing Sally because you're bored?

Instead of saying that out loud, he sat down next to him and said, "It's going to be a long night."

"You know what I'm gonna do with my trillion dollars?"

Ben frowned, unsure whether Chuck was serious or not. "You still think you're going to cure aging?"

"I'm gonna buy my wife an island."

"That's thoughtful of you."

"Nah. I'd do it so she wouldn't bug me on *my* island."

"What's she like?" Ben asked.

"The wife? Bossy. Grumpy. Spends too much money. Like most wives." After a moment he added, "You ain't married?"

Ben shook his head. "Never found the right person, I guess."

"You're lucky."

"I don't think so. I think I'd like to be married. A wife might be a good influence on me."

"You should marry Sally."

Ben stiffened at the remark. Could Sally hear them? He

didn't think so. "What makes you say that?" he asked.

"She likes you. She's hot. What else do you need in a wife?"

"She likes me, does she? Where'd you get that idea?"

"She risked her life coming out here to save you, didn't she?"

"So did you."

"Don't flatter yourself, pal. I came here to get a werewolf."

Ben was happy to change the topic from Sally and said, "Well, now you got one." He glanced briefly at Vlad. "Though he doesn't look much like a werewolf at the moment."

"He will when he's under a microscope."

"Night Moves" by Bob Seger and The Silver Bullet Band began to play from the parking lot, the opening acoustic guitar sounding small and far away.

"Do you think they're being ironic?" Ben asked.

"Huh?" Chuck said.

"Bob Seger. The Silver Bullet Band."

Chuck raised the revolver with his good arm, released the cylinder, and showed him the loaded chamber. "Silver bullets," he said.

"Bullshit."

Chuck nodded. "I had them made years ago."

"In case you encountered werewolves again?"

"It happened, didn't it?" He swung the cylinder closed again with a neat flick of his wrist.

"What do you think is going on down there? The music?"

"They're celebrating, obviously."

"But why?"

"'Cause they get to turn into werewolves tonight."

"And they're celebrating that? Turning into a werewolf is supposed to be a curse."

"Nah, it's a good thing. No stress, no worries. The three Fs of evolution—food, fighting, fucking. That's all that would matter to them. Sounds pretty good to me."

"You forgetting Sheriff Sandberg? You saw him change. That didn't look fun at all."

"I'm not saying *changing* into a werewolf would be fun. I'm saying *being* one would be fun. Big difference."

They were silent for a while.

"Killing Me Softly" began playing.

"They didn't play music in Ryders Field," Ben said eventually.

"How many do you think are down there?" Chuck asked.

"There were thirteen, including Malenia, at their camp north of Camp Verde. Now that she and this guy are dead"—he hooked a thumb a Vlad—"I guess eleven. No reason the others wouldn't have joined however many had been shooting at us."

"And they're all dudes?"

Ben nodded. "Why?"

"Don't you find that odd? One chick and twelve dudes?"

"Got any theories?"

He nodded. "Malenia was the queen bee."

Ben raised an eyebrow. "The queen bee?"

"The leader. Maybe even the first werewolf, the creator of the rest of them. You know, like the vampire called the Mother in Anne Rice's stuff. Think about it. If you were a werewolf, the first werewolf—"

"How do you become the first one?"

"I don't fucking know. But say you were. You'd get to choose who's in your pack because you're the one biting them, turning them."

"You don't think the others have ever bitten a human?"

"Of course they have. But then they eat them. However, you don't eat the ones you want to join the pack."

Ben was hit with a bout of nostalgia by their conversation. It was like no time had passed between now and when he and Chuck had been best friends as kids, hanging out in Ben's garage on a Saturday morning, dissecting the movie they had watched the night before.

Only this is real, he told himself. *And the gypsies/werewolves want us dead.*

"So if you were the queen bee and got to choose the pack," Chuck was saying, "would you let the dudes you bit, would you let them bite and turn younger, hotter chicks than you? I wouldn't if I were her."

"Maybe that's why they want to get us so badly. Because you killed their queen."

"Maybe we can give them Sally? How 'bout that? Let her be their new queen?"

"She mentioned tossing *you* off the cliff to them earlier."

"Fuck her," Chuck said. "Anyway, that's gotta be how it works. And if you're bit, and she lets you live, you gotta be loyal to her. She doesn't want the competition. Look what happened to the sucker in the Captain's Inn."

Ben frowned. "What do you mean?"

"The guy who got his head cut off in Chatham. He was sleeping with one of the inn's chambermaids. Malenia found out and killed him. She was jealous."

"How do you know Malenia killed him?"

Chuck glanced sidelong at him. "Really, pal?"

"What?"

"You really don't know?"

Ben shook his head.

Chuck said, "Your mom and Mr. Zanardo, the teacher who hated your guts, they saw Malenia leave the guy's room right after he was offed."

Ben furrowed his brow. He had heard what Chuck had said, but the words weren't making sense.

"I guess you left town before all this came out," he added. "So your mom and Zanardo were having an affair, right? And one night—"

"Whoa, slow down. I suspected that, but nothing was ever proved—"

"Proved? She told your dad! We were right there!"

Ben blinked in confusion. He wasn't following any of this. "I have no idea what you're talking about. How about starting from the beginning?"

Chuck made a big show of a sigh. "So there was that day when the sheriff came to your house. You remember that?"

"We were in the kitchen, and there was a knock at the door. It was Malenia—"

"*Malenia?*"

"I mean, I *thought* it was. That's what I remembered. But... well, I guess it couldn't have been her—"

"No, it definitely could not, pal! We didn't meet her until later that day, in Ryders Field. Now let me take over here, because your memory is clearly shit, and I have a photographic one. That day's as clear to me as yesterday. We were at your house, and your mom and dad started fighting in the living room. It was bad. Your dad was grilling her about Zanardo, and she admitted she was having an affair with him. It sounded like your dad knew about the affair because of their night together at the Captain's Inn. And after she admitted everything, she told him she saw the guy who got offed. She and Zanardo heard a loud noise, and when they looked in the hallway, they saw a woman—Malenia, with her weird wrist tattoo—leaving the room where the noise had come from. So after she left, they checked it and found the guy in the bed, decapitated. Anyway, your dad became even madder after this, that she hadn't told anyone she'd witnessed the murder, or at least saw the murderer. The fight started up again, and it got so bad your mom clocked your dad with some little statue, and he had to go to the hospital. When your dad left to get stitched up, your mom started dancing. It was like all her stress about the murder, not saying anything, maybe even the affair, it just got to her, like it did to Zanardo the day earlier. When your dad came back and found her dancing, he called the sheriff, and they put her in the hospital."

Ben was dumbstruck. He didn't recall any of this, at least, not the way Chuck had described it. Yet he had no reason to doubt him. He was just...dumbstruck. "Then what happened?" he asked.

"Your dad told the sheriff about Malenia leaving the room at the Captain's Inn. He didn't actually use her name then, but whatever. And when he told the sheriff about her tattoo, the sheriff said he knew who she was. Said he'd given her a permit to camp in Ryders Field back in the summer, when the gypsies were hawking their gypsy shit in the park for the tourists. The permit was long expired, but he said he would go out there and check for her anyway. We heard that, and we decided to go check out the park too."

Ben needed a moment to digest everything Chuck had told him. Had he been so traumatized by his parents fighting, his mom's admission of an affair, that he'd blocked out what really transpired that day? Had he then made up Malenia coming to the door to explain to himself why his mother had started dancing and why he and Chuck had decided to go to Ryders Field?

Did I make up everything else—Malenia's psychic powers, dancing as the cure for lycanthropy, all of it—simply because I couldn't deal with the knowledge that my mom was screwing that prick Zanardo?

"Holy...shit..." he said slowly.

"You're telling me," Chuck said. "Maybe you should get your brain checked out when we get out of this fucking place?"

"What about other people in town? Why'd they start dancing?"

Chuck shrugged. "I don't know, pal. The chambermaid, she found the body in the morning, she was sleeping with him. That kicked off everything. She was the first to dance. The others? My parents said one of the women was just batshit crazy, a hermit with something like ten cats. The others I don't know."

"Miss Forrester?"

"No idea. But...you probably don't know this either. She killed herself the next year."

"Aw, no. Why?"

"She obviously had some issues."

"Shit..."

"Yeah, shit, all right. And didn't you just write a book about Chatham and everything that happened there? Talk about an unreliable narrator—"

From somewhere below them a haunting, rising howl pierced the night.

PART 4
Full Moon Party

CHAPTER 37

RUN!

The naked men seated in the circle around Amanda were overdosing. At first their bodies jerked and twisted in their chairs as though they were all experiencing the same nightmare at once, although not one of them woke from their morphine-induced stupors. Some began clawing aggressively at their chests, others at their faces. The muscular man with the beard fell out of his seat and curled into the fetal position. Two others followed.

Amanda was elated. They had apparently injected themselves with a bad batch of morphine, and now they were all experiencing seriously bad reactions.

Run! she told herself. *Go! This is your chance!*

She had waited patiently until the man in the denim jacket had shot up, and then until the remaining three sober men who had been talking to each other returned to their seats and shot up too. She had waited patiently for another five minutes to make sure they were all completely zonked out and that this wasn't some bizarre ruse to see if she would attempt an escape.

She silently pushed herself to her feet—and froze in horror.

They weren't overdosing, she realized abruptly. They were *changing*. She could see what was happening to their faces clearly in the silvered light of the full moon: skin tearing, eyes bleeding, bone and cartilage *shifting*, for God's sake. Their bodies were changing too, withering away. Powerful shoulders lost their bulk and roundness, turning into little more than bony knobs. Lean biceps became leaner, the taut, smooth skin pulling tighter, revealing bulging veins and arteries, jutting elbows, and skeletal wrists. Six-packs vanished, the muscle seemingly eaten away from within.

More men fell out of their chairs and kicked and writhed on the ground. Some moaned in agony. Some hissed, the hideous sounds inhuman, ghoulish, filled with excruciating pain.

And then Amanda saw the fur. Tufts of fine grayish hair sprouted from bloodied foreheads and chins, shrunken chests and wilted genitals.

And that was when she realized what was happening—and the true danger she was in.

They were turning into werewolves! For the love of God, they were turning into living, breathing werewolves right before her eyes!

We like working for our food.

That thought, that recollection of what the shirtless man had told her, was what finally broke her paralysis.

Amanda ran for her life.

CHAPTER 38

BITTEN

C huck opened his eyes. The room in which he sat was dark and silent, yet something was wrong. He realized what was amiss a moment later.

The werewolf he'd shot in the chest was gone.

Gripping the Colt tightly in his good hand, he got quickly to his feet, went to the hole in the floor, and peered down. He couldn't see anything in the inky shadows. He went to the first room. Sally lay sprawled out on the floor. He thought she was sleeping until he got close enough to see her blue dress was shredded in places. However, she didn't appear to be injured; there were no wounds to her flesh beneath the torn fabric.

Chuck continued past Sally and stuck his head out the main entrance. To his surprise he found Ben sitting on the ledge near the top ladder, smoking a cigarette.

Without looking at Chuck, he said, "Always feel like one of these after a good romp in the sack."

Jealousy stirred within Chuck, though he kept it from his voice. "You and Sally had sex?"

"What does it look like?"

"It looks like she's dead."

"Nah. Werewolf sex gets a little violent."

The admission surprised Chuck, but it didn't frighten him. "You're both werewolves?"

"Can't you tell?" Now Ben did look at him. He wore a silver

Venetian carnival mask, a headband supporting fluffy black ears, and furry gloves with long plastic claws.

The costume was identical to the one Chuck had bought his eldest daughter, Cherry, for Halloween a few years ago. Nevertheless, he didn't doubt Ben was a real-life werewolf.

His eyes glowed a malevolent red in the darkness.

"You think I could have a go at her then?" Chuck asked.

"You want to have sex with Sally?"

"If she wouldn't mind…"

"I don't think she'd let you. You're not very nice to her."

"That's because I like her."

"You're mean to her because you like her?"

"Because I can't have her."

"I got it." Ben shrugged. "Guess you have to go ask her then."

Chuck returned to the room. To his alarm Sally was no longer there. He rushed to the next room and the hole in the floor and peered into the black pool of shadows—out of which lunged the werewolf he had shot through the chest. He turned and ran, but powerful, rotten arms gripped him from behind, squeezing the breath from his lungs.

The last thing he saw was a slobbering mouth filled with sharp teeth closing in on his neck—

△△△

Chuck snapped awake, breathless.

A *dream*, he told himself thankfully…but also with some regret. He'd been about to shag Sally. Why couldn't the fucking werewolf have waited to get him until *after* he'd done that?

He looked at the lifeless body of the gypsy a few feet away from him. It was exactly where it should be, draped in a burial shroud of shadows.

Then it moved.

A shoulder had flinched—at least Chuck thought it had.

He got to his feet, aimed the revolver at the body, and took a cautious step toward it.

Another shoulder-flinch.

Chuck leaped backward.

"Ben!" he shouted. "Get your ass in here!"

A moment later Sally hurried into the room, the rifle held across her chest as though she were some sort of GI Jane. Ben followed a couple of seconds later.

"What is it?" Sally demanded.

"He moved." Chuck wiggled the revolver at the body.

"*Moved?* He's dead!"

"I saw him move! There he goes again!"

This time the gypsy's head shook from side to side and one leg spasmed.

"Impossible!" Ben said. "You killed him!"

"Apparently not," Chuck said.

"You didn't cut off his head," Sally stated. Her voice was calm, matter-of-fact—and full of terror.

Chuck knew she was right. Malenia had entered the yellow circus wagon the morning after the night in Ryders Field with a hacksaw. They hadn't seen her cut off Sheriff Sandberg's head because she'd drawn the wagon's curtains across the bars. But what else would she have been doing in there?

"It's how you kill them for good," Ben said. "You have to cut off their heads."

The gypsy's entire body began to convulse until it appeared he was having a full-on seizure: flailing limbs, jackknifing hips and back and knees, thrashing head. What might have been blood began dripping from his mouth, perhaps from an involuntary bite to the inside of his cheeks or his tongue. A deep, guttural sound escaped his clenched jaw.

Chuck would have sworn it was a growl.

"He's changing into a fucking werewolf!" he blurted.

"Cut off its head, Chuck!" Sally said. "Hurry!"

"Why me?"

"You're a doctor!"

"And that makes me qualified to decapitate a werewolf?"

Ben dropped next to the gypsy and pinned his left arm

beneath his knees. "Sally, hold down the other arm! Chuck, find something sharp! A rock! Anything!"

Cursing explosively, Chuck went looking for a rock. He found one with a tapered edge, though it was bulkier than he would have preferred. He carried it in both hands back to the gypsy, doing his best to ignore the throbbing pain in his injured shoulder.

The gypsy's face had begun to bleed from the orifices and swell as its flesh and skin underwent the metamorphosis into the menacing beast it would soon become. Its bloodied lips skinned back in a snarl from teeth and gums that were no longer entirely human. Bloodshot eyes swam with fever and baleful hate and what might have been madness.

Chuck had never witnessed anything so appalling yet marvelous in his life.

Ben and Sally were shouting at him. He ignored them; he knew what he had to do. Straddling the werewolf's chest, he pressed the tapered edge of the rock against its throat and worked it back and forth. The growling dissolved into a guttural, strangled susurration. Its head thrashed faster, inadvertently assisting the beheading. Its jaws snapped madly, searching for anything to rip a bite out of. Hot blood gushed over Chuck's hands as he continued to saw back and forth.

Suddenly the werewolf freed its arm from beneath Sally. It lurched forward and its teeth sank into Chuck's right hand.

"Fuck!" he cried out. He tried yanking his hand free. "It won't let go!"

Ben snatched the cutting stone, which Chuck had dropped when he was attacked, and bashed it down on the creature's forehead.

It went still.

Chuck tugged his hand free from its slackened jaw. "You motherfucking cocksucker!" he said, grabbing the rock from Ben and getting to his feet. "You guys might wanna back away," he added as he raised the rock above his head.

Ben and Sally rose and backed away.

Chuck heaved the rock down on the werewolf's head with all the force he could muster.

Bone and brain exploded beneath the impact. The rock bounced away to the side. The werewolf's face was an unrecognizable, concaved mess.

Sally spun away from the gruesome sight and said, "Jesus, Chuck!"

Ben averted his eyes and said, "You were supposed to cut off its head, Chuck, not pulverize it."

Chuck grinned down proudly at his accomplishment. "No head or smushed head, what's the difference? That motherfucker ain't ever coming back to life again."

CHAPTER 39

TRIPPIN'

Scooby had no idea where he and Lizzy were, only that they were on a road that (hopefully) led to Montezuma Castle National Monument. All he cared about right then was that there were stars in the sky above him instead of the concrete ceiling of a jail cell, and by sometime tomorrow they were going to be chilling out on some beach in Mexico.

Monster hadn't been happy when he'd discovered Scooby and Lizzy had done a hit of acid at his place. But after he'd finished his streaming he popped a tab too, and everything had been cool for the next eight hours while they tripped out. As soon as they'd started to come down from the high, however, Monster had kicked them out. Luckily it had been dark by then, so Scooby and Lizzy had been able to reach the desert without being recognized by anyone.

And now here they were, in the middle of glorious nature, high as kites—thanks to the second tabs of acid he and Lizzy had dropped about half an hour ago...which were just kicking in now.

Although these thoughts were running in the background of Scooby's mind, what he was mostly focused on right then was the big-ass full moon in the sky. It was huge and glowing like a son of a bitch, and he was having a hard time remembering the science behind why it wasn't crashing down to the Earth. It was a giant rock, after all. Nobody else but him thought it was weird it was just hanging out up there in the sky?

"The moon, girl," he said to Lizzy, breathing in the fresh night air. "Check it out. It's *huge*, you know what I'm sayin'?"

"My feet are huge," she replied distractedly.

Scooby looked at her feet. She wore a pair of white Converse with fluorescent green laces, which made them easy to see in the dark. "Your feet ain't huge," he said. "They're normal feet."

"No, they're huge," she insisted. "Not to you. But to the bugs down there on the ground. I wonder how many ants I've stepped on tonight."

"Shit, girl. Who cares about ants? They don't even have brains, so they don't know they're being stepped on."

"They do too have brains. They're just tiny. But imagine giants were walking around Arizona, and one of them randomly stepped on you. How would you feel?"

"Nobody steps on Scoob."

"A giant might."

"No chance. I'd dive between the treads on the bottom of his shoe, you know what I'm sayin'?"

"Giants would suck. Seriously. We'd probably have to go live underground."

"There are no giants, yo. Why do you keep talking about giants?"

"I'm saying *if* there were giants."

Scooby looked at Lizzy for a long moment, and before he changed his mind he said, "You want to know something?"

She looked back at him. "What?"

"I always tell you that you're ugly. But you're not really. You're...kinda hot."

Lizzy shrugged. "I know I am. You're the only one who doesn't think so. Monster has a crush on me."

"Bullshit he does!"

"He does! But anyway, if you think I'm pretty, why do you call me ugly?"

He shrugged. "I don't know. It's just fun calling you ugly, I guess."

"It's not fun for me."

"Maybe I won't call you ugly no more."

"That would be nice. And you already promised to stop calling me bitch. You have to call me babe from now on. You promised."

"Shit, girl. You know what this is like? This kind of talking and promising and all that? It's like being married. This is what those married suckers do."

She grinned. "Are you proposing to me?"

"Hell no! I'm just saying—we hang out so much, it's *like* we're married."

"Do you want to get married?"

He shook his head. "Scoob doesn't marry bitches."

"I'm not a bitch anymore, remember? And we're going to be living in Mexico together. Maybe we *should* get married?"

He kept shaking his head even as he considered the idea. "Nah, we're too young."

"What if *I* want to get married? Lizzy Adams. Sounds okay to me."

Scooby was surprised Lizzy knew his last name. He had simply been Scooby to everyone for as long as he could remember. "We ain't getting married."

"If we have to get fake ID, that's the name I'm going to use. Lizzy Adams."

"Don't be stupid. You can't use real names when you're a fugitive. That's why we need aliases."

She was quiet for a bit before saying, "You think we'll really be safe when we're in Mexico, Scoob?"

"Hell yeah," he said confidently.

"But don't, you know, US Marshals have connections with other countries. Like high-up connections, and they share information and find people hiding in those countries and stuff."

"You can cut your hair and dye it blonde. I'll grow a stache—" He squinted in the dark. "Is that the parking lot up ahead, yo?"

"We're here!" she said. Then, "Are those *cars*?"

Scooby wasn't sure if he was hallucinating or not. There was Lizzy's car, right where they'd left it. But a little further down the parking lot was a big white van that looked as though it had run straight into the stone retaining wall built into the hill. And beyond that there were some larger shapes that might have been buses.

"Do you see what I'm seeing?" he asked.

"Why are there so many people here?" She stopped suddenly and gripped his arm. "Scoob," she whispered. "They're here for *us*. They're waiting for us."

He stopped too and tried to make sense of that. How would anyone know they were coming out here? Had someone recognized Lizzy's car? Had Monster ratted them out?

He began to feel sick to his stomach. "What should we do?" He realized he was whispering too.

Lizzy's eyes were wide and white in the dark. "We gotta go back!"

"Go back where? We got nowhere to go." He shook his head, clearing his paranoia. "They ain't here for us. Why'd they crash that van if they were just waiting here for us?"

Lizzy didn't say anything.

"We gotta get to your car," he insisted. "It's the only way we're getting to Mexico."

They continued forward. Scooby's eyes darted back and forth, scanning for movement, seeing every bush and tree he had been oblivious to moments before.

Lizzy stopped again. "Look!" she whispered, pointing. "That's a cop car!"

She was right. Up ahead by several RVs—not buses, he could now tell—was a white police SUV, and not only that, it had SHERIFF written along the flank.

Scooby ducked into a squat, pulling Lizzy down with him.

"It's Sheriff Shithead's car," he said quietly. "What the fuck's he doing here?"

"I don't like this, Scoob. It's a trap. We gotta turn back."

"You're just tripping. It's no trap."

He hurried forward in a crouch. He heard Lizzy hiss his name, but he kept going without looking back, knowing she would follow. When he reached her car, he finally looked back and saw her not far behind. He waved her on encouragingly.

She stopped next to him, breathing heavily.

"Told you they ain't here for us," he said. "Now get in the car. Don't slam the door."

Scooby opened the passenger-side door, wincing at the creaky, groaning noise the thing made. Lizzy's door wasn't any quieter. They closed both doors—whump, whump—and Scooby grinned at her.

"We made it, yo. Now let's get outta here."

Lizzy started up the old BMW, shifted into reverse—and cried out in alarm.

Scooby jumped so high his head hit the roof. A second later he saw what had frightened her.

A woman's face was pressed up against Lizzy's window. Her eyes were crazy, and he couldn't tell if she was terrified or psychotic. She banged the glass with her palms. "Help me!" she mouthed—like she was afraid someone might hear her.

Scooby reached in front of Lizzy and hit the push-lock home.

The woman was shocked into stillness. Then quick as a cat she went for the back door. Scooby, a split second quicker, lunged between the seats and locked the back doors too.

The crazy bitch banged on the glass and said in a whisper bordering on a scream, "Please! Let me in! They're coming!"

Scooby didn't know who the psycho was, but he wasn't letting her in the car.

"No!" she sobbed, slapping the window so hard he thought her hand might go straight through it. Then she was gone, running away into the night.

Scooby looked at Lizzy. "What the *fuck* was that, yo?"

"She said someone's after her! Who's after her? Who's out there?"

"I don't know, but we gotta split—"

A harrowing sound cut him off. It rose octave after spine-chilling octave for several terrifying seconds before silence reclaimed the night. It had originated from somewhere very close by.

"Was that a wolf?" Lizzy asked in a small voice.

"There ain't no wolves in the desert. A coyote, probably."

"That wasn't a coyote. That *wasn't* a coyote."

"There ain't no wolves in the desert!"

Lizzy began shaking her head from side to side while her breathing became louder and quicker.

Scooby looked past her out her window. He saw nothing. Even so, he felt eyes in the darkness and shadows, watching them. He didn't like the feeling one bit.

"Calm your shit down," he told Lizzy. "You're having a bad trip, that's all. Everything's fine. We just need to leave. Right now."

Lizzy had stalled the car when the woman had banged against her window, and now she reached slowly, almost blindly, for the ignition. She turned the key, from which dangled a green plastic fob in the shape of a cactus above the words CAN'T TOUCH THIS. The engine turned over, then immediately shut off.

"What are you doing?" Scooby snapped.

Lizzy was still shaking her head. Her hand hovered above the ignition.

"What are you *doing*, bitch? Drive!"

"I c-can't," she stammered. "I can't drive right now. I can't drive right now. I can't drive right now..."

Scooby knew she was having a total meltdown.

"Babe," he said evenly but sternly. "We. Need. To. Go. You hearing me?"

She began slapping the steering wheel with her hands. Tears spilled from her eyes and streaked down her cheeks.

"Babe!" he shouted, grabbing her wrists.

Shrieking as if his touch were fire, she snatched her wrists free, crossed her arms on the steering wheel, buried her head in them, and began sobbing.

The car shook.

Scooby went perfectly still. He didn't breathe. Couldn't.

The roof groaned as something moved up there.

Lizzy lifted her head from her arms. Her eyes were almost all whites as she looked up at the roof. Her mouth hung open dumbly. Tears plastered her cheeks, and a string of snot hung from her nose.

Metal buckling.

Nothing more for a few seconds. Then:

Clink...Clink.

Scooby couldn't fathom what might be up there. But whatever it was, it had big motherfucking claws.

The car shook again.

Scooby and Lizzy both cried out, and he closed his eyes in fright. When he opened them, he found himself staring at some horror from the old *Chamber of Chills* comic books he read while hanging out in his tree. It crouched on two sinewy, furry legs. It had the limbs and upright body of a man but the features of a wolf...though not any ordinary wolf. This motherfucking monstrosity was more like what you'd get if a wolf and a demon had a baby that was aborted early and lived.

And it's got a dick, he thought absurdly. *Holy shit, it's got a swinging, shriveled dick.*

That detail shot down the theories his mind was whipping up: that the abomination was just a man in a costume, that the cops were pranking him, having a laugh at Scooby's expense before they locked him up for murder. Because nobody would make a costume like that and pin a fucking dick on it.

"Start the car, Lizzy," he said out of the side of his mouth without moving his lips.

She said nothing, did nothing.

He could hear her breathing faster and louder than before.

"Lizzy..."

The Wolf Man that was crouched on the hood pressed its deformed, hellish muzzle against the windshield. Its breath condensed on the glass and turned it foggy.

Its blood-red eyes went from Scooby to Lizzy and back to Scooby.

Its lips (which were not really lips at all but strips of ragged flesh) pulled slowly back to form a devilish rictus filled with man-eater teeth. The two upper canines, each an inch long, dripped with bloodied saliva.

Scooby felt heat spread down his inner thighs and realized he had pissed himself.

The Wolf Man raised a knuckly, furry hand and tapped a blackened and curved claw against the windshield.

Once...twice...three times...

Lizzy moaned.

A growl rose from the beast's throat, a rumbling, primeval, hungry sound.

Lizzy mewled.

Scooby wanted to scream but couldn't.

Another howl, farther away than the one they'd heard earlier, stabbed the night.

The creature on the hood of Lizzy's car threw back its head and howled in response. Three more howls, distant but piercingly clear, joined in to create a dissonant, hair-raising symphony.

Abruptly the car shook once more, and then the werewolf was gone.

CHAPTER 40

CHUNK 2.0

After Chuck had finished his two-hour shift, he told Ben he was going to check out the upper floors of Montezuma Castle. The truth was, he didn't give a shit about the upper floors. He'd started feeling...different after being bit by the werewolf. At first he'd thought it was his anxiety acting up, and fearful of having a panic attack, he'd swallowed three Xanax. But the feeling not only persisted, it multiplied in intensity. That was bad enough, but then everything inside him was suddenly racing at the same time, the experience not so much concerning but electrifying. He felt like a million bucks. His thoughts were laser-focused and free of distractions. His eyesight jumped from analog to 4k. The world looked unreal. Everything popped: every contour and crack in the stone walls, every fine hair on the back of his hands, every pore in his skin, every thread in his clothing. And the dark was no longer...dark. It was not daylight, but it certainly didn't impede his vision.

These changes extended to his other senses as well. Two floors down he had passed through a room littered with dead rodents. Yet he could smell them now, from where he sat on the rooftop of the monument, despite the fact they had been dead for months (if not years). He could smell Sally and Ben on the first floor, their fear, their pheromones, their chemistries. He could smell not only the dirt and stones and sycamores used in the construction of the primitive building, but he could also smell their *age*. He could smell water from a nearby river, even though he had previously not known it existed.

His hearing was no less miraculous. If he closed his eyes and concentrated on the direction from which the music was coming, the clarity and range and emotion of each note played, of each lyric sung, were as vivid as if he were listening to the song through headphones. He had no food or drink to test his tastebuds, but no doubt even a plump little grub would be a gastronomical explosion of texture and flavor.

Who would have ever thought that changing into a werewolf could be so much fun?

CHAPTER 41

MORE CLARIFICATION

Ben was seated by the hole in the floor, lost in his own thoughts, when Sally entered the dark, dank room. She was little more than a silhouette in the doorway.

"Hey," he said, surprised she'd left her post at the front entrance. "Is something wrong?"

"No, not really," she said, but he could tell by her tone that something was in fact bothering her. "Where's Chuck?"

"He wanted to check out the other floors."

"Was he...okay?"

Ben shrugged. "Aside from the bullet hole in his shoulder, and the bite torn out of his hand, he seemed good enough."

"The bite is what I was wondering about. He was bitten by a werewolf, Ben. I've been thinking... I'm worried that..."

"You think he's going to turn into one too?"

"What if he does? That's how you said they turn in your book—by a bite or intercourse."

"That was my theory," he said. "And it's been debunked. You debunked it yourself, Sally, you knew better, even before we arrived in Camp Verde."

She shook her head. "Not that part of it. Not how they turn people into things like themselves. Some of their folklore is true. They transform on full moons, that's pretty clear. So who's to say they don't infect people with a bite? How else would they turn others?"

"Don't you remember what happened when we were locked up in the wagon, when I was bitten, after they got my dad...?" Ben unconsciously rubbed his right forearm, where a wormy white scar reminded him in perpetuity of his father's final screams, the ghastly way he had died, and how Ben had been helpless to save him. "I used to think the reason I didn't turn into a werewolf was because you danced with me," he continued.

"Danced with you? I never danced with you, Ben...not in the circus wagon, anyway."

"I know that now. It was just another one of my false memories, my attempt to shoehorn everything that happened into a narrative I wanted to believe. But I *was* bitten. That's for sure. I have the scar to prove it. So why didn't I change?"

"I've considered that myself over the years," Sally said. "I figured children can't change into werewolves. They're immune to the virus, or at least more resistant to it. Think about chickenpox or even Covid. Kids have milder symptoms than adults, and in the case of Covid, it's almost never fatal."

Ben was slightly amused. "You're comparing lycanthropy to Covid?"

"They're both viruses, aren't they? In any event, you definitely were infected, even if the symptoms never fully developed. And that happened right after you were bitten."

"Are you sure about that, Sally? I don't trust any of my recollections of what happened that night..."

"One hundred percent, Ben. You were on the verge of transforming. You... How do I put this kindly? You weren't yourself. No, to be honest, you were pretty frightening. You didn't do anything, but it was the way you were sitting, your eyes, the look in them. Chuck kept blabbing over and over that you were going to eat us or something."

"And what happened?"

"Nothing," she said simply. "You ended up going to sleep, or passing out, and when you woke up you were fine."

Ben recalled why they'd started on this topic, and he stared deeper into the monument, where the ladder to the upper floors was located. He saw only blackness and got to his feet. "I better go check on Chunk. See how he's...feeling. I won't be long."

Sally stepped toward him. "Do you want me to come with you?"

He shook his head. "I'll be fine. You need to watch the entrance—"

As if to underscore his point, a howl resounded through the night, a long, slow otherworldly note that was almost immediately answered by two others.

Goosebumps broke out along his flesh, and he gripped the rifle tighter.

Sally nodded and said, "Be careful then. If Chuck is infected, and he bites you..."

"He's probably fine. But, yeah..." He nodded too. "Yeah, I'll be careful."

CHAPTER 42

THE ATTACK

Sally was gazing out the main entrance of Montezuma Castle, mesmerized by the stars twinkling like diamonds on the black velvet sky; the ethereal full moon; the vast, flat desert; and the distant, silhouetted foothills looming like the gatekeepers to a different realm. The sublime view could have been described as magical...had it not been for the ungodly horrors prowling below, as at home in their beastly bodies as the devil in his serpent skin and cloven hooves, no doubt hunting and butchering and feasting on the blood and flesh of whatever hapless animals crossed their paths.

While Sally didn't feel safe, exactly, high up in the monument, she was becoming cautiously optimistic they might just make it through the night until morning. So far the werewolves had made no attempt to reach them. Judging by their howling, they weren't even anywhere close by. Whatever vendettas they'd held while in human form apparently didn't carry over to their werewolf form.

Which was why she was regretting not going with Ben to check on Chuck. If he was turning into a werewolf—

We'd have heard him by now if he was turning into a werewolf. It's not exactly a pleasant process, is it?

No, it wasn't. At least, it hadn't been for Sheriff Sandberg.

Chuck is fine. Ben is fine. Stop worrying.

Sally tried to take her own advice. Indeed, even if lycanthropy, like rabies, was transmitted through a bite, perhaps infection was not guaranteed, the same way two people can be standing next to somebody with the flu, and only one of them might catch it and fall ill.

So Ben was okay. Chuck had simply been bored. That was why he'd decided to—

A large rock struck the narrow ledge a few yards in front of her.

Frowning, Sally looked up the steep cliff face, her eyes probing the inky darkness. She saw nothing at first—and then movement a moment later, a shadow deeper and blacker than all the others. It was descending the cliff face, maybe fifty feet above her.

Sally's heart slipped into her stomach, and she took a small step backward so she was partly concealed in the doorway. She gripped the heavy revolver in both hands and raised the barrel. Even as she did this, she felt woefully inadequate and vulnerable. She had never fired a gun before. She would have a difficult time hitting a stationary target, let alone a moving one.

A handful of smaller rocks spilled down from above, bouncing over the ledge to the ground far below.

Sally looked back up the cliff. The shadowy werewolf appeared to be moving on all fours, headfirst, the way a cat descends out of a tree.

Forty feet away now.

Had it seen her?

If it hadn't, it must have smelled her or heard her. Why else would it risk such a perilous route to the monument? She decided the real question should be: Did it *know* her? Had it been randomly roaming the top of the cliff, searching for prey, when it caught her scent? Was it simply looking for an easy meal? Or had it intentionally chosen to come after her? Despite its transformation and regression into a (perhaps not so much) mindless beast, had it retained knowledge of her and Ben and Chuck hiding out in the monument? Was it coming now to settle its score with them?

More rocks fell, a small landslide of pebbles and stones the size of tennis balls and melons.

Thirty feet away.

For the first time Sally could make out the werewolf's grotesque, Golem-like body, its misshapen limbs, its abhorrent face and glowing, catlike eyes, which were not green or copper or amber but a vengeful, hateful red.

Sally realized she was holding her breath. She exhaled, adjusted her aim to follow the moving monstrosity, and squeezed the trigger.

The report was like a firecracker going off inside her head.

Reckless with adrenaline, she blindly fired two more shots and stumbled back inside the monument. In her haste she tripped up on her own feet and fell on her butt, hard. The revolver flew from her hand and skipped across the stone ground.

The werewolf appeared at the entrance where she had been only moments before, its pointy ears pressed flush to its furry skull, its chest heaving with each wheezing breath, and its black nose twitching at the end of its wrinkled snout.

Baring its fangs in a mockery of a smile, it came toward her.

CHAPTER 43

THE THING IN THE NIGHT

Gabriela wished she had closed the van's side door earlier. After the two men had opened it, looked inside the vehicle, and left, she'd thought about slipping from her hiding spot to close it again. But she'd feared that as soon as she crawled out from behind the box and beneath the table someone would see her. That was what had always happened when she'd played hide-and-seek with her father on the ranch in Guadalajara. She would be hiding in a perfectly good spot where her father couldn't find her, but then she'd grow bored and try to sneak to a different spot...and as soon as she did that, her father would cry out, "*Te veo!*" So she'd remained exactly where she was for the last several hours, hardly moving except to stretch a cramped arm or leg.

Nevertheless, now it was nighttime, it was cold, and there were wolves outside. One of them had come by earlier and had dragged the driver off the front seat and away into the night.

So should she close the door? she wondered now.

It would prevent the wolves from dragging *her* away into the night, and it might make the van a little warmer.

Yet her fear persisted. The Bad Men would see her as soon as she left her hiding spot. That, or they would notice the door had been closed and search the vehicle for her.

Gabriela stayed put, cold, afraid, miserable.

She missed her father.

She missed Mexico.

But mostly she missed her mother. How was it possible she was no longer alive? It wasn't fair. People were supposed to die when they were old. Her mother was young and pretty.

Tears came to Gabriela's eyes as warm memories played inside her head: her *mamá* singing in the kitchen while she made her favorite breakfast casserole on the weekend; hugging Gabriela every morning before Gabriela left for school, and every afternoon when she returned home; taking Gabriela to the movie theater to see *The King's Daughter* not long after they'd moved to Camp Verde, and getting ice cream cones afterward; tucking Gabriela into bed and reading her a chapter of *Prince Caspian* every night.

Now none of that would ever happen again, and it wasn't fair.

And what was going to become of Gabriela? Was she going to be locked up in a *perreras* as she'd previously feared? If not, would she be sent back to Mexico? She would prefer that... except she no longer had any family there. Where would she live? In a box in an alleyway like some of the really poor people? How would she make money? How would she eat?

She had nobody.

Gabriela remembered trekking through the desert to America like it had happened only yesterday. The sun that day had beat down on her like a scorched hammer, stinging her already sunburned face and hands. Thankfully her mom had had the foresight to pack her a long-sleeve sweater. Although uncomfortably hot and damp with sweat, it had protected her upper body from the sun's vicious rays. Her mom had also packed her a bottle of water. The water had been warm but it had tasted so good, and Gabriela had to keep reminding herself not to gulp it all down recklessly. Instead, she'd taken only occasional and tiny sips, just enough to wet the inside of her mouth. She would leave the water on her tongue for as long as she could until the temptation became too great, her thirst too demanding, and she would swallow the precious liquid and almost immediately begin thinking about how long she would wait until she took her next tiny sip...

At some point Gabriela sank into a light doze, and her waking thoughts about the treacherous border crossing followed her into the basement of her mind where her dreams lived.

$$\triangle\triangle\triangle$$

The coyote leading the way through the shimmering desert had been following a path only he knew. The man didn't look anything like the Wile E. Coyote that was always trying to catch and eat the faster and smarter Road Runner in the cartoons, but "coyote" was what Gabriela's mother called him. Gabriela hoped he knew where he was going. They had been walking for most of the day, ever since first light, and the United States was still nowhere in sight.

The coyote kept up a brisk pace, which surprised Gabriela since he was middle-aged and paunchy. A straw sombrero and sunglasses shaded his face. Huge sweat stains formed dark circles on his tan shirt beneath his armpits and down the small of his back. The rear pockets on his pants bulged with bulbs of garlic, which he'd told them would ward off the rattlesnakes. Gabriela thought it must be working; they had yet to cross paths with one.

Gabriela's mother followed behind the coyote. She was short, only a little taller than Gabriela, who was twelve years old. Her curly black hair fell all the way to her lower back and was mostly concealed by the large backpack she wore. She was one of the prettiest people Gabriela knew, and Gabriela hoped she grew up to be just as pretty.

While Gabriela occasionally scanned the horizon for America, she mostly kept her eyes on the scrubby, thorny ground, partly so she didn't step on a rattlesnake or scorpion, but mostly because the searing light hurt her eyes. To distract herself from the relentless heat and her sore feet and legs, she preoccupied her mind with thoughts of what the United States would look like when they finally arrived. She envisioned tall, shiny buildings and clean streets and brand-new vehicles. That was what she'd seen on the occasional TV show, or the odd magazine she'd gotten her hands on back in Guadalajara, where she'd lived her entire life until just a few days ago.

She also wondered what her life would be like there. Her mother told her she would attend school. That would be a first. In Guadalajara she had been needed around the family ranch from dawn to dusk, seven days a week. She was excited about getting an education, but nervous too. She would have to meet new friends, kids that would be unlike her. What worried her the most was that she would have to speak English all the time. She could understand most of what she heard in the foreign language, but she found speaking it much more difficult. Often there would be something she would want to say when she practiced with her mother, but she could only think of the Spanish word. She hoped her poor fluency wouldn't alert people to the fact that she had come into the country illegally. Her mom cautioned her that if anybody ever asked, she was to tell them that they had driven across the border with their proper documents in order, and that they had family members in the country—

The coyote said something excitedly in Spanish. Gabriela's mind had been so far elsewhere she didn't catch what it was. Her mom threw her arms around her and said, "We're here, *nena*! We made it!"

When her mom let go of her, Gabriela squinted at the harsh desert landscape but only saw a bridge, and beyond that, what might have been a tall fence. It was hard to be certain through the heat haze.

Where were all the tall buildings and cars and people?

She didn't have time to ask this, though, since the coyote was moving again, faster than before, his stubby legs working overtime. Gabriela's mom took her hand, and they had to almost run to keep pace with him. They passed beneath the bridge—the shadows felt wonderfully cool on her skin—and when they emerged into the oven-like heat on the other side, Gabriela could now clearly make out the fence. It soared into the blue sky and was topped with loops of razor wire, like the fences that surround a prison.

"See there?" the coyote said, pointing to a spot where the chain links were cut. "That is where you must climb through."

Gabriela swallowed. The spot was really high up.

"Aren't you coming with us?" her mom asked him, her typically smooth forehead furrowed with lines.

He shook his head. "I said I would help you cross the border, and that's where you cross. That's all."

"Where do we go when we're on the other side?"

"North for three hours. You'll see a gas pipeline. Follow that northeast until you reach a small town. From there..." He shrugged. "That is up to you, *señorita*."

She squeezed Gabriela's hand. "I'll go first so you can watch what I do. Then you follow. You can do this, *nena*."

Gabriela nodded.

Her mom gave her hand another affectionate squeeze, then hurried to the fence. She climbed it quickly and easily. When she reached the spot where the chain links were cut, she shoved her backpack through. It dropped twenty feet onto American soil. She followed it through and climbed down the other side of the fence, dropping the final few feet to the ground.

"See? No problem!" She was grinning, even though a red line of blood was dripping from a thin wound on her cheek where she must have scraped it on one of the cut chain links. "Your turn—"

"*Mierda!*" the coyote shouted suddenly. "They're here!" He turned and ran.

"Who's here?" Gabriela's mom called after him.

"*¡La Migra!*" he yelled over his shoulder as he disappeared into the shadows beneath the bridge, one hand gluing his sombrero to his head.

Gabriela glanced at her mom, who held a hand above her eyes like a visor. Gabriela looked in the same direction.

A man was speeding toward them on a galloping horse. The contrail of dust blowing up in his wake resembled the Tasmanian Devil on one of his temper tantrums.

"Hurry *nena!*" her mother cried. "Climb the fence! Hurry!"

Gabriela latched onto the fence and began climbing. Her heart pounded painfully in her small chest. Her entire body trembled. She didn't know who *La Migra* was or what they would do to her if they caught her, but she was certain it would be nothing good.

Ten feet up the toe of one of her sneakers slipped from the link it had been tucked into. Crying out, she dangled in the air with a single hand. From somewhere close but yet so far away she heard her mother urging her on. She twisted and flailed and kicked her feet, trying her best to regain her purchase.

Her burning fingers gave out and she smacked into the ground with jarring force.

The galloping horse whinnied to a stop next to her in a cloud of disturbed dust, its piston-like hooves nearly trampling her beneath them. A huge man wearing an olive-green uniform and a broad-brimmed hat looked down at her, his eyes hidden behind mirrored sunglasses.

He barked something in English, and Gabriela burst into tears.

Gabriela couldn't understand anything the huge man on the horse was asking her. Her mind was too rattled, she was too scared, to think straight, let alone translate English.

The man alighted from the horse with the swing of a large black boot and crouched before her. A holstered gun hung from his big black belt. A yellow badge above his left breast pocket read: US PATROL AGENT. The nametag above the other pocket identified him as M MORRIS.

He removed his mirrored sunglasses and glared at her with icy blue eyes. Behind a red beard, the edges of his mouth tugged downward in a frown.

Beyond him, Gabriela's mother was attacking the chain-link fence with all her strength while unleashing eternal damnation on the man in a free-for-all of English and Spanish.

The man ignored her and said in Spanish: "*¿Tu nombre?*" His voice was deep, no-nonsense, emotionless.

She wiped the tears from her eyes. "Gabriela."

"Gabriela," he repeated.

"*Sí.*"

He cupped her cheeks with his large hands. He held her eyes with his for an extended moment. Then he spoke a single word: "*Ve.*"

Gabriela stared at him, uncomprehending.

He jabbed a finger at the fence. "*¡Ve, ve! ¡Go!*"

She got slowly to her feet. She started toward the fence. Her mom was crying or laughing, she couldn't tell which. She glanced back at the man, uncertain, confused.

He was standing now, next to his horse. His blue eyes remained fixed on her.

She turned back to her mom, the fence.

She ran the last few steps and began to climb.

△△△

Gabriela woke from the dream to a terrifying sound: snorty, phlegmy breathing by the van's sliding door. This was punctuated by loud sniffs, like someone with a runny nose. Of course, Gabriela knew a person wasn't making those noises; it was the wolf from before. It had come back for her.

I knew I should have closed the door! she thought wildly. *Now it's going to get me!*

The wolf continued sniffing—*sniff sniff*, pause, *sniff sniff*—over and over again.

Although Gabriela was hidden from sight, she knew she wasn't hidden from smell, and the wolf was going to zero in on her any second now. Which meant she had to run. She wasn't faster than a wolf, but she had to try to get to the other car.

She'd heard a boy and girl talking earlier, then the doors to the car next to the van opened and closed. She'd heard the engine start, but then it turned off again, so she knew the car hadn't gone anywhere. So they were still in the car, probably hiding from the Bad Men like she was, or maybe just the boy was there now. Either way, that was her only hope. She needed to get to that car.

Go! Run! Now!

Without thinking anymore, Gabriela shoved the box away from her and scrambled out from beneath the table.

She caught a glimpse of the wolf at the side door and wished she hadn't.

Because it wasn't a wolf.

It was a *werewolf*.

A gasp escaped Gabriela's lips as she slipped between the front seats. With a part bark, part growl, the werewolf lunged for her—but missed. The passenger-side door—the one the wolf (werewolf) must have pulled the dead driver through earlier—hung wide open. She leaped through it just as the werewolf lunged, and missed, again.

She ran around the back of the van and saw the car parked three spots down. The boy was staring out his window at her with eyes almost as wide as his gaping mouth, but she knew she would never reach the car before the werewolf caught her. Instead, she leaped back into the van through the side door and heaved it closed with all her strength. It slammed home just as the werewolf smashed into it from the other side.

Slipping between the front seats once more, she reached out into the night, grabbed the door pull, and yanked it shut too. She pressed the lock, then pressed the lock on the driver-side door too.

Just in time.

The werewolf was looking through the window at her, its red eyes burning like fire.

Gabriela couldn't move, think, or breathe. It was so close, its face inches from hers. She was paralyzed with fear.

They stared at each other for what felt like forever—an eight-year-old girl and a bloodied, sickly werewolf—until abruptly the terrible creature turned and loped away into the night.

CHAPTER 44

THE MANIACAL SURGEON

C hanging into a werewolf wasn't so fun, after all.

The physical transformation started with a fever unlike anything Chuck had experienced before. His skin was not merely hot to the touch; it was almost scalding. In a matter of minutes his clothes were drenched with perspiration, and he couldn't yank them off fast enough. Yet that was no relief. The heat was coming from within him. If he didn't know better, he would have sworn his blood was literally boiling.

Then came the pain.

Chuck had had a severe, incapacitating case of food poisoning while in medical school that had caused him to curl up in the fetal position and clutch his abdomen for hours on end. He hadn't had the strength to sit up, and each subsequent, frequent cramp had felt like a dagger stabbing his bowels.

What he was experiencing now was ten times worse. It was as though a maniacal surgeon had slit him open from navel to throat and was joyfully tearing out and rearranging his organs.

Chuck wanted to pass out, he *wished* he could pass out, but he remained conscious, a gold-seat spectator.

He didn't think the agony could possibly get any worse.

It did.

The maniacal surgeon started work on his face.

A fresh memory surfaced in his mind, a mind that was now

flirting with madness. It was the summer of 1989, one year after the events of Ryders Field. He was riding his bike down Main Street. He had forgotten to tighten the quick release on his front tire. When no cars were coming, he cut across the road. A lady and her dog, however, were blocking the ramp, so he went around them and popped a wheelie to get over the curb. To his dismay he watched his front tire scoot away from his bike. The next instant he went headfirst over his handlebars and ate the sidewalk. The impact had felt like Hulk Hogan swinging a baseball bat at his face, and he'd never again felt anything so excruciating in all his life.

Until now.

Because the pain in his face wasn't a one-off, bone-crushing home run. It was punishment after excruciating punishment. Skin, muscles, bones, blood vessels, connective tissue, and nerves felt like they were being torn apart.

Yet even as he thought all this...he began to cease thinking.

The agony persisted, but he no longer had the language to describe the hell he was going through. Only the raw feelings of rage, fear, sadness, disgust, and pain—oh, yes, pain.

An ungodly, primeval howl cut through his soupy insanity, and the person that had been Chuck Hamman realized it had originated from somewhere deep within whatever he had become.

CHAPTER 45

TO THE DEATH

Ben had been on the third floor of the monument, passing through the room with the desiccated rodents, when he heard the gunshot. He immediately backtracked when two more shots rang out.

Sally! was all he could think. And then: *I never should have left her!*

He struck his head on something in the dark, bumped into several walls, but then was once again on the first floor, rushing to the first room. When he burst through the low door, he immediately saw the werewolf standing on two feet at the main entrance, its furry, emaciated body limned with silver moonlight. He saw Sally next, ten feet from the beast, on her butt, backing crab-like away from it.

The werewolf turned to Ben, and its glowing red eyes transported him to the night in Ryders Field, during the midst of the raging storm, when Malenia in beast form, her eyes also burning red, had come right up to the bars of the circus wagon, mere feet from him.

Ben had been beyond terrified then. Now...he still felt fear, yet it was secondary to intense, vengeful rage. These fucking things had killed his father. They'd traumatized his childhood. They'd haunted his nightmares. They'd nearly turned him into a goddamned alcoholic.

He raised Vlad's Remington, pressed the butt firmly against his shoulder, took aim down the sight, and squeezed the trigger.

The .22 caliber round winged the werewolf in the right shoulder, knocking it back a step.

Ben cycled the lever with a hard stroke to load the next cartridge into the chamber and fired again.

The werewolf dropped to all fours, and the bullet sailed through the air where its chest had been a split second before.

Then it was rushing toward him.

Before he could cycle the next cartridge and take proper aim again the beast leaped at him. He rolled out of the way, fired recklessly, missed. Then the werewolf was on top of him, its bared teeth going straight for his throat. He raised the rifle in both hands defensively, parallel to his body, and the slavering creature got a mouthful of the forestock rather than his jugular.

He shoved forward, pushing the werewolf off him while preventing it from loosening its jaws from the rifle. Yet it had a strength that belied its wasted appearance and quickly regained the advantage, sending him flat onto his back. It freed its jaws and tried again for his throat. He abandoned the rifle and gripped its ropey neck with both hands in a stranglehold. It continued to press down on him. Its snapping teeth closed to within inches of his face. Its breath stank like death. Hot drool dripped onto his chin and he squeezed his lips together tightly so it wouldn't get into his mouth.

It was a moot concern. Ben knew the fight was over. The werewolf was impossibly strong. Any second now its canines were going to puncture his flesh—

Sally emerged behind the werewolf with a large rock held in her hands. She drove it down on the back of the creature's skull.

The werewolf sprang off Ben with catlike grace. Landing a few feet away on all fours, it snarled at Sally, who raised the rock above her head threateningly.

"Get away!" she yelled hysterically at it. "Shoo!"

Ben was about to reach for the rifle when a howl, so shrill it was more banshee than canine, chilled his soul.

It had originated from a second werewolf that was now crouched in the doorway to the adjacent room.

CHAPTER 46
SO CLOSE...

Scooby was losing his shit.

Had he just watched a little girl play Ring Around the Rosie (or more accurately, Ring Around the Van) with a werewolf? He could see her right now. She was sitting in the front of the crashed news van a few parking spots over, staring through the window at him. He couldn't bring himself to look away from her. He knew if he did, she would vanish in a puff of smoke. Because she wasn't real. Couldn't be. The acid was fucking with him. The little girl didn't exist, and the werewolf didn't exist either. It was all in his head.

"Ho-lee shit," Scooby said slowly, now prying his eyes away from the apparition. He steepled his hands over his face, rubbed his eyes with the tips of his fingers. "Ho. Lee. Shit. Get it together, bro. Get it together."

Scooby dropped his hands to his lap, took a deep breath. He glanced back at the van. The girl was gone from the window. *Just in my head.* He took another deep breath. And another. He didn't feel too good. His heart was racing, and he felt faint and nauseous. He wasn't sure if he needed to puke or not. The last time he'd felt this way was after he'd snorted a few lines of blow cut with laundry detergent, laxatives, and amphetamines. Deciding he needed some fresh air, he rolled down the window an inch—but only an inch.

Because there was a motherfucking werewolf out there.

It's in your head.

It shook the entire car!

It's in your head.

Scooby had never had an acid trip with such realistic hallucinations before...and he never wanted to have another. He glanced at Lizzy. Her head was buried in her arms, which were folded against the steering wheel. She was still breathing too fast but no longer hyperventilating. She was also making whimpering sounds like she had regressed to two years old. And unfortunately a two-year-old couldn't drive a car. Neither could Scooby. He had never bothered to learn. If the BMW were automatic, he could probably get the job done. But it was manual, and he didn't know shit about driving stick.

In the calmest voice he could muster, he said, "We gotta get outta here, Lizzy. You gotta drive. Can you do that, babe?"

She kept blubbering, and his fear and frustration exploded.

"We gotta go!" he snapped. "You gotta drive!"

She began sobbing.

"Fuck's sake! Get out of the way then."

He grappled her, intent on shoving her between the seats into the back of the car. She screamed and shook her head and batted his hands away.

"Get in the back, bitch! Let Scoob drive!"

But she was too far gone. Hell, she was fucking insane.

Scooby stewed in his seat, thinking, fuming. He knew what he had to do, but he really didn't want to do it.

You don't have a choice, bro.

Counting silently to three, he shoved open the passenger door and climbed out of the car. He scanned the night-veiled parking lot. He didn't see anything moving, but who knew what was lurking in the deeper, blacker shadows?

Go, bro! You're wasting time!

He darted around the BMW and opened the back door. Then he opened the driver's door and yanked Lizzy out of her seat. She screamed bloody murder and clutched the steering wheel, but he was bigger and stronger and dragged her out with brute force. He shoved her onto the back seat, slammed the door closed, then got behind the wheel, pulling the driver's door closed too.

He exhaled deeply. Then he glanced over his shoulder at her. She was sprawled across the backseat, curled in the fetal position, rocking back and forth.

"Werewolf better not have heard you," he mumbled. Then he faced forward and studied the dashboard. "All right, yo. This can't be too hard..."

The key dangled from the ignition. Scooby turned it. The engine rumbled to life, the car jerked back a little, and then the engine stalled.

"Shit!"

He checked the gearbox. The shifter was in reverse from when Lizzy had stalled the car earlier. He attempted to position it to neutral, but it wouldn't budge. He tried a few more times before giving up. He didn't want to break it.

What was he missing?

He peered into the footwell. The skinny gas pedal was on the right. The clutch was on the left, and the brake was between the two. He stepped on the clutch, pressing it all the way to the floorboard, and tried shifting into neutral again.

It worked!

Keeping the clutch depressed with his left foot, he turned the key again. The engine kicked over—and didn't stall.

"Yeah, boy!"

Holding his breath, he removed his foot from the clutch.

The car kept running.

"Hoh-kay," he said, and what came out of his mouth was a word-exhalation hybrid.

He applied pressure to the clutch, shifted to reverse, and pressed the accelerator with his right foot.

The engine revved loudly. Startled, he lifted his foot off the clutch. The car jumped and died.

Scooby slammed the steering wheel with his both fists.

△△△

Ten minutes and countless failed attempts later, he had resigned himself to the fact they weren't going anywhere. He fell into a funk for a while. When he snapped out of it, he realized he had been watching the instrument panels in the dashboard melt into puddly shapes like the clocks in the Dali painting.

Why would anyone make driving a car so difficult?

He channeled his anger at Lizzy. If she had owned a Tesla, he could have just pushed a button, and it would have driven them all the way to Mexico on its own.

He glanced out the window. Some distance away, at the end of the parking lot, there were a whole lot of vehicles, including a couple of RVs and the sheriff's car. None were Teslas. But one of them, he knew, would have an automatic transmission. The unknown was whether any of them would have the key stuck conveniently in the ignition. People only did that in the movies so the guy fleeing the cops could jack a car and kick off some blockbuster chase scene.

Unfortunately, this wasn't a movie.

Then again, those vehicles weren't parked on a street in Brooklyn or South LA; they were parked in the middle of the desert. So maybe someone *had* left the key in the ignition, after all. And if not there, maybe somewhere even more clichéd like behind the sun visor.

There was only one way to find out. He had to get off his ass and go check. However, that meant leaving the safety of the BMW. He would be exposed, vulnerable, a walking snack for the werewolf.

It doesn't exist!

Maybe it didn't. Maybe some rabid Cujo-like dog had jumped on the car and peered in at them through the windshield. Maybe the acid had made him think it was a werewolf.

But that still meant there was a rabid Cujo-like dog out there.

And Scooby had read the book a couple years ago in his tree. Things didn't end well for the dog's owner or the screwdriver-drinking alkie.

He glanced between the seats at Lizzy. She remained curled in a fetal position, but at least she had stopped rocking back and forth.

"I'm gonna jack a car, girl," he told her confidently. "A car I can drive. I'll be back with it in a jiff, and we'll blow this pop stand." She didn't reply, and in a bout of sentimentalism he added, "Scoob loves you, babe. Hang tight."

He got out of the car and closed the door as quietly as he could...though it still squawked like a motherfucker. He scanned the parking lot.

Empty.

He hoped.

The vehicles were about fifty yards away. Scooby used to play junior varsity football before he dropped out of high school, and fifty yards to the end zone had never seemed like a far distance. Now, however, it seemed like miles.

Yet what other options did he have? Sit around in the shitty BMW until dawn? The Cujo-thing could come back any time between now and then. And it might be more determined to get them the next time. It might try smashing the windshield. Then what would they do? They'd be trapped.

And the vehicles were right *there*.

Scooby started across the parking lot. He could see well enough thanks to the moon and all the stars. Even so, he felt in a strange sort of way that he was an actor on a stage, and there was an audience that he couldn't see, sitting there in the dark, watching him...only it was naked, savage wolfmen that wanted to tear him apart limb by limb.

That thought made Scooby stop on the spot.

What if there isn't just one werewolf? What if there's a whole pack of them?

He glanced back at the BMW. Parked there in the moonlight it looked way too much like a stage prop, so much so he began

281

wondering if any of this was real. Not only the werewolf, but this night, his life, everything, reality. Was any of it real? But if it wasn't, then what the hell was it? Was God just a five-year-old infinitely intelligent alien playing a computer game?

He heard something and stiffened.

The wind? He didn't feel any wind. Can wind make a sound if you don't feel it? Or do you need to feel it for it to make a sound? If you don't feel it, is it even wind at all…?

Scooby blinked, and his drug-addled brain focused.

Get moving, fool!

With dread churning in his gut, he continued toward the vehicles. He reached the sheriff's SUV first. He tried the door. Locked. He cupped his hands against the window and peered inside. At first he couldn't see where the key went…and then he realized the vehicle had a keyless ignition, and the push-button was on the dashboard.

He started around the vehicle—and tripped over a pair of cowboy boots.

"What the…?"

When he saw what the boots were attached to, he recoiled in horror. And it was a "what" and not a "who" because all that remained of Sheriff Walker's body was a skeleton resting on a shredded and thoroughly blood-soaked uniform. He'd been *eaten*, goddamned *eaten*, his flesh picked clean from his bones so his carcass now resembled one you might find in the African savannah after the lions and hyenas and vultures had finished with it.

So how did Scooby know it was the sheriff?

Because the mo' fo's face—minus the eyeballs missing from the bloody, gouged sockets—was still intact, frozen in a dumb expression of fear.

Revulsion squeezed Scooby's diaphragm, which shot the contents of his stomach up his esophagus and out his mouth in a powerful spray. He coughed, spat, coughed some more, then wiped the back of his hand across his slimy lips.

Still doubled over, he forced his eyes back to Sheriff

Walker's skeleton—specifically to his leather duty belt, which still encircled his butterfly-shaped pelvis. Attached to it was normal cop stuff: handcuffs, radio, baton, pepper spray, flashlight, holstered firearm, a couple of pouches—and a set of keys, including a black key fob.

Steeling his stomach against another mutinous discharge, he crouched next to the corpse and unclasped the keys from the belt. He stood and pressed the unlock button on the key fob. The SUV bleeped and the headlights flashed.

Scooby nearly jumped in joy.

He hurried around the vehicle to the driver's side and was about to open the door when he detected movement above him.

Crouched on all fours atop the adjacent RV was the werewolf/Cujo-thing/cop eater. In the next instant it leaped through the air and landed on the roof of the SUV with graceful ease. It titled its head, which was less than two feet from Scooby's, as it studied him with its hellish red eyes. A growl scraped up from its furry, mummified chest.

Scooby backed away a step on legs that felt about as sturdy as cooked spaghetti. He took another step, then another—then spun around and ran.

He heard the little girl in the van screaming before realizing the high-pitched, girlish sound was coming from his own mouth. He saw Lizzy's pale face staring out the BMW's backseat window. If he'd had a voice, he would have shouted at her to open the door, but he couldn't find any words, and he knew he was never going to make it to the car before—

Claws sank into his shoulders.

Teeth tore into his neck.

Despite the werewolf clinging to his back, Scooby made it nearly all the way to the car, but inexorably his strength left his body with his gushing blood, and he fell to his hands and knees.

He reached futilely at the jaws chomping at his throat but could do little more than pat the werewolf's wet, cold snout ineffectually before collapsing.

His final thought before the darkness of death claimed him was that he would never get to Mexico, after all.

CHAPTER 47

MERCY

M *alenia!* Ben thought.

The werewolf he had been battling was Malenia. Her attack had happened too fast, and the room had been too dark, for him to recognize her before. Yet in the reprieve created by the arrival of the second werewolf, he'd noticed Malenia's lack of external genitalia (in contrast to the male werewolf's, which was on full display), and a moment after that, the red tattoo on the inside of her right wrist.

The epiphany flashed through his head in the time it took him to retrieve the rifle. He swung the barrel at the werewolves, knowing that if they rushed him simultaneously he was as good as dead. Yet Malenia's full attention was on the male werewolf, which moved further into the room with a stilted, bipedal gait. Both creatures were panting and sniffing and snorting loudly as they sized each other up.

Ben rose to his feet. Sally moved to his side.

"Shoot them," she whispered in his ear.

To do that he would have to cycle the rifle's lever to load another round into the chamber, and he was reluctant to draw any attention to himself. Even so, he pressed the rifle's butt against his shoulder and moved his finger from the guard to the trigger.

Malenia continued to ignore him and to scrutinize—cautiously, it appeared—the newcomer. Ben didn't understand why she was fascinated by the male, and the male by her. Were their minds so completely debased during their transformations into beasts that they no longer recognized members of their own pack—?

Something around the male werewolf's neck glinted in the moonlight.

A necklace.

A gold necklace.

"It's Chunk!" he exclaimed under his breath.

"*What?*"

"His necklace—"

Chuck leapt suddenly, crashing into Malenia. Jaws snapping, limbs intertwined, they shuffled around in a circle, resembling two starved sumo wrestlers trying to shove the other out of the ring.

"Shoot them!" Sally cried.

Ben cycled the lever but he held off taking the shot.

"Shoot them!" she repeated.

"I might hit Chunk!"

"He's a werewolf now!"

And then Chuck flipped Malenia onto her hands and knees. Ben glimpsed his swollen erection a moment before he mounted her from behind. Gripping fistfuls of her mangey black hair, he thrust his hips and entered her doggy style.

Sally was saying something, but Ben's attention was riveted on the grotesque scene.

A few seconds later, Chuck threw his head back and howled in ecstasy as he orgasmed. When he released Malenia's hair, she scrambled away from him.

Ben had a clear shot and he took it.

The bullet obliterated a good bit of Malenia's skull. Even so, she remained in a crouch for a short time, as if in defiance of death, before dropping face first to the ground.

Chuck whirled toward him.

"Shoot him!" Sally said.

Ben aimed the rifle at the monster that had once been his

best friend. And while what he was seeing with his eyes was an atrocity from hell, what he was seeing with his mind's eye was the twelve-year-old Chunk who'd cried out excitedly when he'd discovered a Bent Ben Garbage Pail Kid card at Justin Gee's house; the Chunk who'd thrown a fit after being busted for stealing cupcakes at Vanessa Delaney's birthday party; the Chunk with whom he'd scarfed down pizzas and watched cheesy horror movies at sleepovers until well past midnight on countless occasions.

The werewolf glared at him with spiteful red hate.

Ben closed one eye and lined up the iron sights.

The werewolf dropped to all fours and growled.

Ben's finger took up the slack in the trigger.

Your move, Chuck. What are you going to do?

With a dismissive snort, his friend fled through the monument's entrance and disappeared into the night.

CHAPTER 48
TAKING LEAVE (OF HER SENSES)

Lizzy couldn't watch the werewolf eat Scooby. She looked away and covered her wet eyes with her hands.

This isn't real, she told herself, the same thing she'd been telling herself over and over ever since the creature had peered through the windshield at them earlier. *This isn't real. This isn't real. This isn't real. This* can't *be real.*

Only it was. She had watched the creature tear out Scooby's throat. That wasn't faked. And she'd seen the look in his eyes as he died, how the life in them...faded out, the way music fades out when you gradually turn down the volume knob. No way that had been an act. And why would Scooby be acting anyway?

This isn't real, she told herself again in stubborn defiance.

Then what's happening?

This isn't real.

You're not on some candid camera show.

This isn't real.

It's as real as real gets.

This isn't real!

You need to get out of here, or you're going to be next.

Next?

Dessert.

Knowing she would regret it, but unable to stop, she moved one hand away from her eyes and peered out the window. The werewolf had torn the clothes from Scooby's body, rolled him onto his front, and was feasting on a buffet of blood-soaked offal.

Lizzy didn't think. She simply scooted across the backseat, opened the door on the side of the car opposite the werewolf, climbed out, and ran.

She ran past the crashed news van.

She ran to the end of the parking lot.

She ran down the middle of the road that winded through the desert.

Her legs didn't get tired.

Her lungs didn't protest.

I'm doing it!

I'm escaping—

Movement on her left.

Ten feet from the road a black shape was shadowing her, moving in an easy bounding gait on all four limbs.

Lizzy was too terrified to make a sound. She ran faster—and noticed movement on her right.

Another black shape effortlessly kept pace with her.

There are two of them!

Now she did scream, although little sound escaped her straw-sized throat.

I'm going to die.

I'm going to be eaten.

Fear and despair made her run even faster...faster than she had ever run in her life.

The werewolves remained on either side of her, boxing her in.

The road curved.

She didn't bother following it. Still screaming mutedly, she plowed off it straight into the desert.

With only seconds to live, her mind offered her the only comfort it could:

You'll never have to worry about Mom and Dad disowning you. Or going to jail.

Or living on the lam.
You'll never have to worry about anything again...
The werewolves attacked.

CHAPTER 49
FINAL CLARIFICATION

"Y ou should have shot him," Sally said.

"I couldn't," Ben told her. "It was Chunk."

They stood side by side at the monument's entrance, gazing out at the night. Chuck was long gone. The desert was still and quiet except for the music playing in the parking lot.

"He would have thanked you," she said.

"For killing him?"

"He's infected now. He has to live with the disease. Every month, every full moon, he's going to change into a werewolf."

Ben didn't respond.

Realizing she was unintentionally guilting him, she softened. "On the other hand, perhaps you were right to let him go. Whether he lives or dies isn't up to you. He can make that decision for himself any time he wants. And he certainly seemed to enjoy being a werewolf…"

Ben shook his head. "That was so Chunk." He paused a moment before adding, "I used to collect comics when I was a kid. Mostly *Archie*, but I also had some horror and fantasy stuff like *Creepy*, *Eerie*, *Heavy Metal*. Chunk would flip through them when he came over to my garage and say things like, 'I'd bang her,' about the scantily clad females—no matter if they were vampires, zombies, mummies, swamp monsters, whatever."

"Werewolves?"

"I'm sure he said that about a werewolf too."

"And now he's living out those fantasies..."

"Can I ask you something?"

"Go for it."

Ben glanced briefly behind them at Malenia's body. "Chunk and Malenia...mating..." he said. "It reminded me of something that happened—or didn't happen—in Ryders Field. There was a circus tent there, right?"

Sally nodded. "You didn't imagine that."

"So what I remember...and I know this isn't what happened...but what I remember is that Malenia was in the tent with Sheriff Sandberg..."

"They didn't have sex, Ben."

He blinked at her in surprise.

"That's what you wrote happened in your book," she told him. "Did you forget that I'd read it?"

He smiled faintly. "I did forget, to be honest. But, yes, that's my recollection."

"Because Malenia had hypnotized him with her psychic powers."

"It sounds so foolish when you say it like that..."

"It *was* a foolish theory. I hope your readers are good at suspending their disbelief. In any event, if you want to know what really happened in the tent, the sheriff and deputy were there, yes. Two of Malenia's goons were there too, pointing rifles at them. My memory isn't perfect either, but I recall Malenia was telling the sheriff how handsome he was, something along those lines. She was teasing him, flirting with him, maybe mockingly. When she tried taking his gun from his holster, they got in a tussle and she bit him."

"She *bit* him?"

Sally nodded. "On his hand. Hard enough he started bleeding. That's when Chunky fell over, and they noticed us peeking in through the flap. After Malenia grilled us on what we were doing there, she led us—as well as the sheriff and deputy—to the wagons."

Ben sighed. "I thought it might have been something stupid like that… Chunk fell over?"

"He had practically climbed onto your back so he could see past you and into the tent, and, yeah, he just kinda fell over and made a lot of noise. Any other questions about that night?"

"No, I think that about does it. Why don't you try to get some sleep? I'll keep watch. It's still hours until dawn."

"I'm not tired." She took his hand in hers and squeezed it gently. "Besides…I'd prefer to stay here with you if that's okay."

"Sure," he said, giving her a squeeze back. "I'd like that."

CHAPTER 50

A TIME TO DANCE

When Amanda had fled the Montezuma Castle parking lot the previous night, and the kids in the car had refused to let her in (what they were doing there, she still had no idea), she hadn't followed the road because it meandered east and then north before finally going southwest to Camp Verde. Instead she had doubled back south through the desert and started along the river westward. She hadn't gone far when she'd heard the howling begin in earnest. She'd known that the hunt was on, and she'd also known that even if she ran at a full sprint, she would not reach the safety of the town before she was tracked down and killed

(*we like to work for our meals*)

which was why she'd climbed one of the large cottonwoods that grew along the river's bank.

That decision had saved her life.

Not a minute later she'd heard all sorts of sniffing and growling and barking at the base of the tree. She'd counted a half dozen black shadows circling back and forth in frenzied excitement, yet not one of them had looked up at her, and after another minute or so they'd all dispersed.

Now the sun was rising in the east, its morning rays lightening the sky and returning warmth to Amanda's body and soul. Initially she'd believed it would be best to wait until midday before leaving the safety of the tree, just to be sure no werewolves were lingering around. Yet she'd since changed her mind, fearing that if the werewolves retained their beast memories when they transformed back into human form, they would know where she was and come looking for her.

Carefully she worked her way down the tree, and it felt good to exercise her cramped limbs. She dropped from the lowest branch to the ground and hurried west along the river toward Camp Verde.

△△△

Half an hour later she came to the Cliff Castle Casino. The stone and adobe building, with its giant yellow neon signage above the porte-cochère, was a heavenly sight. Amanda might have only been trapped in the desert for a single night, but she felt as though she'd been roaming the wilderness for years.

Civilization, she thought, was a beautiful thing, and something best appreciated when you were denied its comforts and conveniences.

A gray-haired elderly woman pushing a teal suitcase exited through the front doors of the casino.

Amanda intercepted her. "Hello, please..." It was the first she'd spoken since the day before, and her voice, rusty from neglect, cracked. She cleared her throat and added, "I need to get to the police station. Could you drive me there? It's an emergency."

The woman frowned at her. "What's wrong?"

"There are some men out at Montezuma Castle. They've..." She shook her head. She knew not to mention the word "werewolf" to anybody. Who would believe her? "They've murdered two police officers, and maybe others as well. *Please...*"

"Oh, my." The woman gave Amanda the up and down and apparently accepted her distress—and allegations—as genuine. "Come with me then. I'm parked over that way a little."

ΔΔΔ

As they drove south along Montezuma Castle Highway toward downtown Camp Verde, Amanda found herself wondering what she had been wondering for the entire night: why hadn't the police department sent more officers to Montezuma Castle after the sheriff and deputy didn't return? Surely the sheriff had told someone the day before he was going to question a band of loitering gypsies allegedly linked to the murder of several cops in Massachusetts three decades earlier. When he didn't return to the station, or radio in an update, it would have been standard protocol for a follow-up team to investigate his whereabouts.

Nevertheless, even as Amanda pondered that question, new ones rose in her mind, such as what happened to Sally and Chuck and Ben? Or the little girl who'd accompanied Ralph and her to the monument? She prayed the girl had gotten away, but she had no recollection of anything immediately after the crash...at least, not until the man with the beard had yanked her from the news van.

Moreover, what were the police going to find when they reached Montezuma Castle? A bunch of naked men sleeping off their werewolf hangovers? Or would the men be long gone? Would the cops be nimble enough to organize a state-wide, or even multi-state, manhunt for the caravan before the vehicles split up and faded anonymously into the arteries of traffic across America?

And finally, what was to become of Amanda herself? She'd witnessed living and breathing werewolves, after all. She could hardly believe that was true. Last night...felt like a dream. Yet she knew it had all happened. *Werewolves existed.* How that might change her, she had no idea...only that her life would never be the same again.

A man wearing white pajamas was dancing on the porch of a house.

Amanda had all but forgotten about the dancing plague—the reason she had come to Camp Verde in the first place—and she said, "Did you see that man?"

"What man?" the woman asked.

"He was on the porch of a house we just passed, dancing."

"The dancing bug." She sighed. "Seems there has been an uptick in cases recently."

"An uptick? What do you mean by that?"

"I'm a regular at the casino. I know many of the other regulars. And everybody I spoke with there last night—this morning—seemed to know somebody who'd started dancing in just the last day or so. I don't understand it. I don't know what's happening. I just hope that if I start dancing, somebody will give me a good, hard slap across the face to knock some sense back into me. There's another one."

A twenty-something woman was in the parking lot next to the Copper Canyon Family Health Center. Dressed to the nines in red heels, a black hip skirt, and a leopard-print blouse, she was dancing seductively, all hips and shoulders, as though she were still at whatever bar or club she had presumably been at earlier.

"Should we help her?" Amanda asked, concerned. "Someone like that, young and pretty, shouldn't be left alone on the street in that state..."

"According to the Bible," the old woman said gently, "there's a time to weep, a time to laugh, a time to mourn...and a time to dance. I suppose it's simply these folks' time to dance, and we should leave them to it."

ΔΔΔ

When they pulled into the parking lot of the Yavapai County Detention Center, Amanda thanked the woman for the lift.

"Are you going to be okay?" she asked. "You've clearly been through a lot—"

"Thank you, but I'll be fine now. It'll all be out of my hands in a few minutes."

"I can wait here, if you'd like?"

"No, I'm fine, really. Thank you again."

She got out of the car and hustled up the sidewalk to the double glass doors with SHERIFF stenciled above them. She went to the front desk. It was unmanned.

She rang the bell and called, "Hello...?"

Nobody appeared or replied.

She kept ringing.

Cursing, she glanced around the reception area, which was appointed with waiting chairs, a flag of Arizona, and a map of the county.

Where the hell was everybody? Granted, it was early, but there should at least be a duty officer around somewhere...

In the break room, she thought. *No doubt drinking coffee and eating donuts and doing whatever else cops do.*

Deciding there was no time to wait for the officer to return to his or her post, Amanda went looking for the break room. Before she found it she came to a door labeled DISPATCH COMMUNICATIONS. She knocked, received no reply, and entered. The room featured a state-of-the-art dispatch console mounted with rows of flat-panel monitors. A roundish redhead, presumably the dispatcher, stood in front of the console, her headset and microphone still hooked around her neck, a sleepy look on her cherub face. She was shuffling in a circle and corkscrewing her hips in a solo, lazy version of the Texas two-step, seemingly oblivious to the spilled coffee and the broken shards of a ceramic mug on the tiled floor.

Amanda stared at the woman in dismay and dim understanding until her exhaustion and fear and the totality of horror she'd been through caught up with her, and she burst into laughter until she cried.

And then she too began to dance.

CHAPTER 51

A SAVING GRACE

Chuck cracked open his eyes but didn't move. He didn't have the strength. His body felt made of lead, as did his brain. He could hardly think and had no idea where he was or why he felt so terrible. His tongue stuck to the top of his dry mouth, and his throat ached as if he were in the grip of a fever.

When the stark white light searing his retinas became too much, he gladly let his eyelids sink closed. He drifted back into the dream he'd been having. Running and bounding through a forest alive with a thousand different sounds and smells. Moving with such powerful ease, he almost felt as though he were flying. Following scents that appeared to him as magical colored ribbons, each one leading to a prize at the end: a foraging skunk or ringtail, a surprised fox or bobcat, a cowering porcupine or jackrabbit. The elation that coursed through him as he sank his teeth into their flesh and tasted the hot spray of blood in the back of his throat. The satisfying crunch of bone and the tearing of juicy meat. From one cowering prey to the next he went, an unstoppable, apex predator...

...but it wasn't a forest he was in, was it? It was a desert, cold and vast. And there were other creatures (like him) prowling the night, and he avoided crossing paths with them because...

...they were dangerous. They would attack him. They would kill him if they could. So he continued further and further into the desert, away from his enemies, until he could no longer detect their scents (slag gray and unappetizing). There he came upon a fresh scent (red and tantalizing), which led him to a sleeping elk. He pounced before it could rise and flee, and even as he feasted upon its corpse, he knew it wouldn't be enough to satiate his bottomless hunger...

Chuck cracked open his eyes again. Same stark white light, plus a flattening heat too. He felt as though he were curled up inside an oven. His brittle tongue probed his burnt lips and chalky mouth. He needed water. He had never needed anything more, and the need grew so large it forced him to move his leaden body.

He rolled from his side onto his front. He pushed himself to his knees. His head screamed in protest—right then his skull may as well have been made from broken glass—and blackness washed through him so complete he was sure he was going to pass out. Yet the blackness, and the dizziness that accompanied it, passed within a few seconds and he remained on his knees.

Squinting, his face twisted in agony, the blinding brightness lessened, and he realized he was in fact in a desert that stretched away from him in every direction to a blue and impossibly far away horizon.

He thought of the dream again.

He raised his arms before him.

They were red with dried blood.

He looked down at himself. He wore no clothes. His naked body was caked with dirt and more red-black blood. Yet he saw not a single cut or scratch.

The blood wasn't his.

Running, bounding, hunting, feasting...

The others like him, the enemies...

Werewolves.

The doors to Chuck's memory swung open then, and everything from the day before flooded out at once. Ben, Sally, Malenia, Montezuma Castle, Vlad—being bitten by Vlad.

Turning into a werewolf himself.

No!

You were infected.

No!

You're one of them now.

Chuck felt as though he'd just been fed a small slice of his own heart. His stomach lurched and he retched, but nothing came up his throat.

Moaning, he bent forward onto his elbows.

It was inside him.

The disease.

Lycanthropy.

It was inside him...

Chuck stiffened as his dread and self-pity abruptly turned into—something else.

The disease of lycanthropy was inside him, yes. But so too was the cure. Not for lycanthropy.

For aging.

I'm never going to grow old, he thought with slow, dull wonder. *I'm never going to see my forty-fourth birthday—not in a biological sense, at least. I'm never going to die from cancer or cardiovascular disease or dementia or diabetes.*

I'm...going to live...forever...

A rasping whistle, pitiful and tragic yet rapturous, escaped his cracked and bleeding lips. His sunburnt shoulders trembled in what would wrongly be interpreted as sorrow.

Chuck's laughter rose—if you could call the hideous sound he was making laughter—until he passed out once more beneath the blistering Sonoran Desert sky.

CHAPTER 52

EXPECT THE UNEXPECTED

10:30 a.m.

"You're sure you want to do this?" Ben said. He stood on the narrow ledge, next to the top of the highest ladder.

"We've already talked it through," Sally said. The howling had stopped about an hour before dawn, and the music had ceased half an hour after that. They'd neither seen nor heard anything since. It was possible the gypsies hadn't departed and were in fact waiting in the parking lot for them to leave Montezuma Castle and walk into their arms. Nevertheless, Ben and Sally had decided that was unlikely. They'd murdered people last night. Those people, whoever they were, might have told others where they'd gone, and if so, the police would eventually show up, looking for them. It would be reckless for the gypsies, whose very existence was based on anonymity, to stick around—especially after Ben and Sally had "returned" the bodies of Vlad and Malenia. And by returned Sally meant throwing them off the cliff. That had been her idea. She'd feared the gypsies might attempt a renewed assault on the monument in the morning to retrieve them, or they might risk remaining stubbornly put until they got them back. Either way, the corpses were gone now; she and Ben had watched several of the gypsies whisk them away not long after dawn.

"All right then," Ben said. "I'll go first."

△△△

When both Ben and Sally were on solid ground once more, they started along the path to the visitor center. Neither of them spoke, and they kept their eyes peeled for any sign of an ambush. Ben carried the Remington, which still had nine rounds loaded in the chamber, in a shooting position with the butt pressed firmly against his shoulder. Sally held Chuck's revolver in her right hand even though it was out of bullets. In the worst-case scenario, she could launch it as a projectile.

When they reached the visitor center, Ben said quietly, "Wait here while I check to make sure they're gone."

She shook her head. "I'll come with you—"

"Wait here," he repeated and dashed southeast through the desert before she could argue further. He went from tree to tree until he had a clear view of the full parking lot.

Sally waited with bated breath, praying they had not just foolishly walked into a trap.

But then Ben waved her over. "All clear!" he shouted.

Her knees went weak with relief—she'd always thought that was just a clichéd saying—and she gripped the corner of the building to steady herself. Then she hurried to where Ben waited. The gypsies were indeed gone...although there were three new vehicles. She didn't know what to make of the old BMW, but the police SUV and the abandoned broadcast van each told a heartbreaking story.

"Amanda..." she said, saddened with grief and guilt. "It *was* her they shot at last night. And it's my fault... She came here looking for me..."

Ben wrapped her in a hug and stroked her back affectionately. She gripped him fiercely. When they released each other, she wiped her eyes with the heels of her hands and took a deep breath.

Ben said, "That's the sheriff's car. Wouldn't the police have sent backup when they couldn't get ahold of him?"

"Guess he didn't tell anyone he was coming out here."

"Surely the SUV has a GPS tracking system? Anyway, you said Chunk left the keys in his car's ignition?"

Sally nodded, and they went to the Lexus SUV.

Ben opened the driver-side door and said, "No keys."

"Guess the gypsies took them," she said.

"Doesn't matter." He pointed west. "We'll just walk. And if we cut through the desert, we'll get to Camp Verde faster than following the road—"

The rest of the sentence died on his lips as the passenger-side door of the Channel 7 news van swung open and Gabriela hopped down to the blacktop.

"Hi guys," she said, serving them a timid wave. "Are the monsters all gone now?"

EPILOGUE

TEN YEARS LATER

Ben was seated at the breakfast nook in his Back Bay townhouse, sipping a coffee and reading the Boston Globe, when he heard Sally and Gabriela return. They had gone to the Prudential Center to shop for Christmas presents earlier in the morning.

Ben set aside the newspaper and went to the stove to boil the kettle. Sally would no doubt like tea (it was -10 degrees Fahrenheit outside), and Gabby had been drinking three or four hot chocolates a day since she'd been back visiting over the holidays.

In September she had begun her first semester at Harvard University. She was living on the Allston campus, and her planned major—or "concentration," in Harvard jargon—was Computer Science with a secondary in either Mind Brain Behavior or Machine Learning. She had been fascinated with AI for years, and she planned to become a robotic engineer after graduating.

Ben had missed having her around the house these last few months. While he had lived much of his adult life as a bachelor, his happiest years had been after Sally and Gabby had moved in with him. That had been eight months after the events in Arizona, and about a month following the court hearing that finalized Sally's adoption of Gabby. In the ensuing years Ben had continued to write horror novels, and to his delight one of them (an interpretation of the Navaho skin-walker legend) had been made into a film on Netflix. Sally, meanwhile, had opened a café on Newbury Street near the Boston Common. It was a cozy spot with good coffee and food, and Ben often brought his laptop there to write on weekend mornings. And Gabby had grown into a beautiful, intelligent young woman. She might not be his biological child, but he loved her as much as any parent could love their daughter. Sally, unsurprisingly, had proven to be a fantastic mother, and after the tragic passing of her biological daughter, Valerie, nothing could have been better for her than the second chance she had been given with Gabby.

Ben grabbed two mugs from the cupboard and dropped an Earl Grey teabag into one and a spoonful of cocoa into the other. He was getting a carton of milk from the fridge when Sally and Gabby entered the kitchen, both of them carrying large paper shopping bags.

At fifty-five years old, Sally was still a stunner. She had a few more fine wrinkles than when they had reunited ten years ago, but she turned more heads in her café than the girls in their twenties and thirties who worked for her. Gabby had lopped off her long, black hair in the summer in favor of a short pixie cut. It was trendy and sophisticated and suited her nicely.

"You guys get everything you wanted?" Ben asked, leaning forward to look into one of Gabby's bags.

She pulled it away from him. "No peeking, Papa," she said. "Your Christmas present is in there."

"Just one?" he kidded.

"I think you'll like it. I'll go wrap it now and put it under the tree."

"There's a hot chocolate here for you."

"I'll have it when I come down."

She left the kitchen.

Ben eyed Sally's bags. "Did you get me something too?"

"Nope," she said, kissing him on the cheek. "Everything in these bags is for me. I bought your present weeks ago."

"You mean it's just been sitting somewhere around this house all that time?"

"You won't find it, so don't bother looking."

"Have you forgotten I work from home? I could have this place pulled apart and put back together without you ever the wiser."

"I know that. Which is why I'm keeping it at the café... What? What's wrong?"

Ben was looking past her at the little wall-mounted kitchen TV, hardly believing who was on the screen.

Sally looked too. "My God!" she said. "Is that *Chunky*?"

The scrolling chyron read: FDA APPROVES "MIRACLE DRUG" TO PREVENT AGING.

"No friggin' way," Ben said, grabbing the remote off the counter and unmuting the volume.

"...but it *is* a disease," said Chuck, dressed spiffily in a navy suit, a white dress shirt with French cuffs, and a red silk tie.

Ben had not been in touch with his old friend since the days of Camp Verde. Following the night they were trapped in Montezuma Castle, the cops that hadn't been swept up in the dancing plague ravaging the town had been skeptical of Ben and Sally's story, which had involved everything that had happened—except any mention of werewolves. Their spin was that the gypsies had kidnapped Ben because he was famous and wealthy, and they were looking for a ransom. Amazingly the Phoenix reporter, Amanda Smith, had survived that night (by camping out in a cottonwood, she'd told them when she'd recovered from a bout of the dancing plague) and had been on board with their tale. During an extensive multi-day search of the desert surrounding the monument, the police and local volunteers (including Ben, Sally, and Amanda) didn't find the sheriff, senior deputy, or Chuck, and all three were ultimately presumed dead.

And that was what Ben and Sally had believed to be Chuck's fate—until he contacted Sally through Facebook a week later. They arranged a three-way call, during which Ben and Sally explained the kidnapping story in the event the Camp Verde police discovered he was indeed alive and wanted to question him. Chuck, for his part, made Ben and Sally promise to never reveal his "secret" (no one on that call once mentioned the taboo word "werewolf"), and they had both agreed.

And that had been that. They'd been incommunicado ever since.

"Aging is a disease?" the CNN host replied skeptically.

Chuck nodded. "I know that might seem like an odd thing to say because people have always believed aging is a natural part of growing old. Well, I'm here to tell you it isn't. It's a disease, all right. Just as cancer results from cell mutation, aging is a result of cell information loss."

"Information loss?"

Chuck folded his hands together neatly and said, "Let me lay it out in the simplest way I can, Bruce. Two kinds of information exist in our cells: digital and analog. As you might know, digital information is stored using a finite set of possible values. Computer programs use binary code, represented by a series of zeroes and ones. Our cells use not base 2 but base 4, and it's those four bases that contain the genetic instructions in our DNA required for making complicated living beings like ourselves.

"Now analog information, on the other hand, is the collection of all the epigenetic marks on the DNA in a single cell, which are different between cell types. A blood cell, for example, will have different marks than a liver cell. So say you have a human fertilized egg, composed of billions of stem cells. The epigenetic marks, deposited on those stem cells by specific enzymes, allow those genetically identical cells to assume thousands of different modalities to create a human newborn. In other words, they instruct the newly divided cells on what type of cells they should be. That's why the newborn's brain cells don't become immune cells, and its skin cells don't become kidney cells. So you see, without analog information, your cells and mine would lose their identity. Our new cells would lose their identity too. And if this happened, our tissues and organs would become less and less functional until, ultimately, they failed. Now here's the rub: unlike digital information, which is extremely accurate and doesn't lose quality when it's stored and copied, analog information degrades over time and *does* lose quality when it's copied. And this is what I'm getting at when I say aging is a result of information loss. Consider a CD player from the 1990s. Remember those things?"

The host said, "They played shiny round discs, didn't they?"

Chuck said, "They had a little laser beam that shone down onto the surface of those shiny round discs to find and read the pattern of bumps on them. If you scratched a disc, the laser couldn't read the information stored on it accurately. Metaphorically speaking, aging is like scratches on a compact disc. It prevents the analog information in our cells from reading the digital information accurately. Consequently, our cells become senescent and stop repairing themselves. The result? Inflammation and chronic illnesses such as heart disease, arthritis, Alzheimer's, cancer. Old age."

"Gotcha," the host said. "And so your drug...polishes the scratches on the compact disc?"

"Exactly," Chuck said, smiling proudly. "Clone your dog when it's fourteen—or seventy-five in human years—and the cloned cells of the new dog will be perfectly good. That's because its cells retain their youthful digital information even when they become senescent. The same goes for us. And that is profound. It means the scratches on our DNA—yours, mine, everybody's—can be *removed*. Aging can be *reset*. And it's precisely this kind of cellular reprogramming, Bruce, that we at Life Biotechnology have accomplished with a revolutionary new drug under the brand name Youthe. After years of clinical trials proving the efficacy of it instructing human cells to reread their original blueprint—regenerating hair, skin, bones, joints, and even brain neurons—it's just been FDA approved." He looked directly into the camera. "So go out and buy yourself some Youthe now, folks. Go out and live forever."

Ben hit mute on the remote control and stared at Sally.

She appeared as amazed as he felt. "But *how*?" she said, shaking her head. "Without Malenia's or Vlad's body to study —?"

"He wouldn't have needed either of them," he told her. "It's in him, Sally. Lycanthropy. The power to rejuvenate his cells after each full moon. *It's in him.* He would have used his own anatomy for his research."

"Holy Mother Mary..." she said slowly.

"Yeah, Holy Mother Mary, *shit*. Chunk discovered the cure for aging. Chunk!"

"Do you think...it works?"

"You don't get featured on CNN by selling snake oil..." He didn't like the look he saw in her eyes. "You're not thinking of taking it, are you?"

"If it really prevents aging..."

"You would put werewolf in you?"

"What?"

"Youthe?" Ben scoffed. "He may as well have named it *Wolfe*, with an E. Who knows what side effects that drug might have!"

"It's been FDA approved..."

"I'm sure Chunk never divulged that his research was based on werewolf DNA. Now please tell me you're not going to try it?"

"No," she told him after a brief hesitation. "No, you're right." She shook her head. "I don't know what I was thinking."

△△△

One month later.

12:01 a.m.

Freshly showered, Sally stood in front of the ensuite bathroom's mirrored medicine cabinet, wrapped in a fluffy white towel. Laid out on the marble counter before her were all the products she used for her nightly skincare routine:

cleanser, toner, hydrating serum, eye cream, moisturizer.

Scrutinizing her reflection, she thought: *You're fifty-five. You look good for fifty-five. It's the new forty. You don't need it.*

It.

Just call it what it is.

Youthe.

Reluctantly, guiltily, Sally retrieved the blue-and-white box hidden in the back of the vanity's top drawer. No larger than a typical Aspirin package, it contained thirty of the controversial film-coated red tablets that were taking the world by storm. She had purchased it the other day from a Walgreens in the South End, as all the pharmacies in Back Bay had been sold out.

You would put werewolf in you? Ben's voice chided her.

Scientists are praising it.

You would put werewolf in you?

Chuck is being talked about for the Nobel Prize in Medicine.

You would put werewolf in you?

It's safe! Everybody's taking it! Everybody but me!

You would put werewolf in you...?

Jaw clenched, Sally opened the box and popped a pill from the blister pack. She raised it to her mouth...where it waited for a long moment. Then angrily (but decisively) she tossed it, along with the blue-and-white box, into the trash bin next to the toilet.

She finished the rest of her nightly skincare routine, switched off the bathroom lights, and went to bed, where Ben was sleeping soundly.

She kissed him on the cheek, closed her eyes, and went to sleep too.

[1] In Ben's novelization of the events of his youth in the original *The Dancing Plague*, he changed Chuck Hamman's name to "Chuck Archibald" and Sally Levine's name to "Sally Bishop" to protect their identities.

ABOUT THE AUTHOR

Jeremy Bates

 USA TODAY and #1 AMAZON bestselling author Jeremy Bates has published more than twenty novels and novellas. They have sold more than one million copies, been translated into several languages, and been optioned for film and TV by major studios. Midwest Book Review compares his work to "Stephen King, Joe Lansdale, and other masters of the art." He has won both an Australian Shadows Award and a Canadian Arthur Ellis Award. He was also a finalist in the Goodreads Choice Awards, the only major book awards decided by readers.